ONE SON IS ENOUGH

EGGY WOODFORD grew up in India, in the foothills of the Himalayas, a magical childhood full of jungle picnics, pony-trap journeys and monsoon rains. After she returned to England she studied at Oxford University for three years and had her first novel published at the age of twenty-six. She went on to become a successful author of fiction for older children, and her titles include *Please Don't Go, Backwater War, The Girl with a Voice* and *Monster in our Midst*. Peggy loves travelling and particularly enjoys visiting Turkey, the setting for this story. She lives in London with her husband.

One Son is Enough

peggy woodford

WALKER BOOKS
AND SUBSIDIARIES
LONDON · BOSTON · SYDNEY · AUCKLAND

For Dash

First published 2006 by Walker Books Ltd
87 Vauxhall Walk, London SE11 5HJ

2 4 6 8 10 9 7 5 3

Text © 2006 Peggy Woodford
Illustrations © 2006 Hannah Firmin
Talisman motif by Hannah Firmin, based on a design by Ruth Dupré

This book has been typeset in Cochin.

Printed and bound in Great Britain by Bookmarque Ltd, Croydon, Surrey

British Library Cataloguing in Publication Data:
a catalogue record for this book
is available from the British Library

ISBN-13: 978-1-84428-145-9
ISBN-10: 1-84428-145-0

www.walkerbooks.co.uk

CONTENTS

LIST OF CHARACTERS

The Family
Osman and **Iskander**, twin nomad boys
Leila and **Gul**, their sisters
Ali, their father, called **Baba** by his children
Fatima, their mother, called **Ana**
Yacut, their uncle, or **Amja Yacut**

On Iskander's Journey
Hasan Efendi, the sultan's agent for the youth levy
Selim, a janissary (soldier) in charge of the boys
Ibrahim, **Ismail** and **Yusuf**, boys travelling
with Iskander

The Troupe
Kizilbash, the boss
Ahmed, his trainer

Yildiz, a Greek girl, one of the acrobats
Bulent, Kizilbash's brother and owner
of the karavansarai the troupe stay in
Zubaida, star dancer from Constantinople

IN THE PALACE
Jelal, Iskander's cousin (Yacut's son),
now a page in the sultan's palace
Abdulhamid Hodja, a teacher
Rifat, a gardener
Prince Murad, one of the sultan's sons
Iskander the Greek, a senior page
Yashar, Rifat's cousin

NE SON IS ENOUGH is set in Turkey in the early years of the nineteenth century, and takes place partly in Anatolia, and partly in the sultan's palace in the capital, Constantinople.

TURKISH WORDS USED IN THE STORY:

Amja	Uncle (brother of father)
Ana	Mother
Ayran	Yogurt diluted to make a drink. Salt and chopped mint, or honey, are often added.
Baba	Father
Bostanji	Gardener
Chengi	A special type of dancer – a boy dressed up as a girl. This came about because in Muslim Turkey girls were never allowed to dance in front of men.
Efendi	Sir
Grand Vizir	The sultan's prime minister
Hamam	Bath house with hot pool, steam room and cool area
Harem	Secluded women's section in a house. Only males who were close members of the family were admitted.
Hodja	Teacher
Inshallah	Version of the Arabic for "God willing"

Janissaries	The sultan's elite band of soldiers
Karavan	A company of people – merchants, pilgrims, etc. – travelling together for safety in the days before motor vehicles. Our word "caravan" derives from the carriages, carts and wagons that people rode in.
Karavansarai	A large square building with high walls and a spacious central courtyard, specially built for the use of travellers and their animals and vehicles. "Sarai" means any big building and rhymes with "why".
Kilim	Rug handwoven in Anatolia, always in bright colours with distinctive designs. Unlike carpets, kilims are flat-woven, with no pile.
Selamlik	Men's quarters where women were not allowed to go
Simit	Sesame-coated bread ring sold all over Turkey
Sultan	Rules the Empire from his palace in Constantinople
Yufka	Special dried bread made by nomads

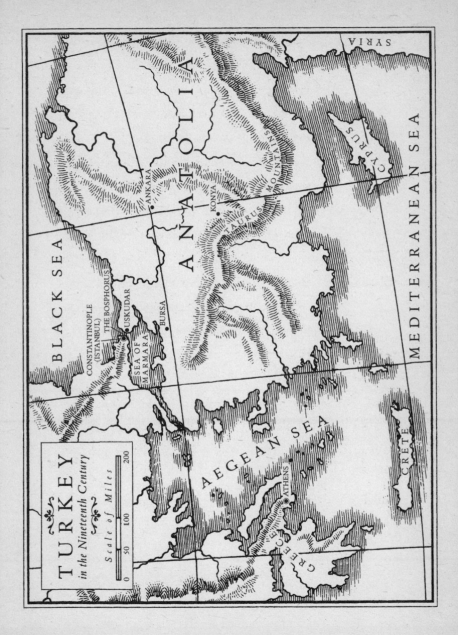

TURKEY *in the Nineteenth Century*

Scale of Miles

0   50   100   200

BLACK SEA

SYRIA

ANATOLIA

CYPRUS

MEDITERRANEAN SEA

ANKARA

KONYA

TAURUS MOUNTAINS

CONSTANTINOPLE
(ISTANBUL)

THE BOSPHORUS

USKUDAR

SEA OF MARMARA

BURSA

AEGEAN SEA

ATHENS

GREECE

CRETE

LEAVING THE MOUNTAIN

VOICES OUTSIDE the tent woke Iskander and Osman as they lay rolled in their blankets.

"What's the matter, Yacut?" Their father sounded surprised to see his brother so early in the morning. "I didn't think we were hunting today."

"The sultan's agents are in the area, Ali." The twins sat up in horror. "I came to warn you. They're bound to want one of your boys."

"You didn't tell them to come here?" The twins could picture their father's angry glare from his tone.

"I didn't have to. They already knew there were boys of the right age in your tribe – they probably heard about the twins when they took Jelal. You can't avoid the youth-levy, Ali." His voice was almost smug. Jelal, his eldest son, had been a slave in the sultan's palace for three years now, and Yacut clearly didn't see why Ali's family shouldn't go through the same pain of separation.

The twins stared at each other, hardly breathing. This was what they'd been afraid of since their cousin left. Silence now descended outside, and when they peeped out, they saw Ali and Yacut arguing at the far end of the encampment, well out of earshot. Then Yacut rode off and Ali came striding back to their tent, scowling. The twins quickly lay down and pretended to be asleep.

"Wake up, boys. Get going. I don't like the look of the weather. Get the flocks in."

"Yes, Baba."

He said nothing to them about Yacut's visit, but as they ate their bread and honey they could hear him talking quietly but urgently to their mother, Fatima, outside. He was obviously trying to calm her down, and when she hurried into the tent she immediately hugged her sons fiercely.

"The janissaries are here again, but don't worry, boys, I'm not going to let the sultan get hold of any son of mine. Baba's agreed we must leave as soon as possible for our winter quarters. If we trek down to the Ruined City now they might never catch up with us. Hurry, get the animals in."

Iskander and Osman grabbed their crooks and ran up the mountainside. The sheep and goats had seemed to sense they were leaving and were scattered far and wide over the slopes, eating as if they'd never see grass again. The twins didn't start work at once. As soon as they were high enough to be out of sight, they sat down in their favourite hollow.

"What do you think Baba's going to do, Iskander?"

"If only we didn't have Yacut for an uncle. He's determined that one of us is going to join Jelal – he goes on and on at Baba about what an honour it is to serve the sultan."

"But Baba doesn't want us to go. He won't give in, surely?"

"I'm afraid Amja Yacut will keep pestering him until he does." Iskander looked at his brother. "Our uncle is a horrible, evil man, Osman. I hate him, I really hate him." He thwacked his stick against a rock as if he was hitting Yacut. Osman had never seen his twin so angry. "And I'm the one who'll be sent to be the sultan's slave."

"Why you? It's just as likely to be me."

"You know that's not true."

They stared at each other, their eyes saying more than their tongues. They both knew Iskander was right – not only was he the eldest by half an hour, but Ali always picked on him: blamed him first and beat him first. He never praised him first. In fact, now that Iskander was almost as tall and strong as his father, Osman suspected Baba feared his brother almost more than he loved him. It hurt Osman to realize he was his father's favourite.

The twins weren't identical. In fact, they looked so different, people were always surprised to learn they were twins. Iskander was a head taller than Osman, and had a reddish tinge to his hair like his mother. Both boys had their father's black eyes, but luckily neither had inherited his big hawked nose or narrow mouth. Osman's face was round and merry, and he was popular with everyone because of his sunny nature. He also had the extraordinary ability to twist his body into strange shapes, or successfully fold himself into a basket that looked far too small, while grinning happily at his audience before he vanished from sight. Iskander was much shyer than his twin, and so reserved some people took him to be haughty.

Osman broke the silence. "Cheer up, Iskander. We've got Ana on our side. It won't happen if she has anything to do with it."

"She's got no power over Baba. He's under Amja Yacut's thumb."

Iskander whacked the rock again for good measure and his herding crook broke in two. They grinned ruefully at each other.

"You start to collect the animals, Osman. I'll go down and get Baba's crook."

Osman watched him bouncing down to their nomad encampment far below. He could see their mother, Fatima, and his sisters, Leila and Gul, busy outside their tent, and signs of activity up and down the lines of black goat-hair tents. Other nomads must have decided to leave early too, since Ali, the chieftain of the tribe, was leaving.

Osman turned to look up at the mountain above him. The faraway peak was always snow-covered and sometimes bit into bright blue sky, but today it wore a heavy ring of dark cloud like a turban. Circling beside the peak was an eagle, and Osman groaned. If it spotted he was on his own it would dive for a kid or a lamb. He willed it to stay high until his twin rejoined him.

Iskander ran into the family tent and stopped short. Ali was crouched on the floor, with his saddle lying upside down beside him revealing a secret hiding place in the pommel. He was stuffing gold coins into a leather pouch, and was clearly furious Iskander had seen him.

"What are you doing here? Get out!" he hissed as he threw some loose wool over the gold to hide it.

"Sorry, Baba, I need to borrow your crook, mine's broken—" gabbled Iskander.

"You've come to spy on me!"

"No, Baba, it was just the crook –" Fear almost made Iskander run, but he needed the crook or he'd be in worse trouble. He edged towards the centre pole but his father grabbed the crook first and hit him with it.

"You saw everything, you little sneak!" He lifted it again.

"I am not a sneak." Iskander stared his father out as he waited for the blow to fall, but Ali slowly lowered the crook before turning away as if ashamed.

"Sit down, sit down."

Iskander slowly sank onto his own kilim, trembling all over. There was a silence while his father calmed down a little before sitting too.

"Now you listen to me, Iskander. I intended to keep this hiding place secret, but now you've seen it. You must promise *never* to tell anyone about it. Not even Osman."

"I promise," whispered Iskander.

"Anyway, maybe it's for the best that one member of the family knows about it besides me." Ali quickly finished stowing the gold in the pouch before stuffing it back into the saddle with some loose wool and tying a flap over it. "See? I turn the saddle over and no one would ever guess anything was hidden there. I made it myself. Clever, isn't it?"

"Very clever, Baba."

"You're wondering where this gold came from, aren't you?"

Iskander nodded nervously. He'd never seen so many little gold coins.

"I found it in an old tomb."

But Iskander wondered why his father was looking so shifty – hunting for treasure was nothing unusual. Lots of men did it, dreaming of gold. He waited as Ali sucked his teeth – he was clearly debating how much to tell his son.

"I don't often find gold, and unfortunately Yacut got wind of it. He was angry because he'd found that tomb first and told me about it. He thought we should share the gold. I refused. Why should I? He hadn't found the gold, only the tomb. We had a blazing row, and then he got violent, so I pretended to give in and took him to where I said I'd hidden the gold. Of course it wasn't there, so I told him it must have been stolen."

"Did he believe you?"

Ali shrugged and sighed. "He doesn't believe anyone when gold is involved."

Iskander began to understand why Yacut was trying so hard to get the janissaries to take away one of Ali's sons: he wanted to punish his younger brother.

"I've never trusted Yacut, Iskander. It's a terrible thing to say, but it's true. He's a greedy man; he'd take my share as well as his. He's a gambler, so he's always short of money. He's cheated me a lot over the years." Ali's whisper was loaded with bitterness. "Just for once, I decided I'd hold out against him."

At that moment they heard footsteps.

"Hush, Ana's coming." Ali swiftly put the saddle in its usual place in front of the hearth where it did duty as his fireside seat.

"She doesn't know about any of this?" Iskander pointed at the saddle.

His father shook his head. "Nobody knows except you, and I'll beat the skin off your back if you tell anyone." Then he pushed the crook at Iskander and waved him out of the door as Fatima and the girls came in.

Iskander ran back up the mountain with his mind in turmoil. This secret frightened him. He thought his father was mad to hide the gold and risk Yacut's fury. And how was he going to keep it from his twin? He'd never held anything back from Osman in his life. Osman would guess something had happened the moment he looked at him. Iskander tried to banish the fear and worry from his face. But luckily all Osman's attention was on the eagle now hovering over the flock, and he began shouting and pointing the moment he saw Iskander.

"Go that way, Iskander, head it off!"

Osman had already starting running while Iskander took the opposite path, so that in no time the two boys were either side of the spread-out flock of sheep and goats. They started to herd the animals together, trying to leave none behind, but as usual the animals panicked and a lamb got separated from its mother. The eagle spotted it at once.

"Over there, Osman! Quick, quick—"

Osman ran as fast as he knew how, but he could see that the eagle had stopped hovering and was coming down like a stone. The lamb was standing still and bleating, its legs quivering as it watched Osman hurtling towards it. When Osman threw himself on the small furry body he was aware of a rush of air and a beating of wings, and claws gripped his shoulders for an agonizing second as the eagle landed before taking off again. He rolled over with the lamb in his arms, and rushed back to his brother.

Iskander stroked the animal to calm it. "We'd have got such a beating if we'd lost you, little lamb." He nuzzled its face.

"The eagle beat me instead." Though his shoulders

hurt, Osman laughed. "I won that time, but that eagle's hungry. He's still up there."

"He'll go on watching – he won't give up until the animals are in their pen. Come on, let's get them down there as quick as we can."

Eagles had already carried away two lambs and one kid, a disaster for the nomad family. Watching the herd closely, they made their way down to the spring near the encampment where their elder sister, Leila, was scrubbing the big copper pot that was the family's proudest possession. It was bigger than anyone else's in the tribe and it usually rode on the lead camel, perched high to show it off, as they travelled down to their winter pastures.

The boys stopped beside Leila as the animals took a drink, noticing that she looked very pleased with herself.

They didn't have to ask why, because immediately Leila announced proudly, "Ana and Baba have decided I'm going to show I'm ready to be married."

They gawped at their sister. Though she was fifteen, nearly three years older than they were, it had never occurred to them she'd be doing the trek tomorrow all dressed up in her best to indicate to other tribes she was open to offers of marriage.

"Well, that's not very gracious, boys. Aren't you going to congratulate me?"

"Didn't know we had to until some man was mad enough to offer to be your husband."

"Don't be so cheeky, Osman—"

There was a sudden rushing, flapping sound behind them, followed by bleating that quickly grew fainter. They swung round and there was the eagle flying triumphantly towards the mountain peak with a young lamb struggling in its talons. Osman started to run up the mountain screaming in rage.

"No, no, no, no! Drop it! Drop it now!"

But though it was still flying low because it found the load heavy, the eagle didn't falter. They heard the lamb bleating desperately until it was out of earshot. Once it was high enough the eagle suddenly dropped the lamb to kill it on the rocks below, immediately plunging after it and rising through the air with the little carcass, its limp legs swinging.

"Now we're in for it." Iskander had gone pale. "I can't take another of Baba's beatings."

Osman returned with tears in his eyes. "That eagle would never have got away with it if we hadn't been talking to you, Leila—"

"Don't worry, boys. I'll explain to Baba." Leila picked up the shining pot and balanced it on her head. "It really wasn't your fault. I'll tell him I distracted you." She started the walk back. "Relax."

"He won't believe you."

She turned and stared at her brothers, her expression fierce under the big copper pot. "Oh, yes, he will. Leave it to me."

As they collected the herd together again, sleet began to fall.

ON THE TREK

THE FAMILY was up before dawn, planning to be packed and on their way long before any janissaries might arrive in search of likely boys. As the sun came round the mountain, they emptied the tent and got ready to load their possessions onto the camels and donkeys.

"It always looks so sad when we've taken all the colour away." Leila stood inside the tent, now like a dark cave of black goat hair. She sparkled in the darkness in her bright clothes and a headscarf edged with shiny gold coins.

"Hurry up, everyone," shouted Ali. "Hand me the stuff. Men's area first."

Outside the tent was a vivid heap of saddlebags and kilims – brown, red, orange, black and yellow in geometric patterns. Fatima had woven the lot, tent included.

Everything was now loaded in a precise order, so that when they unloaded at the Ruined City the bags and kilims would go straight back to their proper places in the tent. Each person had a pair of saddlebags for storage and a kilim to sit or sleep on – Ali and the boys in the main part of the tent, and Fatima and the girls on the other side of the fire.

"Now for the centre pole."

Only Ali was allowed to touch the pole, which he'd carved himself with entwined figures of birds and leaves. On it hung his gun, bullet belts, knives and other possessions, and his sons' knives and herding sticks. With the pole gone, the tent started to droop and the smoke-hole sagged to the floor. Iskander and Osman were still inside when they heard Leila shout "Janissaries!" They froze as the tent collapsed down on them, almost stifling them with its smoky smell.

Leila pulled up a corner of the tent with a giggle, saying she was only teasing them. She stopped laughing when she saw their faces.

"That was not funny, Leila. Not funny at all."

"Sorry, sorry."

The boys scrambled out and went to help Ali, ignoring their sister. Soon everything was loaded on the pack animals, and they were ready to start. Only the beloved family donkey, Karakachan, still lame after a bad slip on a steep path, had no burden. He was black, with a white muzzle and white eye-patches that gave him a permanently surprised and innocent look. In fact he was full of naughty tricks, but always seemed to be saying, "Who, me?" Karakachan was the twins' special responsibility.

"Baba, Karakachan's not ready to make the trek. He'll fall behind." Osman had just bound up the donkey's injured fetlock with a long strip of cotton.

Ali frowned, looking up the mountain – now veiled by a curtain of cloud – and at the sun. "Time's passing, and the weather's changing. We must go. If Karakachan can't keep up, one of you boys will have to go slow with him. We've already lost four animals. We can't afford to lose our donkey."

"No, Baba." This was the only reference Ali made to yesterday's loss of the lamb, with a glare at Osman and a quick glance at Leila. He completely avoided Iskander's eyes. The episode of the hidden gold might never have happened.

"Look at me, Baba!" Leila took his attention away from her brothers by twirling round with a tinkle of the little gold coins sewn to her bright red headscarf. "Don't you think I'm fine enough to attract all the young men for miles around?"

Everyone seeing her would know at once she was ready for marriage. She'd knitted her white socks and covered them with red embroidery, she'd made and embroidered her black skirt, and she wore a fine new shawl tied around her shoulders. Iskander and Osman pretended to swoon with love at her feet, and with much teasing and laughter, the trek finally began.

Except to the newborn animals, it was a familiar journey. As they followed Ali in a long line off the shoulder of the mountain, everyone's heart lifted. The path ahead was empty of soldiers, and the autumn air was fresh but still quite warm – perfect weather for the trek.

Iskander, Osman and Karakachan brought up the rear of the long column snaking down towards the plains. Karakachan hated being last, and the boys had to stop him jockeying for a better position.

"You're still lame, Karakachan," said Osman. "Be a good boy and take it easy. We'll stay back with you."

Karakachan dropped his ears and swung his head, very fed-up. The trekkers settled into a stately pace, the bells on the harnesses tinkling to the rhythm. The lambs and kids quickly learned that they couldn't run off and play, and after the first hour or so Osman and Iskander had little to do except help Karakachan keep up, and keep an eye out for janissaries.

"They must be collecting boys from the other side of the mountain today."

"Let's hope they find enough and go back to Constantinople."

"Not if Amja Yacut has his way."

"Are you all right, Iskander?" Osman looked sharply at his twin. He'd been very edgy today.

"As well as I can be with the levy hanging over me."

By the end of the second day it was clear Karakachan was limping too badly to keep up. Osman ran forward and told Ali.

"We're going to stop soon and make camp for the night, then we'll decide what to do with Karakachan."

Luckily, there was always a gentle slackening of pace as evening approached, until the very end when the animals sensed the spring and sped up in a rush to drink. By the time Karakachan reached the water that evening he had it to himself – all the other animals were now feeding. Osman tried to clean the donkey's tender fetlock while he was busy drinking, but Karakachan objected and managed to kick him.

"Ow! Keep still, you idiot. I'm only trying to make you better." Karakachan gave him a look of disbelief and tried to kick him again. Then Gul came up to fondle

Karakachan's ears and Osman succeeded in putting salve on the wound and rebinding it. Everyone knew that Gul, despite being only seven and born completely deaf and mute, had a wonderful way with animals.

At that moment Ali came up and inspected Karakachan. "That donkey needs to rest, Osman. You'd better stay behind for a couple of days. I think I'll leave Gul with you to help with Karakachan."

"Can't Iskander stay with me?"

"I need him."

Osman felt panic rising at the thought of being without his twin. They'd never been separated before. "What'll I do if the janissaries turn up—"

"Say you're an only son. They won't take you then. I'll say the same about Iskander. It's better this way. Come and give me a hand with the goats, Iskander." Ali walked off with Iskander reluctantly following.

Fatima came up and put an arm round Osman while Gul tapped him on the arm and made her it'll-be-all-right face.

"Can't you persuade him to leave Iskander as well?"

Fatima shook her head as she gave him a quick hug. "He needs him, Osman. I'd stay, but your Baba can't manage without me, either. You'll be fine with Gul – she's grown into a good little helper."

Gul watched them with her bright, clever eyes, lip-reading. Fatima always said the shock of being born in a field surrounded by bleating sheep and goats had made her deaf and mute. But Gul had never felt left out – right from the beginning Leila and the twins had invented their own sign language so she could join in with everything.

Osman loved Gul dearly, but she wasn't Iskander.

The familiar trek routines made it especially hard for Iskander to be without his twin. He'd turn with a joke or comment and there was no Osman to pick it up. He was cold that night because he always slept back to back with Osman, and lay wondering miserably whether his twin was as cold as he was. Sleep took a long time coming. When Ali shook him awake he wandered dazed through the camp, feeling as if he was missing something as basic as a hand or a foot. All their lives, he and Osman had been so close they were like two halves of one person. Ali nagged at him several times to cheer up, concentrate, and put his mind to his work, but it wasn't easy to stop feeling half of him wasn't there.

When Iskander was alone at the spring that evening, Leila came up and whispered, "Baba's feeling bad at leaving the others behind. Ana told him we should have waited together for Karakachan to get better. He wouldn't listen and now he's worried."

"I'll never forgive him if anything happens to them."

"Nothing will happen."

"I've noticed bear prints around."

"Nothing will happen. There are other families following behind. They'll find company. Come on, Iskander. Supper's ready." She smiled. Iskander noticed her bright red scarf was no longer looking quite so fresh and neat, though the gold coins tinkled as merrily as ever.

As Osman watched Iskander and the rest of his family set off with the herd, he felt more alone than he'd ever felt in his life. The landscape was empty and silent. Osman and Gul sat staring blankly at each other while Karakachan lay with his back to them, clearly offended at being left behind. They were in a dell beside a small cave, with supplies of food including some of Fatima's delicious yogurt, a nanny goat to milk accompanied by its kid, and their blankets for the cold nights. The only sound was the cry of an eagle. Even the nanny goat looked a bit uneasy, although the kid ran about unconcerned.

Osman looked at the eagle high above, and tethered the kid to a tree. He made signs Gul must stay on guard while he went off to look for wild honey in some trees nearby. When he looked back, he saw Gul sitting cuddled into the donkey's side, her little face tense, her eyes flicking nervously around. Everyone knew the country-side was full of spirits, which stayed hidden until they thought you were alone. Then they came out and could steal you away. You had to sing and shout to keep them away, but Gul couldn't. He sang extra loud for both of them.

Most of the honey had already been taken, but Osman found the remains of an old comb in one of the trees and carefully dislodged it. He wondered if a bear had taken the rest of the comb, but pushed the thought from his mind; bears didn't usually come so low down the mountain. He ran back knowing that eating yogurt and honey and playing games together would cheer up both of them.

They collected a large pile of wood for the fire, branches and brush for the barricade, and found some mushrooms to cook later. So the day passed. Karaka-chan grazed or slept close to the cave-mouth, and by the end of the day took a little walk to show he was no longer limping. As darkness fell, the whole party squashed itself inside the cave and put the brushwood barricade in place. Osman kept the fire at the cave-mouth fed, and it was on one of his forays to pile more wood on the flames that he spotted the bear. It was standing sniffing at the edge of the dell beyond the barricade, and it was watching him.

Osman did not move, and kept his eyes fixed on the bear's. He knew he must stand and stare it out, and dreaded the possibility of Gul appearing – any quick movement would attract the bear's interest. But there was complete silence behind him, and the only sound came from the crackling of the fresh wood shooting up new flames. At last, after what felt like half the night, the bear seemed to sigh before moving off heavily towards the honey wood. Osman was now so frozen with cold and fear he couldn't move. Then he felt a warm hand take his and lead him back into the cave, and he realized Gul had been watching him as he watched the bear.

The animals were all fast asleep, and Gul made signs that he should sleep too while she kept the fire going. At first he refused, but found his eyes would not stay open. The last thing he saw was his little sister carefully feeding the fire.

He awoke in bright daylight feeling something was very wrong. He lay still, trying to fathom it. There was Gul, asleep now against the donkey. There was the nanny goat and her kid, their eyes wide open, waiting to be let out to graze. Nothing had broken through the barricade. He stood up and moved outside the cave into a fresh clean morning. The countryside around was alive with small animals and birds. No bears. No eagles. But something was still wrong, and the sensation was making him feel slightly sick. He put his hands over his eyes.

Then he realized what it was. He had never woken to a new day without his twin. He visualized Iskander so powerfully he half expected his brother to walk into the dell and join him, and wondered if Iskander too was suffering the same strange sense of loss and disruption.

The nanny goat and kid came out of the cave, and he pulled a hole in the barricade and led them to the spring. While they drank he washed, and then went back into the cave. Gul was still fast asleep and Karakachan had not moved either, though he was awake now. He rolled an eye at Osman as if to say, *Oh well, I'm in no hurry to get up. Let the little thing sleep.*

Ali pushed everyone on as fast as he could, eager to reach the Ruined City. The going became easier – they were now at the edge of the plains, the slopes of the rolling hills were gentle, and the roads full of other travellers. Finally, there they were, arriving at the collapsed walls surrounding the Ruined City, well before dark.

As they'd arrived before the rest of the tribe, they could have chosen any of the ruins for their winter quarters, but Ali usually put his tent up in a particular church, which must have once been near the city centre, long, long ago when this was a real city, full of handsome marble buildings and people and bustle. The ruined church had useful little chapels and annexes where the animals were safe for the night and where Fatima could make her famous cheeses and weave her baskets with reeds from a lake not far away.

When the main tent was up and the animals out in their winter pasture, Iskander persuaded Ali to let him take his mule and ride back to collect Osman and Gul. Ali saddled up the mule with an old broken saddle, avoiding Iskander's eye, and gave the mule a smack on its rump to get it moving. It was most unwilling to retrace its steps after just finishing the trek.

Iskander pushed the mule as hard as he could all day, hoping he'd join up with Osman before dark. A traveller told him he'd seen a boy and a girl with a donkey some way back. His heart lifted. He couldn't wait to see his twin again.

He nearly missed them. They'd fallen in with a group of merchants who'd taken pity on the little party, and invited them to share their overnight stop. When

Iskander saw a large group of men and camels and the signs of an extensive encampment settling in for the night, he decided he'd go on to the next spring, which he knew had a cave near it. It wasn't far away, less than an hour. Surely they'd be there. But when he reached the place, it was empty.

He stopped, gave the mule a good drink, and wondered what to do. The sky was red in the west. It would be dark soon. He had no desire to sleep alone in the cave, and decided to return to the merchants' encampment and park himself at the edge somewhere. He had food for himself and the mule, and his blanket. He only needed the safety given by the crowd of men and animals.

It was totally dark when he finally got back to the merchants' encampment. A big circle of men were watching some spectacle and urging on a performer. Having tethered the mule and tied on its nosebag, Iskander crept closer and saw, in the middle of the circle, an open storage box lying on a rug beside the fire. A boy was folding himself into the box, a space that seemed far too small for his body. He had his back to Iskander and, in a sinuous final movement, he disappeared from sight and pulled the lid shut on himself. Iskander hardly saw the boy, but he knew at once it had to be Osman. No one but Osman could shut himself in such a small box. It was one of his best party tricks. Iskander waited, his whole face alight with anticipation.

The merchants clapped and shouted their praise, but the boy wouldn't come out of the box until they fell silent again. Then, as if on a spring, out jumped Osman with a characteristic whoop that Iskander had heard so many times he thought of it as Osman's sign. He watched his twin laughing and bowing to roars of applause – Osman was clearly pleased he'd earned his supper and repaid the merchants for their kindness. As the applause died down, Iskander pursed his lips and whistled an owl's call. *Hoo hoo. Hoo hoo.*

Like the whoop, this whistle was special. Osman looked wildly round while whistling the same call. He was too near the fire to see the dark edges of the crowd clearly. Iskander whistled again and Osman pushed through the crowd towards his brother. A small figure struggled after him. Gul couldn't hear anything, but she knew from the joy on Osman's face that his twin must have arrived.

There they were, hugging each other and laughing. She went up close and kept tapping on Iskander's arm until he picked her up and swung her in the air.

HOT SPRINGS AND A CHEAT

"RIGHT, BOYS," said Ali one morning. "We need more reeds – and this time you're going to fetch them on your own from Lame Mustafa. If you leave tomorrow at dawn, you'll be at the Lake of Reeds well before dark."

"Do you think that's wise, Ali?" Fatima looked worried. "There might still be janissaries around."

"I'm sure it's safe – I was told in town they'd finished collecting boys and had gone back to the city. You ride the mule, Iskander – Osman goes on Karakachan. And no racing – I don't want my mule coming back lame." Iskander was relieved to see his father put a battered old saddle on the mule.

They didn't exactly race, but they went as fast as they dared because they wanted to swim in the hot springs on the way. This particular place was their favourite – they loved to jump from the white limestone platforms made naturally by the friction of the rushing water on the rock, and sit under the mini-waterfall that fell into the middle pool. The water pushed and pummelled them from pool to pool, down to the last one, which was so calm and shallow they could lie floating with their arms out. Neither boy could swim, but as they could always touch the bottom there was no danger.

"Bathing here is my most favourite thing," said Iskander. "What's yours?"

Osman was watching a buzzard riding the thermals in the sky high above them, and did not answer at first. When the buzzard glided from sight, he looked at his brother. "If I could fly, it would be flying. I'd love to be up there with those birds. It looks so easy."

"Being in water's a bit like flying."

"Mmm." Osman shut his eyes. They bobbed in silence until they heard a sudden wailing cry. They stood up and stared at each other.

"What was that?" whispered Iskander. "It didn't sound like a bird."

"It seemed to come from high up there, near the Cave of the Seven Sleepers. It must have been a bird."

They listened for another cry, but none came. They

could hear the mule and Karakachan chomping grass, but that was all. They lay back down in the water, unwilling to leave, but no longer as relaxed as they'd been.

Osman was staring up at the steam in the top pool, imagining he could see shapes in the cloudy swirls. "Lame Mustafa told me if you come to bathe here at night, you see spirits come up with the steam from deep in the mountain. They are huge and red when they come out, but soon they cool down and shrink into small djinns. At dawn they go back down to the furnaces below, leaving one or two on guard. Lame Mustafa says they're friendly djinns, they've been here for ever and ever, watching over this place—"

"I'm getting out." Iskander didn't like djinns, friendly or not. "I've had enough. Come on, Osman."

They got dressed quickly and started off down the road again.

"Who are the Seven Sleepers?" Iskander asked after a while. Osman always seemed to know these things.

"They were seven wise men from Ephesus who escaped from their enemies by going to sleep in a cave for a hundred years. When they woke up, they found their enemies were dead and the world had changed completely."

"And it happened up there?"

"Lame Mustafa says there are lots of caves with the same name, so it probably didn't."

"But it could have – this road goes to Ephesus after all. And we'd better hurry; look at the sun." Iskander increased the pace of the mule, and Karakachan struggled to keep up.

They'd stayed too long at the hot springs, and if they didn't reach the village beside the Lake of Reeds by sunset, they'd be in trouble. The sun was low enough to make a golden path across the lake when they arrived at Lame Mustafa's, and though he welcomed them warmly enough, he stared beyond them with a frown.

"Where's your father?"

"We've come alone, Lame Mustafa."

"Got lost, eh? How can we feed you if you come so late?"

They hung their heads and stayed silent. In the end there was plenty: an extra fish was grilled, and the pot of chickpeas was big enough to stretch to two hungry boys. Lame Mustafa had always treated them as if they were his own sons – he only had daughters – and tonight seemed no different. They went to sleep in the men's corner of the hut feeling content and unusually clean.

But next day, when they opened up their bundles containing the rugs and saddlebags woven by Fatima for use as barter, Lame Mustafa frowned and sighed and rolled his eyes.

"Boys, boys, this won't do. These days people pay money for their reeds."

"You always take our goods in return for the reeds. Baba gave us no money."

"Times have changed, boys, times have changed. There's no market for rugs and bags these days. Too many around." Lame Mustafa's eyes darted about, looking at the lake, at the walls, at anything but the boys. "I must be paid in cash."

The boys exchanged a quick glance before Osman took the lead. Looking stern, he started to fold up the rugs ready to lay them back on the animals. "I'm sorry you don't like our goods, Lame Mustafa. Everyone else does. Everyone wants Ana's rugs and bags."

"I didn't say it wasn't fine work—"

"Don't worry. We'll find someone willing to give us reeds in exchange for our goods. Thank you for the hospitality, Lame Mustafa. Come on, Iskander. Let's go further round the lake."

"Now, boys, wait a minute. Wait a minute. Don't misunderstand me."

"Baba'll be disappointed to hear we've traded with someone else rather than his old friend, but never mind."

Osman went outside with an armload. Iskander was about to follow with the rest, but Lame Mustafa grabbed his arm.

"Not so fast, boys, not so fast. Come back, Osman. I was just trying to explain how things are changing. Of course I will barter goods with my old friend's sons. Lay it all out properly, let me have a look."

So Osman and Iskander laid everything out again, both watching Lame Mustafa closely.

After a bit he sat back and sighed. "How big a load of reeds do you want?"

"The same as Baba always takes."

Lame Mustafa shook his head from side to side. "I'm sorry to tell you, boys, that reeds are scarce this year, and the price is high. I need more goods than these for a full load. You've still got more bags outside, and a rug. Bring them in."

"We have to do other shopping in the town for Ana."

Lame Mustafa shook a finger at them, his eyes hard. "Get this into your heads, boys. Reeds are more expensive. You pay more. Or you buy a smaller load."

In the end they set off home with a smaller load of reeds, not quite all the spices Fatima asked for, and half the usual amount of the red apples they always bought in the bazaar.

"What are we going to tell Baba?" Iskander was worried. He didn't want another beating.

"The truth. We were cheated. Lame Mustafa saw his chance and took it."

"But perhaps things have changed. Maybe he wasn't lying, Osman."

"And Karakachan can fly."

Iskander laughed despite himself. "Look at poor old Karakachan! I'm sure he'd love to fly right now. He does so hate carrying reeds."

Karakachan resembled a porcupine, with just his gloomy head sticking out of the load of reeds. He ignored their laughter and increased his pace, desperate to get home. They followed the donkey, Osman behind Iskander on the mule's back, hurrying across the wide Anatolian plain. Osman began to doze.

Sometime later, Iskander swerved the mule and donkey off the road so suddenly Osman nearly fell off, and urged the animals to gallop towards the shelter of a wood.

"What's up, Iskander?"

"Janissaries ahead! Can't see how many – they're kicking up too much dust."

"Quick, we don't want them to see us."

When they reached the wood, Osman jumped off to

keep a look-out, while Iskander took the animals deeper in, and tied them up firmly to a tree before creeping back to find his brother. A shepherd boy quietly joined them, curious to see what they were looking at. The wood was slightly above the road, giving the watchers a good view as the cavalcade went by. The white plumes on the soldiers' heads nodded in the sun. There were about a half a dozen janissaries at the front, and behind them marched a group of boys followed by a few more janissaries.

"It must be the levy, Iskander."

"I thought they'd finished collecting and gone."

"So did I. So did Baba or he wouldn't have sent us on our own."

Osman and Iskander fixed their eyes on the group of boys, their hearts cold. Wearing some sort of uniform, the boys walked with shoulders back and heads up, except for one redhead, who shambled along in the rear and seemed to be crying.

"Where are those boys going? Do you know?" the shepherd boy asked Osman in a whisper.

"To Constantinople, of course. Don't you know about the levy?" The shepherd boy shook his head. "The janissaries come round every so often to collect boys to serve the sultan. They only take boys from families with more than one son, and they train them up to be soldiers or servants or whatever the sultan needs." Osman shaded his eyes as he stared at the group. "They tell you it's an honour to be chosen, but I'd rather not be the sultan's slave."

"As if you've got a choice, anyway." Iskander snorted. "So don't go near them, shepherd boy."

"I'm an only son."

"You're lucky then. They won't take you." The shepherd boy smiled and slipped away to look for his flock. Osman and Iskander stayed hidden, watching.

"Poor devils. Bet they didn't want to go."

"They're tied to each other, Iskander."

"To stop them escaping, I imagine. But except for that one at the back, they don't look as if they want to escape. One of them's smiling and talking to a janissary."

"The red-haired boy's miserable."

The group was moving at a good pace towards the Lake of Reeds. A chilly sense of their narrow escape filled the boys.

"Thank goodness you spotted them, Iskander. And they've obviously finished looking for boys in this area."

"We hope." Iskander was always less optimistic than his twin.

Behind them the shepherd boy started calling and

whistling to his flock. Karakachan brayed in response, but the twins did not stir until the cavalcade was no more than a blur of dust in the far distance.

THE SULTAN'S AGENT

LEILA CAME RUNNING out of the Ruined City the moment she saw the twins riding up the road, smiling all over her face.

"What is it, Leila?" called Iskander.

When she got near enough to speak she suddenly went bright red and giggled instead of saying anything. Osman nudged his twin.

"I've guessed – she's found a husband!"

"Who told you?" She tried to sound indignant, but couldn't stop smiling.

"I can tell just by looking at you. Go on, Leila, tell us who's mad enough to think you're worth marrying."

"Don't be so cheeky – I'm an engaged woman now." She giggled again. "He's called Mehmet. He came with his father yesterday to ask Baba, and it's all arranged – I'm to be married in the spring, when we're back up in the mountains!" She spun around, making the coins on her scarf tinkle. "Oh, I'm so happy, boys!"

"So you like him?" Iskander was frowning.

"Yes."

"But how can you say that when you don't know him?"

"He has a kind face. Baba thinks it's a good marriage."

"And Ana?"

Leila stopped smiling. "Ana's pleased, but she doesn't like to think about me going away for ever. Come along, let's take her the reeds and cheer her up." She hurried away ahead of them, while they looked worriedly at each other.

"If Leila hasn't noticed how few reeds there are perhaps Ana and Baba won't either."

"Don't be silly, Osman. Of course they will. There'll be a row and then Baba will beat us."

Just as they feared, Fatima couldn't hide her disappointment over the reeds and the shopping, and Ali was furious about the poor deal they'd made with Lame Mustafa. All his pleasure in the successful agreement he'd come to over Leila's marriage was swallowed by his anger, directed as much at his old friend's behaviour as his sons. The twins stood in silence, knowing that anything they said would simply make him worse.

"Right. Where's my stick? You first this time, Osman. You're the clever one, and you let yourself be cheated." The boys both noticed he sounded half-hearted, and weren't surprised he lowered his stick without beating Osman when, at that moment, he spotted his brother, Yacut, walking towards them. Yacut said news had already reached him about the excellent new family alliance, and suggested the two of them go into town to celebrate.

The whole family was relieved to see Ali ride off. They could be sure he wouldn't be back until late, particularly since he hadn't been able to go to town at all while the mule was away fetching reeds.

Fatima made a delicious meal for the five of them to celebrate the engagement, and they passed the merriest three hours they'd had for months. Fatima was so relaxed and happy that the boys wondered whether she secretly found Ali as repressive as they did. Leila couldn't stop smiling all evening, and Gul did her version of the rabbit dance and made them all laugh. They went to bed late, but Ali still hadn't returned.

"I think it's sad our family is only really happy when Baba isn't around." Iskander and Osman lay snug in their blankets watching the fire as they whispered quietly so the women couldn't hear them from their beds on the other side of the fire.

"It's his fault, not ours."

"It must be our fault a bit too, Osman."

"It's you and me that make him cross. He never gets annoyed with the girls."

Iskander poked the embers from his bed, using a long stick. The fire would now last all night with luck.

"I sometimes think Baba hates me because he likes to rule the roost and he thinks I'm a threat now I'm almost as tall as he is."

But he got no answer. Osman had fallen asleep.

Iskander lay awake for some time, thinking about his father. He could do nothing to please him. His efforts always had the opposite effect. He'd just carved a perfect spoon for him out of a fine piece of cherry wood, but Ali had said it was too small to be of any use to him and immediately gave it to Gul.

Ali did not return that night, and since he'd never done this before without warning his family, Fatima was worried. All morning she wandered fretfully round their ruined church, never really settling to work, and still Ali didn't appear.

"Let me go to the town to find him, Ana. It won't take me long if I ride Karakachan."

"We'll wait until after midday, Iskander. Then you can go."

"He and Amja Yacut have probably met some old friends who've put them up."

"What friends? He never mentions any names. I wish your father wasn't so secretive."

She had tears in her eyes. Iskander took her rough hand in his and patted it. Women had such a hard life: they did most of the work, and were never told anything by their men. He was very glad he wasn't one.

Gul came running through the ruined streets at that moment, waving her arms. She made her hand gesture to signify "Baba" and pointed. Ali was walking between Yacut and a tall, sharp-eyed stranger dressed in smart city clothes. His uncle's expression of smug triumph sent Iskander's heart into his boots. Yacut had his arm round his brother's shoulders, almost as if he didn't want Ali to escape. His father looked so upset Iskander could see something was very wrong.

A trail of nomad boys followed them, and Iskander spotted Osman lurking nearby. He'd obviously been eavesdropping, and as he came close, Iskander could see from his eyes he had bad news.

"That's the sultan's agent. He's come for you." Osman hardly moved his lips as he whispered.

"But they've stopped collecting boys – we saw them marching away…" This new development was so unexpected that Iskander started to panic.

"Calm down and listen, Iskander. I'm going inside the tent to pack our stuff. When I give you a sign, you must escape somehow – I'll run on ahead and wait on the road." Osman slipped into the tent – no one was better than him at moving without being noticed. One moment he was there, the next he wasn't. Iskander was beginning to feel sick. Ali wouldn't meet his eyes and flapped his hands miserably at Fatima, who'd begun to pull at his arm.

Yacut grabbed Iskander. "Come here, Iskander. This gentleman would like to look at you." Iskander had never hated his uncle so much, and knew that if he'd had his knife on him, he'd have tried to use it. "This is the other twin, Efendi. Stand up straight, boy. See, Efendi, he's a good height and strong with it." Yacut smiled his oily smile that never reached his eyes.

"Indeed. Yes, a fine-looking boy. Turn round. He's got a good strong back. Excellent. Open your mouth, please. Wider. Sound teeth too." Iskander snapped his mouth shut again as if he wanted to bite the agent's fingers off. "I can also see he's got some spirit."

"I think he may be a bit too spirited for you," said Ali. He was living in a nightmare. He'd been tricked into this by his brother after a long night's drinking. He should have left the moment the sultan's agent joined them – Yacut had clearly made some underhand agreement with Hasan Efendi, probably for money. Now he'd sobered up he saw how stupid he'd been to agree to part with Iskander – all for the reflected glory of a son being a royal page. He tapped the agent's arm to catch his attention. "And very unreliable and obstinate – he's not suitable."

The agent brushed Ali's objections aside. "We'll train him out of his bad habits. Now, Iskander, please listen carefully. I am Hasan Efendi, the sultan's agent in this part of Anatolia. I am sure you have heard of the youth-levy. Yes?" He stared at Iskander, forcing him to reply.

"Yes, Efendi." Iskander's voice was barely audible.

"Then I'm sure you also know what an honour it is to be chosen, don't you?" Iskander stared wordlessly at him as if hypnotized. "Your uncle, whose son is doing so well in the palace, urged me to come and assess you when he heard we were a little short on numbers. I was unwilling, because winter is approaching and the rest of the boys have already been sent on their way to the collection point near Konya. But your Amja Yacut's very persuasive." He smiled at Iskander, a smile that made his heart freeze. "Now I've seen you, I admit I'm glad I came. You will do very well. But as I explained to your uncle, and of course to your father, now I've chosen you there's no time to waste. Normally boys have a few days to say goodbye to their family and friends, but in this case we must leave as soon as possible. In fact, I want you to pack at once and come with me now."

Iskander was so shocked he couldn't think, but at last managed to shut his eyes and cut off that gaze.

Fatima gave a loud, spine-chilling howl. "No, no, NO! Don't take my son – you can't take my son!" She rushed towards Hasan Efendi. Yacut tried to stop her but she pushed him away, spitting in his face.

"You take your hands off me, you poisonous toad of a man! I know this is all your doing!"

"Fatima, Fatima—" Ali tried to put his arm round her, but she struggled free and flung herself at the agent's feet.

"I beg you, Efendi, on my knees, I beg you! Don't take our lovely son away from us!" She tried to grab the agent's hand but he stepped back from her. She lost her balance and fell on her face on the earth, picking herself up at once. "Don't take him! Twins are not like ordinary brothers – don't separate them!" Again, she tried to grab his hand in her desperation.

Hasan Efendi was losing patience. "One son is enough, woman." He'd obviously said this many times before. "One son is enough. Control yourself. You must accept this. You have no choice."

"Stop him, Ali, stop him – we can't separate the twins – it will break their hearts—" She began screaming dementedly as she was pulled away by Ali, tears now pouring down her face. Leila started to wail and tear at her hair, and Gul was crying too, even though she couldn't really follow what was going on.

"GO AWAY! All you women, please go! This is no place for you—" Yacut started to shout in fury. He hated losing face in front of the agent. "Ali, take your women away!" Ali knew this nightmare had gone beyond his control, so he coaxed his wailing, weeping womenfolk out of earshot.

"Now, Efendi, let us get down to business." Yacut made signs towards the tent.

Iskander at last noticed out of the corner of his eye that Osman had popped his head out of the tent and was making frantic signs to keep them all talking for another minute, before ducking back out of sight.

Yacut again waved a hand towards the open tent flap.

"So, Hasan Efendi, shall we conclude our arrangements in the family tent?"

"Sir, could you tell me more about the training I will get? I am only a nomad boy. I know nothing about the big city." Iskander moved to block the doorway as he fixed his eyes earnestly on the agent's.

"You will learn to read and write, and if you show any particular abilities you will be trained to develop them. What are you good at?"

"I love riding, Efendi."

"Then you might find yourself serving one day in the sultan's mounted corps."

"The janissaries?"

"That's enough, Iskander—"

"Let the boy ask a few questions – he is facing a big change in his life and it's natural he should be curious."

"Where do the boys live, Efendi?"

"In the pages' school in the palace grounds. So you see you'll have the privilege of living near the all-powerful ruler himself." Hasan Efendi smiled, relieved the boy was being sensible. "Of course you will rarely see him."

"How long does it take to get to the big city?" Iskander was running out of questions, and Yacut interrupted angrily.

"That's enough, Iskander."

There was a flash of Osman's hand pointing north, and then it was gone.

"Thank you, Efendi." Iskander backed away from the agent with a bow, and slipped into the tent.

"Come in, Hasan Efendi." Ali had rejoined the men, and trying to make the best of a bad situation, elbowed his older brother aside as he ushered the agent towards the entrance. "Welcome to my humble home."

Iskander was through the back flap and out over the wall so fast he barely touched ground. The interior of the tent was dark, and at first Ali didn't realize that his sons were not sitting in their usual places. He sat on his saddle containing the hidden gold, realizing with a leaden heart that if he hadn't felt guilty about keeping it, he might have had the moral strength to resist what Yacut had done in revenge.

When all the arrangements had been made, Ali shouted for Iskander, sure his sons were outside with the other boys, still waiting to see what would happen next. Silence. He looked out of the front flap. No sign of the twins. He called again, then put his head out of the back flap. No one.

The twins had completely disappeared.

UP THE OAK TREE

A S SOON AS he was safely out of sight of the Ruined City, Osman hid in a ditch at the side of the road to wait for his twin. The minutes went by, each an agony. He was convinced that his father had somehow stopped Iskander from escaping. Then he heard the unmistakable sound of someone running in panic down the road, and leapt out of the ditch. The twins hugged each other as they never had before, despite hearing faint angry shouts as the search for them began.

"Come on, Iskander. Let's hide in the old oak tree and move on when it's dark. If we climb really high up, its leaves are so thick no one will see us from below. Baba won't expect us to hide so near the Ruined City. Quick, up we go. You first."

Osman knew he was far nimbler at climbing trees than his brother, and pushed Iskander up before handing him the two saddlebags full of their stuff. Then he followed so rapidly he overtook his twin through the branches. The tree forked quite high up, and there they made a perch, breaking off small branches to make a nest and camouflage themselves as much as possible from anyone looking up.

"I can hear them. They're coming this way."

Ali was on the mule, and Yacut and Hasan Efendi on horses. They rode by at speed, clearly thinking they'd soon establish whether the boys had used this route. They were back very soon: the boys saw two shepherds with a large flock of goats making their way towards the Ruined City with Yacut, Ali and Hasan Efendi riding beside them asking the shepherds questions. Their voices drifted up the oak tree. The shepherds were repeating they'd seen no one, no one at all, either on the road or running through the countryside nearby. They'd been there all day.

"Shepherds see everything, Efendi. I think it's certain those wretched boys went another way," raged Yacut. Osman winked at his twin.

"Then I suggest we follow the road going from the Ruined City towards the town where we met last night." To their surprise, the boys heard the agent laugh. "I must say, I admire your son's spirit, Ali. Just the sort of boy our sultan needs. I'm keen to catch him.

I'll make it worth your while in gold if we do."

However hard the boys strained, they couldn't hear the rest of the conversation and soon the men galloped away out of sight. But the shepherds stayed, resting under the oak tree while the goats pulled at anything edible within their reach.

"Do you think they're going to spend the night here?" Iskander asked in an almost silent whisper.

Osman rolled his eyes at the prospect. "We must keep very still now they know they'd be paid gold if they found us."

"The agent may bring janissaries to look for us."

"Let's hope they've all gone with those boys we saw."

"Janissaries are so scary."

Iskander had started to shiver in reaction to the tensions of the last hour, and Osman said nothing because there was nothing to say. Half an hour passed, the shepherds stayed put, and Osman began to fidget.

"I'm getting desperate to pee. Go, shepherds. Go."

But they didn't, and the twins began to be really afraid that they were going to stay all night long. Then luckily the wind got up and the tree became a mass of rustles and creaks, and both boys were able to relieve themselves into a convenient hole in the trunk without being heard, after which they felt a lot more comfortable. The shepherds had started to eat something while they chatted. At least they hadn't gone to sleep. The boys willed them to move on, hating them for the way they lolled comfortably and slowly ate and drank.

"Where'll we go when we can finally get down from this tree?" Iskander knew his brother would have thought of something.

"What about hiding in the Cave of the Seven Sleepers above the hot springs?"

"It's a long way to go on foot."

"Well, think of somewhere better then." Osman suddenly prodded his twin. "They're off!"

Having finished their food, the shepherds quickly got to their feet, whistled and called their flock together. Within minutes they were out of sight. The twins didn't dare leave the tree yet, but at least they could move about and jump up and down on the branches to get rid of their stiffness. It had been a long day but it was nearly over. The sun was now much lower in the sky, and it would be dark soon.

"Show me what you packed for us in the bags."

Osman pulled out extra clothing, their sheepskins, and their knives and bowls. He had also managed to steal some food – bread, lentils, goats' cheese, and onions. He'd thrown in the wooden spoons they were in the process of carving, as well as a few prepared but as yet uncarved blocks of cherry wood.

"Why did you bring these?"

"To carve, of course. We can barter spoons for food. Let's face it, Iskander, we might have to hide there for some time."

"I'm still not sure that's the best place."

"Of course it is. There's lots of water, there'll be good hunting around there, and —" Osman stopped. "What's bothering you?"

"Everyone knows the Cave of the Seven Sleepers is haunted, Osman. Even if those sleepers didn't die there, it's full of spirits."

"That's why we should hide there. Baba wouldn't think of looking for us there. He'd expect us to avoid it like everyone else."

Iskander stared at his twin, a smile slowly spreading on his face. "You're a clever devil. That agent got the wrong brother. Had he only known! If you worked for the sultan he'd make you grand vizir in a swish of Karakachan's tail."

"I wish we had Karakachan with us. I thought of it, but he'd bray and give us away."

"Someone's coming down the road." They stopped talking and watched.

"It's only Mad Miriam." The bent old nomad woman from their tribe came up under the tree and started to bang it with her stick as she sang something in a quavery voice. "Let's tease her." He held an acorn above her head.

"Don't, Iskander."

"Why not? She doesn't remember anything."

"Some days she makes more sense than others. It would be just our luck if today was one of them. 'Spirits up in the oak tree threw acorns at me.'" Osman imitated Mad Miriam's voice. "Horrible Amja Yacut would guess at once it was us."

No one came after Mad Miriam had sung her way down the road, and soon the sun disappeared behind the Taurus mountain range and it was dark enough to leave the tree. There was a good moon that night, and the twins walked fast, partly in fear of their uncle, and partly through sheer nerves. The vast empty plains and foothills stretched around them, clear in the moonlight and full of sudden strange screeches and rustles made by the nocturnal wildlife. When dawn came they were exhausted, and hid themselves under an overhang in a patch of rocks well back from the road, where they slept all day, having tied their precious bags to their hands and put them between their two bodies.

BANDIT COUNTRY

A TUG ON HIS HAND woke Iskander. Someone was pulling at his bag. He shot upright, banging his head on the rock above.

"Well, well, what have we here?"

Blocking the light was a large man. He had a gun slung against his body, and his torso was criss-crossed with ammunition belts. Two knives were stuck in his belt.

Iskander was wordless, stunned by the knock on the head and the man's sudden appearance. He turned to wake his brother. Osman's sleepy eyes flooded with horror when he saw the armed man and his breath came out in a hiss of fear. He squeezed Iskander's hand to tell him to keep quiet, and smiled at the man. "Who is it?" Osman yawned, staying curled up and looking as relaxed as he could. "Oh, hullo. Are you a bandit?

I've always wanted to meet a real bandit."

The man threw back his head and laughed.

"What are two fine young fellows like you doing out here all on your own?"

"Waiting for our father. We got bored and fell asleep." Osman sounded very convincing as he yawned again and sat up. Iskander nodded in agreement.

"So where's your father gone?" The man looked at their bags with greedy eyes.

"Baba forgot something and had to go back to the Ruined City. He should be here any minute."

"And where are you heading?"

Osman wanted to say "mind your own business", but Iskander spoke first. "We're going to buy more reeds, but Baba forgot his money." Iskander sounded even more gormless than Osman.

The man's fingers tapped a rhythm on the barrel of his gun. "So what's in your saddlebags, then?"

"Food." Osman pulled out the onions. "Food and clothes for the journey." He rootled around as if he was about to bring out more food, but he could see the bandit was losing interest, particularly when Iskander pulled out some old socks from his bag and dangled them in front of his face.

The bandit stepped away from the boys and whistled

sharply. An answering whistle came.

"So you're part of the nomad tribe that winters in the Ruined City?"

Iskander nodded hard. "We go there every year."

Then suddenly, with quick leaps and bounds up the rocks above, the man was gone. The twins flopped back in relief.

"That worked a treat! Well done, Osman. He and his band now think they're going to ambush Baba and they won't find him."

"All the same, let's leave now. The bandit might come back."

"Why should he? We're no use to him. We must keep to our plan and travel in darkness."

"I suppose you're right. Then let's eat something while we wait."

But neither of them moved. They were both becoming aware that being on their own in an adult world had great dangers. After a long silence, they sat up cautiously and started to eat some bread and onion. Then Iskander said, "How long do you think the sultan's agent will wait for us?"

"I was wondering that too."

"Maybe we should hide until it's real winter and the snow will mean no one will march to Constantinople until the spring. But the agent might come back again next year."

"Then we'll have to hide again."

There was another silence. Iskander was looking more and more depressed, and in the end he gave a big sigh and said, "I'm beginning to think we should go back now, Osman. We're never going to win in the end."

"Yes, we are. When they see how determined we are not to be separated, they'll leave us alone." Osman wasn't sure how true this was, but he knew that he had to give his brother hope, because once Iskander believed something deep in his heart, he was the one who could carry them both through. Osman was quick-witted, resourceful and tough, but Iskander had the steadfast staying power. "We're a good team, Iskander."

"Let's hope we're good enough to win."

They didn't make such fast progress the second night, mainly because they had to hide off the road while a group of bandits galloped by, their horses loaded with goods.

"I wonder if they're the same bandits as before." Osman tried to pick out the man who'd come to the cave, but there was too much dust and movement.

"They've certainly got what they wanted – they look

as if they got quite a haul. They'll be on their way to their hideout in the mountains. Wouldn't it be awful if they used the Cave of the Seven Sleepers?"

"Of course they won't. Bandits are just as superstitious as everyone else. And anyway, they always base themselves miles away from roads in really inaccessible places."

The twins didn't dare return to the road for at least an hour in case other bandits passed by, and when they finally arrived at the hot springs early the next morning they felt in no mood to bathe until they knew for sure the cave above was empty. They followed the path up, a path that only those skilled in tracking would find easily, encouraged by clear signs it hadn't been used recently. The sun was hot by the time they stopped for a rest, after a good hour's clamber. They'd seen no sign whatsoever of a cave.

"Maybe we've passed it."

"The path goes on up so I'm sure we haven't."

But the path didn't go much further. It soon led them out onto a natural platform with a breathtaking view of the valley below. Snaking along the valley floor was the road to the lakes, part of the ancient route known as the King's Road because it took rulers from the Mediterranean coast right across Anatolia to Baghdad. Or so they'd been told. The twins stared down in silence, overcome with surprise at the wide view from their vantage point.

The path clearly ended at this ledge, and there was still no sign of a cave. The twins were surrounded only by rock face. Their hearts sank.

"Maybe there's no Cave of the Seven Sleepers. Maybe it's just one of Lame Mustafa's stories." Iskander looked as if he was about to cry from exhaustion. They had been walking and then climbing for hours and now it was noon. "I've had it, Osman. Let's find some shade and rest for a bit. At least this is a wonderful position. No one could creep up and surprise us here without us seeing them first."

Behind them there was a low thicket of growth round a large old fig tree. The fig had dropped its leaves so offered no shade, but Osman, without knowing quite why, pushed behind it where it was closest to the rock face. Then he stopped dead.

"Iskander, come here."

"Why?" Iskander had seen a more promising shady spot round the corner.

"I think I've found the entrance to the Cave of the Seven Sleepers." Osman stared at the narrow gap ahead of him, concealed from the ledge by the thicket. He realized he didn't want to go in on his own, and felt almost as if someone was restraining him.

Iskander came up beside him. "What's the matter?"

"It's as if there's a hand on my shoulder—"

His twin gave him a push. "It's mine. In we go."

The entrance was deceptive. At first it was so low they had to crouch for a few feet, but then it began to open out into a larger space that in turn led to the cave. They crept along in stages, waiting for their eyes to grow accustomed to the darkness. Then they saw it wasn't as dark as they expected because some light came down through a natural chimney. The cave was dry and smelt of old fires.

Normally the thrill of finding the cave would have kept them awake and exploring, but both boys began to feel leaden with exhaustion. They saw some flat surfaces and put their saddlebags down as pillows. Sleep. They were so desperate to sleep they lay down at once.

Just before oblivion overcame him, Osman tried to say something, but the words came out slurred and he couldn't finish the sentence. "Maybe everyone falls asleep here because the spirits ... make ... you ... sleep..."

Iskander began to answer, "For ... a ... hundred ... years..."

Then both boys fell soundly asleep. Not even the arrival of a troop of bandits would have woken them.

THE CAVE OF THE
SEVEN SLEEPERS

SMAN WOKE FIRST, and lay for a few moments wondering where he was. Then he remembered, and prodded his twin awake when he saw bright daylight pouring through the cave's chimney. They took their food out on the ledge and ate heartily, too hungry to worry about it running out. They finished their supply of water, and explored round the cave hoping to find a spring. But they drew a blank, so they decided to make the trek down to fill their water-skins and have a bathe, if it was safe.

"There's no one on the road. You can see for miles each way."

"It shouldn't take as long to go down as it did to come up."

It took longer, because the shale was slippery and they had to go carefully. This was disappointing: a good two-hour round trip for water was bad news. But their bathe in the hot springs made them forget the hard climb and the twins splashed for hours in every basin until they had to leave in a hurry – travellers were arriving.

They hid themselves in the wood beyond the springs, and sat so still a fat partridge foraging in the undergrowth wandered up too close. Iskander managed to grab it and wring its neck before it could give more than a couple of protesting squawks. They also noticed lots of familiar herbs growing all round them and, as soon as the travellers had left, gathered a couple of handfuls and hurried back up to the cave.

The twins collected a store of dry wood and stacked it in a corner of the cave. They built a fire under the natural chimney, where it was clear from the blackened rock others had done the same before them. When the fire was hot enough to cook their partridge, they found they had a problem. The women of the tribe always did the plucking and cleaning of game birds, and they'd never been taught how to do it. It took a surprisingly long time to pull the feathers off and the guts out, and they were both hungry and cross by the time they had the poor mangled carcass ready for the fire.

"What a mess – we should have done it outside. It looks as though we've had a pillow fight and the pillow burst!" They decided they'd clear it up another day, and went out on the ledge while the partridge cooked.

They sat there staring out at a landscape transformed by the golden glow of the dropping sun. It was beautiful, yet somehow it made them feel sad.

"But we'll be back home before winter sets in, won't we?" Osman spoke in a whisper. He couldn't shake off the feeling they were being watched, though it was clear from all the telltale signs that no one had been near the cave for months.

Iskander wasn't listening. He was watching a long cavalcade of camels, horses, mules, donkeys and men far below, travelling west. Camel trains this long had usually come along the silk road from China, bringing fabrics, porcelain and spices over so many deserts and mountain ranges his mind swam trying to imagine them. The goods would end up in the markets of Constantinople, and the pick of them would go to the sultan's palace. If he'd gone away with the sultan's agent, he'd now be far ahead on this same road.

His brother suddenly stood up and walked to the edge of the ledge, then clambered off it to the left, opposite the original approach. It looked steep and dangerous, but the rocks surprised him by opening up, and through the gap between them was an old path leading downhill.

"This looks like another way down to the springs, Iskander. You can't see it from up there. But it's getting dark. We'll explore it tomorrow. Let's go and have a look at the partridge. It's beginning to smell good."

Now followed a few days of magically easy living for the twins. The new path was indeed a short cut, and not only did it halve the time needed to get to the hot springs, but off it they discovered a little stream with the most delicious-tasting water. Clear, cold, pure – the best the twins had ever drunk. Game was easy to catch, and one morning a young nanny goat with full udders wandered onto the ledge. Osman milked it into his wooden bowl, and the milk tasted like nectar. The next day they found real nectar – a honeycomb, untouched by man or bear.

That same day, Osman made a discovery in the cave. In a dark corner beyond the rock he slept on, something round and whitish gleamed in the dust. It looked like a stone and he ignored it until it occurred to him there hadn't been a stone like that there before. He went to pick it up, and it fitted snugly into his hand.

What an odd little object. He stared at the flattish disc carved with neat zigzag patterns and little circles – like beads – dotted all over it, back and front. Out of the top of the disc peered two small heads. They had beaks and round eager eyes, and long necks that stuck out from the disc as if they were two chicks popping out of an egg. They looked very eager and happy, and Osman smiled at them, half expecting them to smile back.

At that moment Iskander came into the cave.

"Look at this." Osman held it up.

"What is it?"

"I've no idea. I found it in the dust over there. It's really odd we never noticed it before."

"Let me see it."

Osman didn't want to give it up, and almost refused. When Iskander took it, he felt like he'd let go of a precious personal possession.

"It's surprisingly heavy."

"I didn't find it heavy."

"The birds look so – so sweet and so sad."

"I thought they looked happy. But maybe they're not birds…"

"What else could they be?"

"Spirits? Souls of unborn babies?"

The twins stared at each other.

"There's something creepy about this cave, Iskander. I keep feeling that someone is here with me, leading me to things. Like to find the path, and then to look in the corner, and here's this."

"I know just what you mean. A nanny goat suddenly appears – it's really odd. No one's come looking for that goat, as any shepherd would if they lost such a fine one."

"And now there's this talisman. It wasn't there before. I know it wasn't." Osman put his hand out for it, but Iskander didn't pass it over at once.

"Maybe someone brought it here while we were bathing."

"Who? Surely we'd have seen them."

"I don't know." Iskander at last handed the talisman back with a little sigh. "I hate parting with it."

"Me too."

The little heads gazed at Osman as if they were trying to tell him something. He put the talisman down on his saddlebag, and found that wherever he and Iskander were in the cave, those beady eyes watched them. Uneasy, the twins went out on the ledge. Everything looked the same. As usual, the nanny goat was cropping anything it could reach. They hadn't tethered it – they had no rope – but remarkably the goat hadn't strayed. Iskander milked it and they drank from his bowl.

"Since we're both worried about this place, Osman, shall we move on?"

"Where else can we go? We'd never find another place as good as this. What do you think?"

"I don't want to go. You decide – you're the one this spirit is after, not me. You found the cave, the new path and the little spring. And now the talisman."

"You found the nanny goat."

"It found me more like. It seemed to arrive by magic."

Osman suddenly ran back into the cave. The talisman was still there, but now it just looked like an egg-shaped carving with two funny little heads sticking out. He ran out again.

"We're just imagining things. There's nothing to worry about. Come on." Osman pushed his brother towards the path. "Let's go for a swim. We can easily get back before dark if we hurry."

The twins bounced down the secret path, suddenly full of energy. The cool evening air caused the steam from the hot springs to make a thick cloud like a fog, screening off the first pool. They threw off their clothes and dived in. They didn't bother to check if anyone else was there because they would have heard them. At this time of day no one visited the springs unless they were camping overnight – it was too far to get back to any of the nearest villages by nightfall.

So they didn't notice Lame Mustafa arrive. He had a

habit of coming in the late afternoon to bathe there. This evening his leg was more painful than usual, and long ago a wise woman had told him that the waters were especially beneficial at night. He enjoyed having the springs to himself, to float for an hour or two until it was quite dark while the steam made strange twisting shapes like ghosts above his head. He wasn't frightened of them as some were, and he and his horse even liked riding back at night to the Lake of Reeds.

As he approached the hot springs and heard all the noise, Lame Mustafa wondered for a moment whether the spirits of the underworld were angry, but soon realized it was caused by boys playing around. He was about to tell them to shut up when he suddenly checked himself. Lots of boys swam here, but never as late as this. Where did these boys come from?

He'd heard Ali the nomad was looking for his sons and that the sultan's agent was offering a reward for anyone who found Iskander. Lame Mustafa knew there were plenty of caves round here to hide in, the best known being the Cave of the Seven Sleepers. He also knew Osman and Iskander had always loved swimming in the hot springs; but the steam was so thick he couldn't be sure it was them. There seemed to be only two boys in the water despite all the noise they were making.

Lame Mustafa waited. He needed to be sure. The mist grew thicker as the evening got colder and darkness began to fall.

Then he heard one of them shout, "Osman, throw it here!" and a few minutes later the other said, "Hurry up, Iskander, we must go back to the cave – look how dark it's got."

Lame Mustafa crept back to his horse and quietly led it back to the road.

"We're going to the Ruined City as quickly as we can," he whispered as they rode off. "Ali will be very pleased to see us. He might even forgive me for cheating him."

THE TALISMAN

OSMAN AND ISKANDER found scrambling up from the hot springs in darkness very difficult. The path was full of hazards that hadn't been there in the daylight. They got lost a few times and slipped at unexpected places. When they reached the ledge outside the cave, there was no sign of the nanny goat.

"Maybe her owner came and got her at last."

They hurried into the cave and all seemed much as they'd left it. The talisman glowed almost luminously in the semi-darkness like a small moon, and the little bird heads appeared, as usual, to be watching them. Osman picked the talisman up and stroked it.

"I'm beginning to love this thing. I'm sure it's a good omen, Iskander. It means that we won't be separated. Like these two, we'll always stay together."

"Don't talk like that." Iskander snatched the talisman

from him and tossed it back on the saddlebag. "It scares me. And the spirits in this cave won't like it."

"I'm going to light a fire." Osman turned his back on his brother, hurt. Sometimes he didn't understand Iskander. "I'm cold." He went off to the corner where they kept the dry wood, and stopped dead. "Someone's taken our wood."

"That explains the nanny goat disappearing. Maybe someone was looking for firewood, or his goat, and took both."

"Maybe."

"I'm hungry, and we forgot to collect any herbs or berries. We haven't done very well tonight."

Iskander went to the bag to bring out the little packet of yufka, the dry flatbread for which he'd bartered a wooden spoon. "I think it's time to eat some of this. Let's soak a piece in water with salt and make porridge. We've still got some salt, haven't we?"

"Not much." Osman shook a small leather pouch, not seeing he had it upside down, and the few grains of salt inside it fell into the dust and feathers on the cave floor. There was a long silence. Everything was going wrong this evening.

"Let's just eat the yufka dry, Osman. And then go to bed."

"I want to try and make a fire first. I'm cold. I'll go out and find wood. There's still plenty not far away."

"Don't go, Osman. Just accept it – our luck's out tonight."

They stared at each other, and then sat down and quickly ate their small amount of food. Then they lay back to back with their camel-hair blankets over their bodies. It was usually the best way to keep warm, but the cave seemed chilly and dank that night.

"I'm still cold, and I'm still hungry."

"Me too." Iskander sighed. "Wouldn't it be wonderful if we could shut our eyes and then open them to find we were at home with Ana's lamb stew bubbling on the fire and—"

"Don't! I can almost smell it."

"We'd dunk our bread in the gravy—"

"Don't, don't! I can't bear thinking about it I'm so hungry. Tomorrow we'll catch a couple of fat partridges and have a feast."

There was a silence. Normally they would have fallen asleep, but tonight sleep was slow coming, and each could sense the other's brain was still alert.

"Are you still thinking about home, Osman?"

"Yes."

"So am I. I'm wondering how things are without us.

For Ana and Leila and Gul, I mean."

"They'll have a lot of extra work. Baba won't be much help because he'll be busy searching for us. It'll be hard for them."

"It makes me feel mean, Osman. Really mean."

"They understand why we ran away. They'll be pleased we escaped. They'll guess we'll go back when it's safe."

"I wish we could send Ana and the girls a message without Baba knowing."

"It's not worth the risk. We must just stick this out a bit longer. We'll go home with the first snow."

Very soon they were both asleep, and as usual in the Cave of the Seven Sleepers, their sleep was deep and sound, so sound that they'd never wake until the early morning sun streamed down the chimney.

So it was unusual for Osman to wake up suddenly as if a noise had disturbed him. He lay very still with his eyes shut and his heart beating fast, but heard nothing. He slowly opened his eyes and caught sight of a ghostly figure in the half-light of early dawn. A man like no man he had ever seen, with wild hair in a strange style, and a skirt of leather round his waist. His face was old and his beard grey and bushy. He was hovering near the entrance of the cave, but as Osman watched, he disappeared; just faded away without sound or movement. Osman shut his eyes and opened them again. Nothing. No one.

When he finally raised enough courage to crawl out of his cocoon of blanket to investigate, he found the talisman lying in two pieces, broken between the bird heads. The division was so neat it looked like a cut. He stared at it in horror. He felt as if someone had broken the thing he most loved. He found he couldn't move to pick the pieces up, and shut his eyes again.

A strange, sweet smell began to fill the cave, of musk, apples, honey. Osman was sure the figure was back, but was afraid if he opened his eyes, he'd vanish again. He sensed someone moving across the cave towards him.

"Who are you? Why are you here?"

I am always here. I have been here since the mountains rose from the sea. I live in high places, I cover the earth like a mist, I am always here.

"You're one of the old gods of the mountains, aren't you?"

When men first came, I was here. I guided them in the paths of wisdom. I am always here...

The voice was fading and, afraid that he would vanish again, Osman tried asking another question.

"Why did you break the talisman? What does it mean?"

Do not look for answers, my son. Be patient. Do your best and the answer will find you ... find you ... find you... The echo was a dying whisper.

Osman finally opened his eyes and was aware that a wavering, flickering light had faded into the rock above him. The scent had also gone, and now his nostrils were filled with the usual earthy cave-smell. It was a dream, just a dream.

He stood up with a piece of the talisman in each hand. The little heads looked sad and lonely separated. Osman half expected their eyes to swivel sideways to search for each other.

Search for each other... It was only now he realized that Iskander was not in the cave at all.

LAME MUSTAFA'S BETRAYAL

ISKANDER WAS STANDING silhouetted against the rising sun, his body tense.

"What's the matter?"

"I can hear something. Someone's coming up the path."

"Perhaps it's the nanny goat."

"It doesn't sound like a goat. They rustle and crash about, they're only thinking of eating. This sound is cautious. Come and listen, Osman, see what you think."

Osman stood beside his twin. There was absolute silence apart from the early morning birdsong, and then he heard a twig crack. Just one crack, but it was enough. Only a human would make that sharp sound and then freeze.

"You're right. We should pack up and get out. They're quite close."

"You pack. I'll keep watch."

His hands shaking, Osman threw everything into their saddlebags, wrapping both sad little talisman pieces together inside his blanket. Within minutes, they were out on the ledge.

"Let's go down the secret path. The noise is from the main one."

Iskander led the way, but when they rounded the first outcrop of rock that hid the path, all they saw was thick undergrowth and confusing boulders.

They blundered about in desperation, but the path was no longer there. There was no way down that part of the mountain. After five minutes of fruitless searching they stared fearfully at each other.

"It was here last night."

"It wasn't the same, it was much more difficult."

"But it was here. What's going on, Osman? We've been bewitched."

"We'll have to go back to the ledge and try to find some other way down. Come on."

Osman remembered the strange visitor. Maybe he wasn't a dream, maybe he'd appeared as a ghostly warning that things were about to go wrong, but now was not the moment to tell Iskander about him. They started to climb back up to the ledge.

As the boys appeared on one side, Lame Mustafa and Yacut ran in from the other. Ali was just behind them looking apprehensive.

"Got you, you little devils! Got you at last!" shouted Yacut, his eyes bulging with triumph.

Iskander darted across the ledge and leapt on his uncle, knocking him flat, face down on the ground. The attack was so sudden it took the other men by surprise, but before Iskander could jump up again and escape, the other two had fallen on him. They pulled him up and pinioned his arms behind his back. Osman remained frozen in horror at the side of the ledge. Yacut got to his feet, dusting himself off and looking furious as he rubbed his big nose. Then he hit Iskander hard on the face.

"You break my nose and I'll break yours!" He swung his arm back again but Ali stood in front of Iskander.

"Yacut, stop it. Violence doesn't solve anything —"

"Tell that to your son then!" Yacut shook his fist, aiming a kick at Iskander's shins instead.

"There was no need to attack your uncle, Iskander." Ali glared at Iskander, but with an odd look in his eyes that was almost pride. Then he undid the pieces of rope wound round his waist and started to tie up Iskander while Yacut tied up Osman, twisting the rope extra tight on his wrists. Osman stopped himself from crying out as the rope bit.

Soon both boys were standing with their arms pinned behind their backs, Osman's rope held by Yacut, Iskander's by Ali. The boys hadn't said a word. Lame Mustafa was sent into the cave to check it over, and came out at once.

"They've packed everything into those bags, Ali. We can leave."

"You've led us a fine dance, the pair of you. But it's a good hiding place, I do admit. You go first, Lame Mustafa." Ali led Iskander gently towards the path, unlike Yacut, who gave Osman a brutal tug which nearly pulled him over.

Iskander's face was expressionless as he passed Osman. He didn't need to say anything, but there was a flicker in his eyes that showed he still hoped he was too late for the levy. Osman's heart went cold; he was afraid from Yacut's gloating expression that some arrangement had been made with the sultan's agent, and he was going to lose his twin. With feet like lead, he was dragged after Iskander.

Negotiating the path without the use of their hands was difficult, and both boys fell painfully several times. They gathered from the men's chatter on the way down that it was Lame Mustafa who had betrayed them after he'd heard them bathing late the evening before. They also gathered that their escape and ability to evade capture for so long had simply made Hasan Efendi even more eager to enslave Iskander for his sultan.

Hateful Lame Mustafa – neither twin could bear to look at him. He was almost as bad as their horrible uncle. When they reached the bottom of the path, they walked past the hot springs without a second glance and ignored Lame Mustafa when he bid them all goodbye and rode off to the Lake of Reeds, his job done and the reward in his pocket.

Ali then turned round to his sons, took a deep breath and put on the blustery tone they knew only too well. It meant he was going to do whatever had been decided on, even though his heart wasn't in it. His pride would never allow him to seem weak in front of his brother.

"Right, Iskander. I am taking you straight to Hasan Efendi."

"I'm taking him. I don't trust you."

"No, Yacut. You've done enough." The two brothers glared at each other.

"You'll give in at the last minute."

"I will not. I promised Iskander to Hasan Efendi and I don't break my promises. But I'm going to need your horse – my mule can't carry both of us."

"I refuse. Give me your mule and let me take Iskander."

"NO!" Something snapped in Ali, and he ran towards his brother's horse. Yacut dashed after him, and they started to fight. The twins watched in horror – their uncle was much stronger than Ali, and was now in one of his blind rages, punching Ali with sickening thuds. Suddenly their father pulled out a knife.

"Yacut, I've had enough. Iskander is my son. Either I take him or the deal's off."

Yacut saw that for once Ali was not going to give in. He wanted to scream with rage. He'd set up this whole business, it had already caused him a great deal of trouble and he'd lose face if they let down the agent. He tried to stare Ali down. The knife stayed ready to strike.

The boys looked quickly at each other with the sudden hope that their uncle would refuse to give up his horse, but not wanting their father to be hurt which he surely would be if the fight went on.

"You'll ruin his mouth, you only ride mules and donkeys."

"I ride as well as you do and you know it."

"Oh, take my horse then!" Yacut shouted. Ali lowered his knife. "But what am I supposed to do? Walk back unprepared? It's a long way!"

"What's in those saddlebags, boys? Water and food, I'm sure."

"Baba, please untie my hands and I'll sort out the stuff. I know what's in the bags. Please."

"No, Osman. I'll do it."

"It's quicker if I do it. Everything's in a muddle, I packed in such a rush. Iskander will need his own things and they're all mixed up with mine. Please, Baba." Osman stared in desperation at his father. He could only think of the broken talisman, convinced that he and Iskander must have half each when they were parted. It meant one day they'd be together again and be able to join the broken pieces. If Iskander didn't have his piece – Osman gulped in panic.

Suddenly Ali untied his hands without meeting his eyes. "Do it quickly then. Let's give the animals a drink, Yacut."

Ali tied Iskander to a tree and led an unwilling Yacut towards the nearby spring. Osman got the distinct impression his father was giving the twins a chance to have a final talk together. He started to sort the bags out close to Iskander, and showed him the broken talisman.

"I found it like this when you'd gone outside this morning. Like it had been cut in half by somebody so that we could have a bit each." Iskander's eyes had gone blank, as if his brain were dead. "Listen to me, Iskander. It's important. You've got to keep your half safe. One day we'll join them up. Look. I've put it inside one of your socks." Osman stared at the pale empty face of his twin. "Iskander, say something."

"What's there to say? We'll never meet again."

"You mustn't say that – of course we'll meet again. I promise I'll come and find you and get you out. You've got to believe me!"

"I can't. It's impossible. Look how far it is."

Iskander's eyes turned to the distant line of mountains leading to plains and more mountains, all part of the unimaginable distance that lay between them and Constantinople.

"Don't ask me how. I'll do it somehow."

"It's no good, Osman. Once I'm in that palace I'll be there for the rest of my life."

"No, no, you mustn't talk like that. And you must keep that half of talisman safe."

"You don't need to go on and on about the talisman. I'll take it, and I won't lose it."

"I'll find you, Iskander, I promise – however long it takes. And I'll help you escape."

"I'm afraid, Osman."

"I'm afraid too."

"I don't know how I'll manage without you. You're the strong one."

"You're much stronger—"

"No, I'm not. I may have the muscles, but you're strong in spirit. You keep me going..." Iskander had tears in his eyes, as Ali and Yacut led the animals back from the spring.

"Have you finished sorting the stuff, Osman?"

Osman held up Iskander's bag. "There. All done."

"Now I'm going to I tie you up again. I don't trust you – you might run away from Yacut."

"Tie me if you like, Baba, but I won't run away again, I promise."

"It's your uncle's decision."

"Tie him. I can always untie him later on." Yacut glared at Osman. "Or not."

"You'll have to untie my hands, Baba." Iskander's voice was suddenly much firmer, and his tears had stopped. "You know it's impossible to ride that mule with no hands. He'll throw me off."

"You'll escape again."

"I promise I won't."

Ali glared suspiciously at his son. The boy looked so downcast and beaten that he decided to risk it and untied his wrists. Iskander swung himself lightly up onto the mule's saddle, watched with trepidation by Ali and Yacut. Neither boy nor mule moved. Ali quickly mounted Yacut's horse and turned it ready to set off.

Iskander turned and stared numbly at his twin. The dead look had returned to his eyes. Osman tried to say something but couldn't. With tears pouring down his cheeks he watched Iskander wheel the mule to follow Ali. As horse and mule broke into a canter and disappeared from sight round a bend, Yacut gave a vicious tug on Osman's rope and led him in silence along the dusty, empty road towards the Ruined City.

ISKANDER'S JOURNEY

WHEN ISKANDER LOOKED UP from his corner in the hot, crowded room, his father had left. One minute he was there talking to Hasan Efendi, and then he wasn't. Iskander jumped to his feet and looked round in panic before starting to push through the crowd to the door. Hasan Efendi ordered him to sit down again. Iskander froze as he met the agent's impassive stare. That was when Iskander realized he'd believed in his heart of hearts that despite the fact his father had said goodbye, somehow he'd be able to get Hasan Efendi to release him and take him back to the Ruined City. Ali had clearly been very upset at parting from him, and had hovered around for ages until he was taken aside by Hasan Efendi. Now he was gone, and all hope was gone too.

Slowly, his heart in ashes, Iskander sank back onto

the floor, put his arms round his knees and his head on them, and refused to move, eat, or speak. Faint from lack of food after a long day that had begun at dawn and ended in the most stressful ride of his life, he was past thinking or feeling, and remained folded up in the position he and Osman used to call the rolled-up caterpillar until he finally fell asleep.

Some hours later a firm hand squeezed his shoulder.

"Wake up. It's time to leave, Iskander. But please have some breakfast first." Hasan Efendi had obviously come straight from the hamam, he looked and smelt so clean and fresh. He handed Iskander a bowl of ayran – thin yogurt flavoured with mint – and a piece of flat bread with some hard goat's cheese. As Iskander lifted his hands to take the food he saw that someone had locked a metal clasp on his wrist while he'd been asleep. A longish chain now joined him to a boy nearby, a dark-skinned, plump boy with bright nervous eyes.

"This is Yusuf. He will be your travelling partner on the journey to the city. Now we must hurry and join the other group of boys. You're lucky – we're so short of time you'll be riding the first leg to Konya. Since you're the good rider, Yusuf will be seated behind you. From Konya onwards you'll be walking. I see you've got good shoes, Iskander. I'm going to have to do something about Yusuf's."

As Iskander rode away from the little town heading westwards, he felt as if he was now dead inside, his whole being as cold as the earth under the flying hooves of the mule. He did not look back.

It was nearly dark when they saw the high walls and turrets of the karavansarai outside Konya. As soon as they rode through the great gate into the vast inner courtyard, Hasan Efendi handed the two boys over to a large janissary called Selim, who, though he looked fearsome, had kindly eyes. Selim fetched food for them, stood nearby while they went to the toilets at the back of the building, and then took them to a room filled with sleeping boys. He prodded a couple to make them move over, and left Iskander and Yusuf to bed down for the night, locking the door behind him.

"We've been waiting for you," came a whisper in the total darkness. "What are your names?"

"Yusuf."

But Iskander didn't speak.

"I'm Ismail. I'm the youngest. I'm from Adana – where are you from?"

"Belt up, Ismail. Some of us need to sleep even if you

don't." This was said in a tough, gruff voice and Iskander imagined him to be big and overbearing. The morning light proved him right: the speaker was Ibrahim, a butcher's son, taller even than Iskander and much heavier. He eyed Iskander as they packed up before hurrying downstairs to breakfast and the next leg of their long journey.

"What's your name, big boy?"

Iskander said nothing. He thought of his little sister, and decided that for the moment he'd be like Gul – mute.

"I see – the strong silent type. I'll ask Selim instead." Ibrahim had strange yellowish eyes, one darker than the other. He seemed to barge deliberately into Iskander as he left to go into the courtyard with Ismail, the partner he was chained to. Ismail looked faintly familiar – red-haired, skinny, peaky faced. Suddenly Iskander remembered where he'd seen him before. This was the boy he and Osman had seen weeping as he trailed behind the group of boys being marched across the plain.

He and Yusuf followed the last pair of boys, Greeks from the coast called Leonidas and Petros. They collected their bowls of food, ate quickly, and then were taken out to the pack animals to load their bags. Iskander had to part with his bag, but managed to slip his half of the talisman inside his cloth belt before the bag was slung with the others. He'd have to find a better place for it. The best thing would be to slip it into the lining of his coat when he had the chance.

The boys were roped together loosely, and the cavalcade set off with a group of janissaries in the lead, and one or two riding up and down the column. For the first time in his life, Iskander found himself totally surrounded by strangers. The one person he knew, Hasan Efendi, was not travelling with them. Selim marched beside his charges, keeping a close eye on them and discouraging any chatter. He didn't mind the fact that Iskander refused to speak. Hasan Efendi would not have chosen the boy if he'd been born dumb, and if he preferred to remain silent on the journey it made life easier for Selim.

Then came days of forced marching, following river valleys through mountains, then crossing dusty plains. The janissaries were in a hurry to reach Constantinople before the weather deteriorated, and the boys had no choice but to keep up. Iskander was grateful for the punishing pace, which left them all so tired at the end of each day they hardly had the energy to help put up the tents on the nights when there was no karavansarai en route. There was no opportunity for anyone to feel homesick. The pace didn't worry Iskander – he was used to walking miles every day, and did not suffer the way Yusuf or Ismail did. Their blisters and exhaustion at the beginning were distressing to see, but they hardened up quickly, and soon Selim praised all the boys for their speed and endurance.

"It won't be too many days before we reach the Sea of Marmara. And tonight you're all in for a treat – we're staying at a very comfortable karavansarai in the royal city of Bursa. You'll have the chance of a good bath in the hamam, and from the smell around me, you boys certainly need it."

A hamam in a royal city. As the other boys buzzed over this delightful prospect, Iskander remembered the one occasion he'd been in a proper hamam. Ali had taken the twins to the small bath complex in the town near the Ruined City, and though they'd enjoyed the process, to them it didn't compare with the delights of the hot springs.

The hot springs… Iskander tried in vain to push them out of his mind. It was agony to think about the last evening swim there with Osman, and how everything had gone so wrong afterwards. Up to now he'd frozen his mind as he'd frozen his tongue, but he could feel that his pent-up pain was waiting to pour out, and hoped that splashing in the hamam pool and lying in the steam room would give his tears a chance to flow unseen.

He fingered the rough edge of his half of the talisman, which was now tucked into the inner pocket of his coat. He'd have to take all his clothes off at the hamam, and he didn't want anyone going through his pockets. He must now hide the talisman in the lining for safety. His fingers worked at a gap already growing in the pocket seam, making the hole big enough for the talisman to slip down out of sight between the coat and its lining. Fatima had sewn the coat so well it took him some time, but at last the talisman disappeared downwards out of the pocket. He pictured the little head with its two searching eyes trying to pierce the darkness.

Just at that moment Ibrahim tripped him up so that he fell against Yusuf, nearly knocking him over. "Now tell Yusuf you're sorry like a good boy, Iskander."

Iskander silently put an apologetic hand on Yusuf's shoulder.

"Open that stupid mouth of yours and SAY SOME-THING!" shouted Ibrahim, and received a clip round the ear from Selim.

"Shut up, Ibrahim. You talk far too much. You're going to find life difficult in the palace – the rule of silence applies there all the time." Selim stuck his face close to Ibrahim's. "ALL THE TIME. And I'm not joking." He walked up the column to the front.

"Silent *all* the time?" whispered Ibrahim to another janissary walking beside him.

"Silence is required in the courtyards and public spaces, and in the presence of our sultan. But you are allowed to talk when you're inside your quarters."

"That's a relief. Selim got me worried." He fell silent when he saw Selim coming back down the line.

Iskander had not said a word to anyone throughout the journey.

The boys were cowed by the bustle and richness of Bursa. The narrow hilly streets were lined with fine buildings and full of confident men going about their business. They all looked rich as pashas and stared in pity at the ragged, dirty group of boys being marched through the city to the karavansarai.

This was more enormous than usual, and was packed with prosperous travellers. To Iskander's surprise, Hasan Efendi suddenly appeared and came forward to greet them. He'd obviously ridden on ahead. Iskander could not help having a joyful reaction to this familiar face, the last link with his family. But Hasan Efendi ignored him, and after talking to Selim, disappeared again.

Despite the splendour of the karavansarai, the boys had been allotted a grim dank room at the back. They left their baggage and, still chained together, were taken to the large imposing hamam next door. Once inside, their manacles were removed along with all their clothing and, supervised by Hasan Efendi, the boys were vigorously scrubbed and their heads shaved with painful thoroughness by the hamam attendants. By the time Iskander was sent to float in the hot pool of the main hall, he felt as if all his skin had been peeled off.

He moved his hands about in the water, staring at the red weal on his left wrist. This was the first time he'd been free of his manacle, and it felt wonderful. The tears he'd expected to pour out didn't come – the relief and sense of freedom in the water banished them. While splashing around he checked out the doors of the main hall. There was only one exit – the door through which they'd come. The other doors led to the hot steam chamber and the cold pool. If he leapt out and sprinted he might make the exit before Selim did, but how far would he get escaping stark naked?

Almost as if Selim was reading his mind, the janissary moved to stand in front of the door with his arms folded, watching his charges. He was joined a minute later by Hasan Efendi. They were taking no chances. Iskander dived down through the water to hide his annoyance. When he reached the steam room and lay on a stone ledge hidden by the thick clouds of hot vapour, at last his tears started to flow. He wasn't the only one. Ismail was lying nearby, choking on his sobs. Then they were all summoned to take a quick dip in the cold pool, and the hamam session was over.

"Everyone has new clothes now," announced Hasan Efendi as the boys were being led back to the room they'd undressed in. "We want you to arrive in the city looking presentable."

Iskander was last coming out of the main hall and didn't hear. When he saw the hook he'd hung his clothes on was empty, he turned round in dismay. "Nice new clothes for us," whispered Yusuf, nudging him. "Over there."

Iskander ignored him and marched up to Selim. "I want my own clothes, please."

"You are being given better clothes." Selim made no sign he was surprised to hear Iskander speak at last, but in the background Ibrahim made a cock-crowing noise.

"I'd prefer to wear my own."

"They are filthy, tattered, full of lice, and no good for anything. They've been sent to be burned."

Iskander could feel panic building up and turned to Hasan Efendi.

"At least let me keep my embroidered coat, Efendi. It's a fine coat. My mother made it for me." He tried to keep his voice calm, and was aware of titters from the other boys. "I beg you, Efendi. I won't wear it, but I'd like to keep it to remind me of home."

"Fetch the coat, Selim. Let's inspect this precious garment."

"It's probably already burned." Selim wandered off, shaking his head at this pointless exercise.

Iskander stood naked, waiting, eyes shut. The searching gaze of the little bird bored into his mind, as if it was begging to be saved from the flames. Then the boys all started to hoot and laugh, and Iskander opened his eyes again to see Selim coming in holding the coat out by one finger and closing his nose with two fingers of the other hand.

"Not only dirty, but crawling with lice too, I'm sure." He dropped it on the floor near Iskander's feet.

"Now put the new uniform on at once, Iskander, and in future keep that coat right out of our sight." Hasan Efendi stared at Iskander, frowning. "You're not at all like your cousin Jelal – he couldn't wait to throw out his old clothes." The boys suddenly went silent and stared in surprise at Iskander. Hasan Efendi noticed. "Yes,

Iskander has a relative amongst the senior pages. Jelal has done extremely well and will no doubt go far in the sultan's service. Not that this will help you, Iskander – every new page is judged on his own merits."

"Yes, Efendi." Iskander hesitated before going on, "Does Jelal know I am coming?"

"Of course not. He probably won't even recognize you after three years, nor you him. Hurry up, everybody. Get going." He and Selim put the manacles back on the boys, and roped them together to return to the karavansarai.

Iskander kept his rolled-up coat close to his side when he went to bed, extra aware in his cleansed state of its strong, smoky tent-smell. He wept again silently as he thought of his family sitting snugly round the fire on this cold evening, eating his mother's good chickpea stew and listening to the wind as it moaned through the decayed walls of the Ruined City.

The sea. There it was; a thin line twinkling in the far distance. Iskander thought it looked like the Lake of Reeds, and was at first rather disappointed. Then it disappeared again as the marchers descended into a valley, and when it finally reappeared after they'd climbed the shoulder of the next mountain, it was right below them.

Hasan Efendi galloped up and halted them. "Look well, boys. That's the Sea of Marmara." He pointed from his horse as he spoke. "And there is the royal palace of Topkapi on its promontory, and behind it the great city of Constantinople. Over there is the Golden Horn. And that channel there is the Bosphorus. What a glorious setting for a royal palace."

The boys stared down, all silent for once, even Ibrahim. The sea was full of ships, large and small, sailing in all directions. Beyond them, the countless minarets and domes of the city gleamed among red-tiled roofs of houses and dark cypress trees. The sun was so bright above the city it made the boys half close their eyes, and the scene quivered as if it was a mirage too beautiful to last. But the awe-inspiring city was real, and as they trudged down the road that would eventually lead them to the shore, the sun started to set behind the minarets and domes through a cloud-streaked sky of orange, red and purple. Soon the details of the buildings became too dark to see.

To Iskander, the shadowy promontory bearing the sultan's palace looked like a huge crouching dragon, growing ever darker against the blazing sunset, a dragon ready and eager to consume them all.

TOPKAPI PALACE

"I CAN'T HELP LAUGHING." Ibrahim nudged Iskander. "You're all as green as cucumbers!"

Iskander took no notice. He was desperately trying not to be sick. No one had ever told him the sea was like a bucking mule, only much worse, because once the boat set sail you couldn't get off and there was nothing you could do to control the rocking. As each wave passed under it, the boat made a horrid quivering lurch, and boy after boy would lean over the side and puke his heart out. When they finally arrived at the jetty beside the palace walls, they were all ready to die, except for Ibrahim, the only one who hadn't been affected. He stepped out of the boat looking cocky, but immediately slipped on some seaweed – to the delight of his companions, who lost no time telling him his arse was as green as their faces.

Still manacled and roped together, the boys were led towards the tall forbidding walls. They'd been dropped near a large gate guarded by janissaries whose plumed hats streamed in the stiff breeze. A small postern door was opened and the boys found themselves on a path beside a large vegetable garden.

Iskander stared at a heap of orange and yellow gourds, such a common sight all over the country at this time of year – late October – and thought how odd it was they were the first things he saw inside the fabled palace. He and Osman used gourds to play ball. He turned to look up at a splendid row of domes. Surely they were the sultan's own quarters? But no, said Selim, they were the palace kitchens. Nothing was quite as Iskander expected, except for the fierce-looking janissaries on guard everywhere.

"Now listen to me everyone. From the moment we enter the courtyards you walk in absolute silence until we're indoors. And that means not a word – you hear me, Ibrahim? You'll find yourself clapped in prison if you so much as open your mouth."

They were led up into a massive courtyard full of men standing in groups, totally silent. Hasan Efendi left the boys without a second glance, his job done, and walked away on business of his own. Selim took them through an imposing gateway into another courtyard, empty of crowds, but filled with fountains and pretty trees dotted amongst the handsome buildings. Again, complete silence reigned except for the water tumbling from the fountains and the screeches of some strange large birds strutting about, which they later learned were peacocks.

Iskander was used to silence, but this wasn't like the silence on the mountain. This was uncanny, even frightening. There was a sense of tension amongst the people walking about, as if the air was full of unspoken things. Then he spotted a couple of finely dressed young men communicating with sign language, rather as he and Osman and Gul did. *So that's how everyone manages...* Thinking of Osman brought home to him how far away he was now, and he felt almost giddy with a piercingly sudden sense of loss.

Selim led the boys round a corner, crossed a smaller courtyard, opened a door, and ushered them into a large hall. Dozens of boys with shaven heads, each covered with a small cap, turned to look briefly at the new arrivals, and then ignored them again. They were all sitting in close groups on square raised platforms, each group working with its own teacher.

Iskander tried to pick out his cousin – a familiar face would be a comfort – but he couldn't see Jelal anywhere. Maybe he'd changed so much he was unrecognizable. Jelal used to be arrogant, bossy and cruel, and Iskander and Osman had particularly hated his habit of torturing animals; he thought nothing was funnier than to blind a chicken and watch it blunder about, or to tie the legs of a sheep and a goat together and see them struggle and fight to free themselves. He hoped life in the palace had changed Jelal in character as well as looks.

At this moment Selim pushed Iskander roughly, making him move on with the other boys to an empty platform at the far end of the pages' hall, and showed them the cupboards that held everything they would need, including mattresses and bedding, where they could also put their few possessions.

"This platform is your home now, where you'll spend a lot of your day, sleep at night, and where you can talk when it isn't lesson time. This is the bottom class, and if you do well you'll move up to the next class." He pointed to a nearby platform, where a group of boys were sitting cross-legged, laboriously copying something onto writing blocks resting on their knees. "The top class is over there by the stove."

"What happens if we don't do well?" Ibrahim asked, looking nervously round.

"Then you'll be sent elsewhere to learn to do something more suitable for thickheads. Now, I'm going to take off those manacles." They fell with a clatter as Selim unlocked them. "But don't get any ideas. You'll never be able to escape, so don't even think of it. Any boy caught trying to get out of Topkapi Palace is executed."

They stood rubbing their wrists as they watched Selim make a great pile of the manacles and ropes and then put them into a sack. Their skin underneath had hardened during the journey, except for Yusuf's whose wrist looked horribly inflamed.

"Right, boys, this is where I bid you goodbye."

They gazed at him in consternation. They'd all got used to Selim and assumed he'd remain with them. He shouldered the sack and went off laughing, leaving them uneasily waiting for something to happen.

Yusuf crept up to Iskander and whispered, "I can't read or write."

"Nor can I."

"I'm scared." Yusuf looked round at the long hall full of industrious boys who were being closely supervised by their teachers. Some were writing, some were reading, some learning to chant something by heart. One class was answering their teacher's questions.

"Cheer up, Yusuf." Iskander tried not to sound

impatient, but he was heartily sick of being Yusuf's partner. He preferred Ismail, but it was Ibrahim who most interested him. Although he could be a bully, and never stopped talking unless he was forced to, he had plenty of spirit and a good brain.

The new group of boys stood and waited. Nothing happened. Ibrahim moved first. "Let's sit down and look expectant, and perhaps someone will remember we're here." He lowered himself and sat with his legs crossed.

Iskander immediately took the space beside him. Ismail quickly sat the other side of Iskander and Yusuf had to find another spot. They went on waiting and still nothing happened.

"Bet this is part of the training," whispered Iskander. "They want to see how we cope."

"What should we do to impress them?" Ibrahim answered, hardly moving his lips. He was almost as good as the twins at silent whispering.

"Keep still and look totally calm."

"Fat chance. Look at Yusuf."

Tears were running down Yusuf's face as he rubbed his sore wrist.

After what seemed a long time, but was actually no more than ten minutes, a tall bearded man strode through the main door and stopped at their platform.

The boys stood up and bowed their heads.

"I am Abdulhamid Hodja, your teacher. Hasan Efendi tells me he has brought me a good batch of boys this time – now you have to prove to me he was right. Sit down, sit down." The hodja saw Yusuf's tears, and the sore wrist. "If you are crying from real pain, please endure it until the end of the morning's lessons, and I will arrange some salve. If you are crying for any other reason, I'm not interested."

Yusuf stopped crying.

"Now, tell me your names. If any of you are Christians, we will rename you now. Leonidas and Petros – are you Greek boys the only ones? You will be known as Hasan, Leonidas, after your protector Hasan Efendi, and you Petros will be…" he paused while they all watched him. "You will be Halil. Hasan and Halil. You will not use your old names again."

Iskander was relieved that although he was a nomad and not regarded as a proper Muslim by those who were, his name was Muslim so he wouldn't have to change it. He looked at the two Greek boys and saw how pale they were. They had obviously not expected this name change, and he wondered why Selim hadn't warned them.

The hodja had hard black eyes above his thick beard

and, from the way he described the regime of lessons, lectures, prayers five times a day, exercise sessions and meals, a hard heart too. There was little free time in their schedule because the hodja believed that boys didn't need it. If they had it they just got up to mischief.

And so the boys were plunged straight into the palace school routine and within a week they felt as if they'd been there a year. Iskander was so busy and tired by the end of the day, he hardly had time to think about Osman. He put off trying to work out which of the older pages was Jelal, but a couple of weeks after Iskander's arrival, Jelal himself made the first move. He'd heard Ismail call Iskander's name out on the archery ground, stared hard at the new boy's face, and came over to him later after they'd all finished their archery practice.

"You look very like Iskander, the son of my Amja Ali."

"Yes, that's me – and you must be my cousin Jelal!" Iskander stared, bemused by this tall, broad young man with signs of a closely-shaved beard and a deep voice. "I wanted to tell you I was here, but I didn't recognize you." He gulped, tears suddenly collecting in his eyes.

Jelal laughed, pleased with himself as always, and put a comforting arm round Iskander's shoulder. "I'm not surprised – I don't think even my father would recognize me now. So where's Osman?" He stared round.

"He's at home helping Baba."

"But you two did everything together."

"Not any more," whispered Iskander, afraid the tears would come back.

Jelal heard his name called, and gave his cousin's shoulder another squeeze before removing his arm. "I'm really glad to see you, Iskander, but I've got to go. I'll come and find you again soon – I can't wait to hear all about my folks at home." Someone shouted again for him. "Senior pages don't have much to do with new arrivals, so it might not be for a few days." Head high, he walked off with that particularly arrogant swagger of his, which Iskander remembered only too well.

When Jelal did finally find an opportunity to talk, Iskander noticed it was when they were unobserved by the others. Jelal asked lots of questions about his family, but seemed so detached from what Iskander told him they might almost have been talking about strangers.

"Well, I'm glad to hear my parents and brothers are doing fine." Jelal yawned and stretched. "But I tell you, Iskander, all that nomadic stuff – the tents, the herds, the trekking from plain to mountain – it seems like another world."

"Do you miss it, Jelal?"

"No. Not at all. And I'll tell you something else, cousin. When you've been here a few months you won't either." He yawned again and patted Iskander's hand condescendingly. "This is much better than a nomad's life. We're the lucky ones, Iskander. Don't forget that. Now I must go and practise jerid – I'm hoping to be chosen for the prince's team. Have you seen jerid played yet? No? It's very exciting. You have to gallop down the pitch and hurl your javelin through a hoop. You need to be a good rider and have a steady aim – but I doubt they'll teach boys like you to play it because you've only ridden donkeys." He made a sweeping movement with his arm as if he was aiming his javelin right at Iskander's heart, and walked off laughing.

Iskander watched him go, full of a mixture of feelings, the uppermost being an intense dislike of Jelal. Nothing had changed, either in his cousin or himself. And he vowed he'd never despise his former life the way his cousin did, however much he enjoyed all the new things he was learning. And if he ever played this jerid game, he'd show Jelal what a good rider he was.

Iskander showed a natural aptitude for reading and writing, although he wasn't as good as the Greek boys who were already able to do a bit of both. He began to learn both the Turkish and the Arabic scripts; he studied the Koran and had to learn passages of it by heart. He liked learning to write numbers and add up, and thought how much Osman would like this system instead of having to mark tallies to count their flocks. He'd teach it to him. And he'd teach him to read and write.

Above all, Iskander enjoyed the sport – the wrestling, archery and javelin throwing. He and Ibrahim were chosen to learn jerid and discovered how hard it was to throw a javelin through a small hoop from a galloping horse. Ibrahim's aim was phenomenal – he said it was because a butcher had to aim precisely otherwise he'd cut off a finger, or even a hand, with his cleaver.

As the winter grew colder and December turned to January, the boys loathed the moment just before dawn when the muezzin chanting from a hundred minarets throughout the city called all the sultan's subjects to prayer. However warmly cocooned you were in your bedding, you had to get up.

"It's a good life here, except for this," whispered Ismail, as they got up in the icy dark.

Iskander didn't answer. It frightened him how quickly palace life had swallowed him. He had little time to think about Osman during the day and by nightfall he was often so tired he fell straight to sleep. But on the nights he did lie awake, Osman came so vividly to life in his mind he sometimes felt if he turned his head very quickly, he'd be asleep beside him. But there was never Osman's warm back against his, no embers burning nearby, no snores from Ali or quiet breathing beyond the fire from the women. He burned to escape then and there, to fly through the air and find himself at home with Osman.

Often moonlight came through the high window above him and lit the pages' hall. One night, when the moon was full, he stared at it for ages, wondering if Osman was doing the same thing and missing him as much as he missed Osman. Then a new thought came into his mind: maybe Osman was suffering *more* than he was. Maybe it was more painful to stay at home amongst all the familiar things and people. Osman had to do the things they'd always done together on his own now, so surely that meant if the person you did them with wasn't there, you missed them all the time? Iskander was consumed with guilt for not thinking of this, and filled with such a longing to comfort Osman he couldn't stop himself sitting up. He got out his half piece of talisman from its hiding place in his old coat and held it against his cheek to comfort himself. Would he ever see his twin again? How could they possibly overcome the huge obstacles of every sort that lay between them?

And even if Osman managed to reach Constantinople, how could he do anything? The sultan's janissaries guarded every corner of the palace, inside and out. Iskander had begun to realize that his only possible escape route would be to find an ally within the palace who had access to the outside world and, as a powerless new boy, how was he to do that? That he'd get no help from his cousin was absolutely clear. Jelal would say he was mad and probably report him. Iskander also now knew for sure he was the only boy in his group who wanted to escape. He never stopped yearning to get out, but the others clearly found their new lives better than their old.

Clank, scrunch, clank. He could hear the janissary patrol marching by the pages' hall on its nightly round. He cradled the talisman in his hand, staring at the little head with its hypnotic black eyes. They held his gaze as if they longed to speak, but could give him no message.

OSMAN IN WINTER

NOW CAME EARLY that year. Not the heavy crushing snow of full winter, but a light fluffy powdering of the Ruined City's walls and the nomad tents within them. Soon after sunrise, Osman walked out through the gates to the oak tree and sat under its shelter to think about Iskander. Though he'd been gone six months, Osman sometimes pretended Iskander was still around, that he was just finishing some job and in a minute he'd be coming to join him so that they could go tobogganing together on one of their mother's washboards.

Osman watched the snow falling, and put his hand out to catch a flake. Before it melted away, he looked at its perfect shape and thought of the marvel that there were uncountable numbers of flakes drifting out of the sky. Where did they come from, how did it happen?

He remembered his mother's story that the mother of the sky god was plucking birds to feed her son, and letting all the feathers fall from her lap to make snow. Iskander's theory was that the gods didn't like the sight of the mud and mess of winter and covered it up with snow. Osman thought it was more likely they got tired of seeing the world brightly-coloured and made it white for a change.

A breeze loosened snowflakes lying on the oak leaves and they floated delicately down. Osman tipped his head back and caught them on his tongue. Like Iskander, he always expected snow to taste sweet. Perhaps Iskander was looking out at falling snow like him and catching it on his tongue somewhere in the sultan's palace. Osman tried to imagine what a palace might look like, and didn't get beyond a vague idea of domes and minarets. He'd never seen a palace. He knew that Topkapi Palace was beside the sea, but he'd never seen the sea either. He shut his eyes, sharply aware that trying to imagine what Iskander saw every day was useless, yet not being able to stop doing it. They'd seen the same things all their lives and shared everything to such a degree that their mental maps had been almost identical. But not any more.

Osman put his head on his knees and rocked himself.

"Don't cry, boy." A cracked, high voice made him jump. Mad Miriam had crept up on him, her footsteps silent in the snow.

"I'm not crying." Osman kept his face hidden.

"Tears are cold in winter. Cold." Mad Miriam waved her stick vaguely at the snow. She always wore the same rags, winter and summer, and never seemed aware of the weather. "Cold in winter. Bitter in summer. Best not to cry, boy." She started to sing her habitual wordless song as she moved away.

Osman watched her for a few minutes, and then leapt to his feet. At least his life was better than Mad Miriam's. He ran back to the ruined church, and saw Gul standing in the tent doorway, the worried look on her face wiped away by her smile of relief when she caught sight of Osman. He hadn't realized that every time he disappeared on his own she was afraid he'd gone for ever, gone to look for his twin.

He hugged her and signed to ask whether breakfast was ready. She nodded, and he followed her into the tent. The smoke from the hearth was extra acrid this morning; but their eyes were used to it. Ali had already eaten and left with his gun to go hunting with Yacut. Fatima wouldn't let Yacut near the tent since Iskander's departure – and she let everyone know she blamed him.

"Eat, boy, eat. You've got Baba's share to do today. Do you want me to help you?"

"It's all right, Ana. You've enough work here." There was a large pile of reeds, several half-finished baskets, and a carpet on the loom that she had just started. Osman grinned at his mother. "At least you lucky things can keep warm while you work."

Fatima gave him some extra soup and sighed. "One son is certainly not enough for us. What a lie that was. You have too much work to do and it worries me."

"I worry more about Iskander, Ana."

"Don't, my dear. It achieves nothing except to make you sad."

"But don't you worry about him too?"

His mother started work on a basket before replying at last. "I hold him in my heart and pray every day for him." Tears ran down her cheeks as her hands flew, twisting the reeds.

Osman sat staring into the fire, putting off the moment when he'd have to go and let out the animals, which always played up when they saw he was on his own. Suddenly he burst out, "I feel trapped here, Ana. Trapped by the winter, the snow, the hard work that never ends. But the worst thing is the big hole in my life. Nothing will ever fill it except him. I want to go and find Iskander."

She didn't look up, but her hands went still. When she raised her eyes, Osman had gone.

He was running blindly towards the animal pen, tears freezing on his cheeks.

The snow's got into my brain, Iskander. The winter makes me feel I'm trapped here for ever.

Leila glowed all winter while she prepared her trousseau. She made and embroidered skirts and blouses for herself, shirts for Mehmet, and socks for them both. Fatima was making a kilim for Leila using the traditional pattern known as the Golden Slipper, which would be given to Mehmet's family to spread in front of their hearth as a welcome to the new bride.

"I like Golden Slipper, but I prefer the design of One Hand and One Place, Ana. Why didn't you make that one? Your mother made it for you when you married Baba."

"I'll make it for you a year after the wedding, not before. And you'll come to love the pattern of Golden Slipper when you're sitting with your new family and missing us. The first few months can be difficult, my dear. We've no idea what Mehmet's mother's like."

Leila went quiet. She knew how strict the tribal rules were. She knew she wouldn't be able to speak or join in with anything, work or play, until invited to do so by her new in-laws. And they might watch and wait, to test their new daughter-in-law's strength of character.

"I heard of a bride who said and did nothing for a whole year. Her in-laws criticized her for being stuck-up and lazy, but really they had totally forgotten to ask her to join in!" Leila laughed. She clearly thought it would never happen to her.

"I can't imagine you being silent for five minutes, Leila." said Osman. He was carving a spoon. He could see the handle was slightly crooked, and didn't care. His usual skill had deserted him.

"She'll have no choice."

A silence fell, broken only by the soft sounds of their fingers working and the crackles of wood burning on the fire. Osman had never noticed these long silences before, because he'd be sitting working beside Iskander, and they'd communicate with glances and a quick sign. The silences were part of family life in winter, when the evenings were long and everyone worked near the fire. Now that there was no one at the end of the rug he'd shared with Iskander, the blank space and the silence made his heart ache.

He tried to carve away the bend in the handle and the spoon broke in two. He looked up and met Fatima's eyes. She gave him a little smile and held out her hand.

"Quick, give me the pieces. I can hear your father coming." She tucked them well into the hottest part of the fire, and when Ali came in, only the extra puffs of new smoke gave their presence away.

"It's late to be putting fresh wood on the fire."

"We were cold."

Nothing more was said, and everyone started to put their work away and prepare for bed.

Osman decided to make a special hidden pocket inside his sheepskin coat to keep his half of the talisman safe. He actually wanted to sew it in, because he found the lonely bird's head painful to look at. Its eyes seemed to ask, "When are you going to find my brother?" and he couldn't answer it. He felt in his bones that when the right moment arrived, he would know it. He couldn't plan it. *Do not look for answers, my son.* He couldn't forget what that ghostly visitor had said. *The answer will find you.* The words went round and round his brain. He just had to be patient, do his best, and wait.

He tucked the little questioning eyes out of sight again, and tried to imagine what hiding place Iskander had devised for his half of the talisman. It comforted him to think that perhaps his brother had done exactly the same as him, and sewed the talisman into his coat.

Ali came up behind him. "What on earth are you sewing for, Osman? I need a son not a seamstress! Come and help me fetch the flocks in. There's a storm coming."

"Yes, Baba."

"And then I want you to mend the camel shelter. That wooden roof is about to blow off."

"Yes, Baba."

"You're a good son, Osman." He thwacked his leg with his crook as if he was about to say something else but couldn't find the words, and the two of them went off to gather the animals in silence. Since Iskander left, Ali hadn't beaten Osman once. His rages seemed to have disappeared. He would sometimes stand and stare blankly into space, and then sigh and walk away. Osman wondered how much his father missed Iskander, but knew better than to ask.

LUCKY SNOWBALL

"IT'S SNOWING REALLY HARD! Look, Iskander!" Ismail pointed up at the high windows in the hall. "We can play snowballs when we go down to the games field."

Ismail always sat close to Iskander, and treated him like an older brother. Though he was by far the youngest in the group, six months younger than Yusuf, he'd settled in much better because he was highly intelligent and shone in class. Poor Yusuf wasn't at all intelligent, and struggled with everything they were set to do. So it wasn't surprising that, by chance on the day when the snow first fell, Abdulhamid Hodja told Yusuf he was to be transferred to be trained in the palace kitchens. When Yusuf started to cry, the hodja explained that Yusuf would be much happier doing something he was good at, and would find life easier than it was in the palace school.

"You don't need to feel ashamed, Yusuf – we always move a few of the new boys. It's better to go sooner than later. And they'll treat you very well in the kitchen school."

"When do I have to leave?" whispered Yusuf.

"No point waiting – I'm taking you over now. Just bring your bag. Someone will fetch your bedding later. Don't worry, Yusuf, you're not going far. Right, back to work the rest of you. I want all that copying done before I get back."

And just like that, Yusuf was gone. Iskander felt bad because he hadn't been very nice to him recently, and hadn't had time to make up for it. He also saw how ruthless the palace system could be when necessary. If he didn't work hard, he might find himself transferred too. This might give him more chance to escape, but how would Osman ever find him if he was moved from the palace? Turkey was so big. He couldn't risk it. He'd have to wait until Osman arrived in the city and somehow made contact.

"Travel outside the palace? Don't think of it, Iskander. You have to become a royal page, and only a few boys make it." Jelal had looked down his nose at his cousin when Iskander had asked him about it. "*Very* few. Getting into the prince's jerid team is the best way, and you haven't a hope of that."

Iskander knew Jelal was desperate to be chosen by the prince, so he said, "I hope it happens to you soon."

"Oh, it will, it will. There's a match coming up—" Jelal saw a boy in the distance who had already been chosen, and rushed off mid-sentence.

Iskander stared up at the snowflakes floating past the window. Snow always made him think of his twin, of how they both loved the first heavy snowfall on the Ruined City, which masked its broken walls and muddy tracks. He thought of his sisters mixing the snow with honey to make a delicious snack you had to eat quickly before the snow melted.

His sisters. His mother. He looked round at the pages' hall, full of boys and men. Outside in the courtyards, more men. There was never a single woman, even a veiled one, because the royal women and their servants were not allowed in the men's part of the palace, the selamlik. They lived in a secluded harem area of the palace where only the sultan and his sons had access. Iskander had been brought up very differently in his tribe, and was used to nomad women walking about freely amongst the men-folk. They never had to veil their faces.

How he missed them all, their laughter, quick jokes,

and bright eyes as they greeted you. It was as if a natural part of his world was missing, and he'd only just realized it. Perhaps the Greek boys felt the same – after all, they'd been brought up with free, unveiled women too – he must ask them some time. He watched the flakes flutter down, seeing his mother in his mind's eye as she swept away the loose snow outside their tent and scolded her twins if they carelessly brought more in.

At that moment the door of the pages' hall opened and a flurry of snowflakes came in as the person entered. Iskander looked round almost expecting it to be Fatima, she was so present in his mind, but it was the bad-tempered teacher of the class on the next platform. As he turned back, his eye caught Jelal's for the first time since their conversation about the jerid team. Jelal glowered at him, and Iskander wondered what he'd done to offend him, but could think of nothing. They hadn't even spoken since Jelal had sought him out to learn about his family.

Soon the whole city was thickly blanketed in snow. Marooned within the palace, everyone who could sat wrapped in quilts near the few huge fireplaces and the many small dangerous braziers. The pages' hall was especially chilly because there was only one fireplace, and sitting close to it went by seniority. The new recruits got used to being permanently cold, and ran about whenever they could to get warm. Iskander began to feel he was frozen in time, trapped in a white prison from which there would be no escape.

It was a snowball that brought Iskander the first ray of hope. Ismail had thrown one hard at him when they were in a corner of the exercise ground in the free time after games, and as he ducked there was a shout from behind. An old man shook his fist at them. The snowball had knocked off his red conical cap, the sort worn by all the palace gardeners.

"Sorry, sorry, sorry." Both boys ran to retrieve the cap, and noticed his eyes were twinkling even though his face remained stern.

"At least you didn't hit my face. You're from the last new batch, aren't you? What are your names?"

"I'm Ismail and he's Iskander."

"My name's Rifat, and I've been here longer than anyone else in the palace. You look a bit alike – are you brothers?"

"No fear." Iskander looked at Ismail and couldn't see any likeness, but noticed how pleased the younger boy was at the mistake. "I only have one – my twin back at home." Saying the word twin out loud to this friendly old man suddenly brought tears to his eyes. He hoped the other two thought they were caused by the cold wind.

"Ah, a twin." Rifat's pale grey eyes had missed nothing, but he pretended not to notice. He rummaged in his baggy blue trousers and pulled out an apple, a perfect red apple. "Watch this, boys." He broke the apple in half with a sharp twist of his hands, and gave them the two pieces. "Eat it quickly, or the others will see and want some too. If you come here tomorrow, I might have something else for you."

And so Rifat became their friend, and often gave them little titbits while he chatted to them. They learned that the bostanjis like him were not only gardeners and woodcutters, but also rowed the sultan's skiffs up the Bosphorus or the Golden Horn. They did police duty occasionally in the suburbs of the city and on the shorelines round the palace. Iskander listened intently.

"I've been a bostanji for years – never regretted it. So if they decide to make you boys bostanjis instead of keeping you on to train you as pages, don't look at it as demotion. Think yourselves lucky. That's my view anyway, but maybe you lads are cleverer than I was. What are you hoping for, Iskander?"

"I haven't been here long enough to know." Iskander looked at his feet, then out at the grey Sea of Marmara beyond the palace walls. "Being a bostanji sounds fun."

"I want to look after the sultan's money in the treasury," piped up Ismail. "I love arithmetic."

"Well then you probably will." But Rifat was staring at Iskander. The boy had a shadow in his eyes, as if he carried some sort of heavy inner burden. He clearly wasn't happy, like little Ismail.

A shout summoned the boys at that moment and Rifat quickly gave them a pomegranate to share before going back to stacking logs of wood. As they ate the fiddly orange seeds, Iskander inwardly blessed Ismail's lucky snowball. At last he'd met someone who had access to the outside world, someone who was friendly and seemed to like him.

January turned to February and the bitter weather continued. Iskander and Ismail ran about in the snow as often as they could to warm up, and always looked out for Rifat; but the bostanjis were kept so busy cutting wood to keep the palace warm there was rarely an opportunity for gossip. Everyone longed for the hard winter to end, yet the weeks went slowly by with no change for the better. It seemed as if time itself was frozen.

OSMAN IN SPRING

AS SPRING APPROACHED, every eye in the Ruined City began to turn and look towards the distant mountains. The snows were retreating up the slopes, and all the nomads longed increasingly to leave the exhausted winter pastures and cramped winter conditions, and return to the wide-open spaces above. But this year, Osman didn't know what he felt. He wanted to go back up to the summer pastures, yet he knew this would take him further from the route to the city. If he was going to follow Iskander, he knew he should do it before the trek started; but he didn't feel it was the right moment yet, and dithered, miserable. If only he knew for sure when to escape.

Suddenly, it was too late – the winds turned light and fresh and, almost as one, the families of the tribe started to pack up their tents with much laughter and chat.

Nothing could stop them now, not even the fact that one woman was about to have a new baby. After all, it was said babies born on the trek had good luck all their lives – if they survived the trek in the first place. Everyone was gone within the week.

Arrival in the summer pasture was usually pure pleasure for both people and animals. Every foot moved faster as the final slopes came in sight, with heartbeats quickening and noses full of the smell of fresh young grass and sharp mountain air. Only Osman had a heavy heart. Feeling more lost than ever without his brother, he followed the happy sheep and goats to the upper pasture. He and Iskander had always loved the mountains best, so it was much more painful to be without him here than in the Ruined City.

Osman went and sat in their usual dell high up the shoulder of the mountain, and wept quietly on his own. His favourite ewe came up close and pushed her face into his, half knocking him over. Her strange yellow eyes with their sharp black slit of pupil were expressionless as usual, but she nuzzled him for a moment before giving a little baa and moving off to start cropping grass nearby. Sure that she understood he was sad because he was alone, he couldn't help being cheered by her. Baba always said that sheep were not nearly as stupid as they looked.

He heard his father calling angrily from below, and knew he'd be in trouble for disappearing whilst everyone else was unpacking and putting up the tent. He might even get beaten — Ali always seemed keener on beating when up in the mountains. Osman didn't care. After the long trek, he desperately needed to get away from the family. He sat for a little while longer before going down.

Leila came running up to meet him as he neared the tent-site.

"The centre pole is broken." Her eyes were frightened.

"It can't be. I loaded it carefully, just as we always do." A broken centre pole was a very bad omen. Osman began to feel frightened too.

"Baba is wild about it. He says it's all your fault."

"It isn't, but I'm not going to argue with him." Osman walked straight up to his father and said he was very sorry if he'd been the cause of it.

"Who else? Who else? Do you think the camel bit it in half?"

"I'll put a splint on it, Baba. It'll last until we can make another."

"This took me a whole winter to carve. A whole winter." Ali was almost screaming. "Get your shirt off,

I'm going to beat you."

"Let me mend it first and then beat me." But Ali couldn't be made to see sense, and he beat Osman as he used to sometimes beat Iskander, quickly losing control.

You're a pathetic, stupid, violent idiot. Pathetic. Stupid. Violent. Idiot. Pathetic. Stupid. Violent. Idiot. Osman sent his silent words up into the mountains, one with each stroke, until his father eventually stopped. Then he stood up as steadily as he could, put his shirt back on and went to find some good seasoned wood to make a splint. He could feel the blood seeping through his clothes, but almost enjoyed it. Poor Iskander had felt like this more than once, but for Osman this was the first time. *We're quits now, Iskander,* he thought. *I'll have a back with as many scars as yours.*

As he worked at binding the splint to the pole with long thin strips of leather, his mother and sisters finished unloading the pack animals and put everything in orderly rows ready to be installed in the tent once it was up. Ali had disappeared, as he always did after giving a bad beating.

"He's gone off because he's ashamed," said Leila, touching her brother's arm in sympathy. "Poor Osman. We all know it wasn't your fault."

"To hell with his shame. It was crazy to beat me

before I mended the pole. I never want to be like him." He remembered Iskander once saying exactly the same thing after a beating, and had the brief illusion that his twin was beside him, comforting him, not his sister. Then Fatima came up, holding a pot of ointment. "Did Baba always have a temper like this, Ana?"

She shook her head but didn't meet his eyes, and Osman didn't believe her. She kissed him and then made him take his shirt off again, and her gentle hands smoothed the salve onto his back to take the edge off his pain and start the healing process. To his surprise, he slept well that night and felt almost back to normal in the morning, if doing the work of two sons day after day could be called normal.

It was Leila's wedding not long after, and fortunately the splinted centre pole was well hidden by all the guns and belts of the guests hung on it.

Ali was in his element on occasions like this. He loved being an expansive host, but as Osman watched him swaggering about with his friends and showing off, he knew that when it was all over Ali would be complaining about the expense of it all and blaming his family for their extravagance.

"Come here, Osman. I want a word with you."

Osman found himself being pulled behind their tent by his mother. "Now listen to me. I know why you're miserable, but you mustn't spoil your sister's wedding by glowering and being gloomy all the time. Be happy for her. We're going to have plenty of time to feel sad when she's gone."

"I'm sorry, Ana. I'll try."

"Now come and help me prepare the fire-pit. Your father's killed two beautiful fat yearling sheep. No one will forget this wedding."

It was indeed a fine wedding feast. The two sheep carcasses were stuffed with herbs and slowly roasted over the fire, filling the camp with a tantalizing and delicious smell for several hours. Fatima and Leila had spent days making bread and yoghurt to eat with the lamb, along with heaps of rice pilav and rich vegetable stews. Other women had helped by making mounds of traditional sweetmeats. When the meat was cooked, all the food was laid out round the family tent for people to help themselves.

Everyone was dressed in their best embroidered clothes; the children had flowers in their hair, even the camels and donkeys wore beads and ribbons and tinkling bells. Men fired guns in the air in celebration, and birds wheeled in alarm and flew ever higher. Musicians played, there was dancing by the young girls, a sword dance by one of the boys, and a wrestling match with the young men from Mehmet's tribe. After three days of celebration, Leila left with her new family, proudly leading the wedding gift of a fine young camel. Fatima cried, Gul cried, but not Leila, even though everyone expected her to. Osman ran with Gul to the edge of the plateau to see her off, and soon the guests and Leila were small specks on the hillside. Leila's new village was on the other side of the mountain, a two-day journey on foot.

The family tent was so silent that night that they all turned in early, and then lay with their eyes open, each thinking that life was going to be painfully quiet now. It would always be silent: Gul couldn't talk, Osman wouldn't talk much without his twin, and Fatima would grieve that her firstborn had left the family tent for ever. Next morning, Ali decided he needed a break from his depressing family and went off hunting, saying he might not be back for a day or two.

There was a vivid sunset that night, red and orange and purple, and as Osman watched the fiery sky slowly fade to darkness, he was sure that somehow, somewhere, Iskander was watching it too. Later, when he crept into the tent, Fatima and Gul were already asleep. He found his coat, carefully loosened a couple of stitches, took out the broken piece of talisman and carried it outside to the moonlight. The eyes in the bird-like head gazed eagerly at him.

What shall I do, little bird? What shall I do? Your master told me not to ask questions, that the answer would find me, but how? How will I know the moment has come? Has it come now? You and I could escape easily while my father is away hunting, but how can I leave my mother and little sister to do everything? It wouldn't be right. They couldn't cope.

The bird looked sad, but then it always did. It was incomplete, like him. And as usual, it gave him no answer.

THE ACCIDENT

WHEN ALI WENT HUNTING he was sometimes gone for three days, particularly
when he was with Yacut. So Fatima didn't
worry until she heard he hadn't been with Yacut at all.
No one in the tribe had seen him. Fatima put her hands
to her face. The men in the tribe took the view that Ali
always wandered further than he meant to, and would
be back any time. No one offered to search for him yet –
it was too soon.

Later that afternoon, Osman found Fatima standing
outside the tent, staring up the mountain. He took his
mother's hand in his.

"Baba won't be back now, Ana. It's nearly dark. Shall
I go and look for him tomorrow?"

"Wait another day. Your father always says wait
three whole days and only start to worry on the fourth.

He'll be angry if you waste your time looking for him too soon." Her eyes filled with worry, Fatima went back to her weaving, and Osman to his herds.

When there was still no sign of him by the next afternoon, Osman started to make preparations for a dawn start the following day. He cut plenty of fodder so that the animals didn't need to be put out for a couple of days, and Fatima made him a bag of food and drink.

"Do you want to take Gul with you?"

"No. I'll go faster on my own. Anyway you need her. There's a ewe missing – she can try and find her." They looked at each other, both with the same thought in their heads: if only Iskander were here.

It was raining hard at dawn next morning, and there were ominous storm clouds building up round the mountain peak. "I think you should wait until the storm's passed." As Fatima spoke, sheet lightning ripped across the sky, followed by a deafening clap of thunder. "There, it's right overhead."

It was a fearsome storm, and no one was able to leave the tents until well after midday when, at last, the wind dropped and the rain became a drizzle. Osman looked at his mother, wondering whether it was now too late in the day to start a search. She sent him instead to talk to one of the elders of the tribe and ask his advice.

"I'm sure Ali's sheltering in a cave somewhere." The elder clearly thought they were fussing needlessly – in his view, a man could be gone a week and it shouldn't worry his wife. As Osman left the tent, the old man added that if Ali still hadn't turned up in a couple of days the tribe would have to organize a search party. Everyone knew that wouldn't be very popular – men hated losing a day wandering the mountains looking for someone who'd probably turn up at some point anyway.

Osman decided it was worth doing a short search in the few hours left of daylight, but didn't find any signs of Ali, and the silent, tense family hardly slept that night. Osman kept being filled with a fearful panic that seem to settle round his lungs and stop him breathing, and he'd have to sit up to control it. He'd have given anything to find Iskander there beside him, an ally in this crisis. How was he going to cope if something had happened to Baba? He'd never felt so alone in his life. His mother was a capable woman, strong and full of energy, but she had plenty to do already. And Gul was only seven.

Both Fatima and Gul were up at dawn, ready with Osman's breakfast, a coil of rope and his pack of supplies.

"You must come back tomorrow evening, Osman."

"What happens if I haven't found him?"

"The men can go in a proper search party whether

they want to or not." Fatima looked fierce. "I'll make sure they do."

He set off in the calm, soft dawn, with all the penned animals bleating in their eagerness to get back to their pastures after the storm. Fatima and Gul would have to do that, and spend the day on the mountain shepherding them.

Osman headed straight for the most dangerous section of the mountain range. It was full of unexpected ravines and sudden shale-covered cliffs, and though the hunting was good there, no one took their flocks anywhere near it even though there were pockets of rich grass between the ravines. He peered nervously over steep drops, he whistled and shouted, he searched the ravines he could climb into. Nothing. He was about to give up and move to another area when he suddenly heard a faint bleating in response to one of his whistles. His heart jumped, and he returned to the last ravine, too deep and dangerous to climb down. He whistled again, and unmistakably heard a sheep bleat. A very weak, whispery sound, but it could be the lost ewe.

Osman tied the rope to the toughest little tree he could find, and started to let himself down into the ravine with the other end tied securely round his waist. He reached a firm ledge, and carefully looked over, sickened by the enormous drop below him. There, on another wider ledge not far down, lay the ewe, looking as if she had broken one of her back legs and possibly her spine. She saw him and bleated again. Osman knew he couldn't do anything on his own. He'd have to go back and get help. And should he do that before going out again to look for his father? In two minds, he was about to work his way up the cliff again when he caught sight of something far below on the ravine floor. It was a man's leg. The rest of the man was out of sight, hidden by a bulge in the cliff, but Osman knew that leg, that boot. He shut his eyes and opened them again, hoping he'd made a mistake. He hadn't. It was Ali down there. He felt sick.

"Baba! Baba!" His frantic shouts made a couple of rooks rise cawing in alarm, but the leg didn't move and there was no other sound. Even the ewe had gone silent, exhausted by bleating in her weakened state. "Baba! Baba! Baba!" The echo repeated Osman's shouts and magnified them. If his father had been conscious, he would have made some response or twitched his foot. Ali didn't move. He was dead, or very near death.

Osman could feel himself panicking, and took some deep breaths before climbing back up the cliff. It was too dangerous to go down. He left his rope to mark the spot, and ran back to the nomad encampment without stopping once during the hour it took him. Sometimes, as he leapt from rock to rock he felt he was near flying, and back into his mind came his conversation with Iskander at the hot springs.

"Oh, Iskander, Iskander. I need you, Iskander, I need you…" As he ran he found he was repeating "Iskander I need you" in rhythm with his steps and it helped him keep up his pace until he could see Gul high up the mountainside with the sheep and goats. He ran on past her until he found Fatima.

Yacut galloped over from his village the minute a messenger told him the bad news. A party of men under his guidance brought back Ali's body, which was laid down just outside the encampment to be prepared for burial at once by the women, as Ali had clearly been dead for several days. When the women had finished, the washed and shrouded body was laid on a wicker bier and carried to the small burial ground nearby.

Osman walked behind the bier beside his uncle. Dry-eyed, he watched as the body of his father was consigned to the earth. He was sure that if Iskander had been there with him, he'd have been able to weep. Never in all their months apart had he missed his twin so sharply as he had during the last twenty-four hours.

As was customary, Fatima, Gul and the other women stayed behind in the camp and mourned aloud together, the traditional laments echoing across the plateau. When the men returned from the burial, the women left Fatima and went back to their own tents. The communal mourning rituals were now over, and Ali's family was left to deal with the grief and loss in private.

Fatima needed to channel her grief into practical action, and immediately turned her attention to the ewe, which had been brought back alive even though everyone expected her to die. Fatima was determined to save her – Ali had lost his life trying to rescue her, and survive she must. As Osman watched his mother's almost manic determination to save the animal, he understood that this was her way of coping with the loss of her husband. Life had to go on, and the ewe must live.

Fatima was known for her knowledge of bones and her ability to manipulate and set them, and she managed to splint the ewe's broken legs (her back was luckily not broken) and keep her immobile long enough for them to mend. As the weeks passed, it was clear the ewe would walk again. The day the ewe finally trotted unsteadily about the camp everyone cheered her.

It was also the day that Yacut returned. He'd hurried back to his village immediately the funeral was over, and they hadn't seen him since. He rode up just as Osman was tethering the ewe again after its walk, and handed him his horse as if Osman was a groom. Though he was used to his uncle's arrogant ways, Osman almost gave in to the temptation to give the horse a smack on its rump and send it galloping off. Almost, but not quite. Unfortunately, he needed his uncle now.

He heard raised voices and hurried to the family tent. Yacut was sitting inside on Ali's saddle instead of in the guest's place. Offended, Osman remained standing at the back, unwilling to sit beside his uncle. He could see that his mother was very distressed. Yacut turned at once to his nephew, his close-set black eyes fierce and his face flushed with anger.

"Your mother tells me she knows nothing about – about a sum of gold that I believe your father has hidden here somewhere. It came from a tomb I found and it belongs to me."

"Gold?" Osman stared at his uncle in surprise. Gold wasn't something that figured in his family life.

"Gold, gold! Don't play the innocent. You know what gold is, Osman. And don't pretend you don't know where it's hidden." He was breathing heavily.

"I'm afraid I don't, Amja Yacut. I didn't even know Baba had any gold."

Yacut stood up, kicking the saddle aside. "Don't lie to me."

"I'm not lying."

"You are lying! I can see it in your eyes. I'll beat the truth out of you." He took the horse whip from his belt. "Right, Osman. The truth or—" He cracked the whip across Osman's shins and was about to do it again when Fatima gave a little moan.

"Don't beat the boy, Yacut. He knows nothing."

Yacut swung round on Fatima. "So he knows nothing, eh? How can you be so sure of that, unless there's something you're not telling me?"

"Ali never mentioned any gold to me. All he said was, that if – that if anything happened to him, I was to ask Iskander—" She wiped her tears.

"Ask Iskander – go on, woman. Ask Iskander what?"

"To tell me the secret." Her voice was a whisper. They all stared at her. "Ali didn't say what the secret was, but it might have been where the gold was hidden." Fatima started to sob. "But that was before Iskander was taken away from us."

Yacut swung round on Osman. "So you know too! You twins never kept anything from each other." He brought the whip down on Osman's shoulders this time, and Osman couldn't help flinching. But he was more hurt by the knowledge that Iskander had kept a secret from him.

"Iskander never told me. I know you won't believe me, but however much you beat me, there's nothing I can tell you because I know nothing. If Baba made Iskander promise to keep his word about something, he'd never break that promise." There was a long silence, at the end of which Yacut groaned with frustration and sat down again on the saddle. Osman sat down too and waited.

"So only Iskander knows. And we all know where Iskander is." Another pause, and then suddenly Yacut smiled.

His smile is far worse than his frown, thought Osman, hating him from the bottom of his heart.

"Well, well, I didn't come only to talk about gold, I came to give you comfort and help. It would be quite wrong if I didn't do all I could for Ali's family. As you know, it's customary for a man to take responsibility for his brother's widow, and this of course means I will take you, Fatima, as my second wife and look after all of you when the mourning period is over." He paused for a moment as he looked round, very pleased with himself and completely unaware of the consternation he had created. Fatima put her hands over her face, Osman was openly horrified, and Gul, who'd been trying to lip-read, started rocking her body from side to side in distress.

The silence lengthened. Yacut got to his feet, still smiling, and Fatima uncovered her face and did her best to force a smile too. Yacut patted her shoulder. "I know you'll find life hard while you wait, but when the time is right I will fetch you to live with me and my family." His smile faded. "That's why I need to know where the gold is hidden – to cover the expense of all the extra mouths to feed and care for." He glared at Osman while flicking his whip, but Osman met his eye so openly and steadily that Yacut at last seemed to accept his innocence.

"Maybe Baba spent it all on the wedding." Osman waited for his uncle to explode again, but all he did was shake his head, collect his horse, and bid them all good-bye before he galloped off in a hurry.

"You can't let that horrible man marry you!" Osman exploded. "You hate him as much as I hate him!"

"It was easier to let him think I would. I haven't decided what to do now there are just three of us." There were tears in her eyes as she turned to put her arms round Gul and calm her down with kisses and cuddles. Osman was about to leave the tent when his mother stopped him.

"Wait, Osman. Wait. I want to talk to you."

At that moment the ewe bleated loudly outside, demanding food and attention. Osman went to the tent entrance. He couldn't cope with any more.

"I'm going to cut the ewe some fodder, then I'll come back," he managed to say before running up the hillside. He found a place out of sight, flung himself down and howled, grief for his father finally pouring from him. When his racking sobs ended at last, he rolled over and looked at the pale blue sky above him. High on a thermal swung an eagle watching for lambs, but he didn't care. He must go and find Iskander, get to him before his uncle did, to tell him about his father's death and this problem about the hidden gold. He must leave tonight. He'd take Karakachan…

"Osman." Fatima had come up to find him. "Don't despair."

"I absolutely refuse to live with Amja Yacut. Not that he wants me anyway."

"I'm not asking you to. I have a better idea." She sat on a rock beside Osman. "You can guess what Yacut is going to do now."

"Rush to Constantinople to get the secret from Iskander."

"Precisely. That's why he suddenly hurried off. He'll tell everyone he's going to visit his son at last, but that won't be the real reason." Osman sat up, surprised at his mother for being so sharp. "So I think you should leave at once for the city and try to see your brother first. After all, families are allowed one visit a year. I want Iskander to hear about his Baba's death from you, not his uncle."

"I intend to get him out of the palace, Ana."

She shook her head, her eyes troubled. "You'll never succeed in doing that." An inquisitive goat came up and sniffed her.

"I usually succeed when I say I'm going to do something. When I hold up a small box and say I'm going to squash myself into it, everyone says no, it's impossible. And I do it."

Fatima laughed as she pushed away the goat. "Oh, Osman, you'll never change! I know if you've made up your mind to do something, no one will be able to stop you." They looked at each other for a long moment.

"I must leave tonight. I don't want anyone in the tribe to see me go."

His mother hugged him. "Good luck, dearest Osman. Of course you must take the mule—"

"No, I want Karakachan. He'll be better company even if he's slower."

Fatima looked into Osman's eyes, so like her own. "And bring Iskander back so that we can all be together again." She kissed his forehead and then hugged him.

"I'll do my best. But Ana, how are you going to manage without me? You can't look after all the animals with only Gul to help."

"I've decided to sell a lot of them, Osman. I need the money. I'll just keep a few animals – only what Gul and I can look after. Then we'll go back to my own tribe and family, and that's where you'll find us." She gave Osman a sly smile. "I'll never marry Yacut, but it would be good to know the hiding place of this wretched gold. If it exists at all, which I doubt."

Osman grinned back. "Anything to stop Amja Yacut grabbing it, if it does."

She stood up. "I'll go down and prepare a pack for you. There's no time to lose. I have a feeling your uncle will set off as soon as he can."

"*Inshallah.*"

"*Inshallah.*"

Osman watched his mother hurry down the slope back to their tent, and then lay back again for a moment, losing himself in the limitless sky above.

Do not look for answers, my son. The answer will find you... It had. He was beginning to trust that strange spirit in the Cave of the Seven Sleepers.

Then he jumped up and went to cut fodder for the ewe.

JELAL SHOWS HIS HAND

SPRING AT LAST. The palace gardens were suddenly full of flowering cherry trees and timid, leggy gazelles running about beneath them. Iskander had only seen autumn and winter weather since his arrival and was surprised at the freshness and greenness of the palace gardens, and the amount of birdsong from the trees. His heart lifted a little. It was hard to feel hopeless in this burst of colour and activity.

His shoes were now too small and his trousers and sleeves too short. Without being aware of it, he had grown so fast during the winter he was now the size of many of the oldest pages. He was a couple of fingers taller than Ibrahim, and little Ismail came only to his shoulders. Iskander's voice was making odd noises out of his control, and a faint down had appeared on his upper lip.

"You're becoming a man," said Rifat. "Look at you. I wonder what they'll do with you now."

"What do you mean, 'what they'll they do'?" Squeak, growl.

"You'll be promoted to a higher class soon for sure. But they might decide to send you off to train as a janissary."

Iskander was horrified. "I don't want that at all. I'd much rather be a bostanji like you, Rifat."

"Anything's possible, but you won't be able to choose and there's nothing you can do about it. Have some peas and stop worrying about the future. It'll just make you miserable and get you nowhere."

Iskander walked back from the games ground munching the tender peas – pods and all – and wishing he'd had the courage to tell Rifat about Osman and his hopes that, now spring was here, his twin might soon arrive in the city and come up with a plan to free him. The last thing Iskander wanted was to be posted elsewhere.

The change in Iskander's life came within days, and was caused by his skill at the game of jerid. His height and strength now gave him a natural advantage, and his aim had improved with practice and Ibrahim's expert tuition. Once a week there was a contest between the older and younger pages, and this time to the older team's dismay (and especially Jelal's), the younger team won.

Iskander didn't know it, but watching that match closely from a nearby pavilion was one of the sultan's sons, Prince Murad. The fifteen-year-old prince loved all sports and jerid in particular. He was determined to form a strong enough team to beat his father's, but was short of two players. After the match, he sent one of his pages to say he had chosen Jelal from the seniors and Iskander from the juniors to join his team, the Cabbages. The sultan's team was called the Leeks, vegetable team names being a palace tradition.

Iskander was nervous about being chosen, particularly when he saw Jelal's face change from pleasure at his place in the team to a look of stunned disbelief and then fury. Iskander hurried away before Jelal could get hold of him. He tried to discuss the match with Ibrahim, thinking he'd be delighted about the win over the other team. Ibrahim just grunted and didn't meet his eye.

"Anyway, the prince should have chosen you from the juniors, Ibrahim. You've got the best aim of anyone."

"I'm glad he didn't."

"Why?"

"You can be very thick, Iskander. Because the prince

should have chosen his team only from the senior pages, that's why. That's the tradition. Look how angry they all are with you."

Ibrahim turned away and started talking to someone else, and Iskander saw he was right: Jelal and his friends were staring at him with cold, hard eyes as they muttered together. Iskander started to say he didn't deserve to be chosen, it was just luck, but Jelal simply leaned forward and hissed at him.

"You'd better watch out, you creepy little toad. You always were too big for your boots, and now you're going to pay for it."

Iskander felt a shiver of the same nauseous fear he remembered feeling during a beating by his father when it seemed Ali would never stop.

The very next day, Iskander found himself walking behind a haughty, silent Jelal – they'd been summoned to the first practice of the prince's new team. Iskander had decided to play so badly he'd be deselected, so that one of Jelal's friends could take his place. But he found this harder than he expected, mainly because Prince Murad was playing beside him in the team and constantly shouting encouragement and instructions to everyone. Besides, Iskander really loved playing jerid.

He loved the excitement of galloping down the pitch to score, loved the weight of the javelin in his hand and the sight of it arching clean through the hoop when his aim was true. He forgot his decision to play badly, and knew that by the end of that first practice he'd impressed the prince. He also saw that Jelal had been unseated by one of Prince Murad's regular teammates, and suspected this had been done on purpose to curb Jelal's arrogance. Jelal now looked utterly thunderous, so Iskander wasn't surprised when his cousin came up close behind him and clamped a hand on his shoulder on the way back to the pages' hall.

"Mind your back, big boots – I saw you sucking up to the prince." He ground a finger hard into Iskander's ribs as if it was the tip of a dagger.

Iskander didn't have time to answer because a large, angry janissary came up and clipped Jelal's ear smartly to remind him he'd broken the silence rule. Both boys hurried back to the pages' hall while the janissary watched them, and once inside Iskander escaped to the safety of his own platform. He told Ismail what had happened, and Ismail pulled a face.

"Jelal will hate you even more because he was caught breaking the rules."

"Part of me wants to say stuff him and his threats."

"Jelal's always violent when he's annoyed. He's said he expects to be chosen as a page for Prince Murad, and he won't let anyone get in his way."

"I'm not in his way. I don't want to be Prince Murad's page."

"Be careful, Iskander. Angry people don't think straight."

"What do you think he'll do?"

Ismail wagged his head in his funny solemn way. "Hurt you badly enough to stop you playing jerid. Keep your knife on you in future."

"It's only a small knife."

"Better than nothing."

Iskander got his knife out of the cupboard and wished he had a big knife like that one of Ali's always hanging on the carved tent post at home. The thought of this brought back all the other things that hung there in the smoky tent, and the memory was so sharp he shut his eyes and turned away. His mother would be cooking the evening meal now. He could almost smell fried onions and new bread and the sharp scent of her yogurt. She'd be singing if the cooking was going well. Osman would be bringing in the herds before dark, shouting "heh-heh-heh" in his special way to control them. Poor Osman would have so much extra work Iskander ached to think of it. Ali might be helping Osman (unlikely), or smoking with the other men in his tent (more likely), or riding back over the mountain after a day of hunting with his brother Yacut (most likely). Leila would be fetching water with little Gul. But no – Leila might be married and gone.

"Iskander." His mind was so far away Ismail had to shake him. "Stop dreaming – it's time for evening prayers. Didn't you hear the muezzin? Hurry up or we'll be late."

As the two of them scurried through the silent third courtyard to the mosque, they realized Jelal and his friends were just ahead of them. They slowed down but Jelal had spotted them. He made a deliberate gesture, drawing an imaginary knife and jabbing it in Iskander's direction.

But it wasn't by stabbing that Jelal got his revenge.

The prince held daily practice sessions during the next few weeks as he knocked his team into shape. When he was satisfied with their progress, he announced that a match against the Leeks would take place the following day, and though he assured his team he didn't expect them to win, it was clear from the excitement in his eyes he was hoping they had a chance.

On the way to dawn prayers next morning, when everyone had eyes full of sleep and moved in slow motion, Iskander, who happened to be near the end of the column, noticed Jelal and three other senior pages dropping back to walk close beside him. They made sure he was last, then suddenly pinioned his arms, put a hand on his mouth, and dragged him struggling towards a parapet. He thought they were going to throw him straight over and braced himself, but instead while two boys gripped his rigid body tightly, Jelal and the remaining boy grabbed his right arm and brought it down with a crack on the metalwork on top of the wall. In horror Iskander watched his forearm bend and break before the pain hit him and he doubled over, faint with shock. The boys threw him over the parapet and walked on to dawn prayers as if nothing had happened.

All this took place without a word, the only sounds being the grunts of the boys, the crack of bone, the thud of Iskander's body landing in the garden below, and the dawn chorus of birds greeting a new day.

OSMAN'S JOURNEY BEGINS

K ARAKACHAN BRAYED with indignation about being woken and made to travel at night, but calmed down when Fatima fondled his ears and put Ali's fine saddle on his back instead of the makeshift one the donkey was used to.

"This is an important journey, Karakachan. Do your best," whispered Fatima. She turned to Osman and patted his saddlebag. "When you look in there, you'll find your father's big knife."

They stared at each other, knowing how much Ali had prized it. Then Fatima pushed a small purse at him. "Oh, Osman, I wish I had more money than this to give you."

"Don't worry, Ana. I'll earn what I need. People always give me coins when I do my tricks."

"Go now, my son. I will pray for you every sunrise.

And one day we'll all be together again, *Inshallah*."
Fatima gave him a short fierce hug as tears began to run
down her cheeks, and hurried back to the sleeping Gul.

Osman and Karakachan made the journey down to
the plains in record time, but this section was the safe
part. Osman knew that the biggest danger he would face
was from bandits on the main road. They would steal
Karakachan from him as soon as they saw he was travelling alone. He hoped he could join a big caravan heading
west, and for this reason needed to travel by day after
this first night journey. As dawn broke, he saw a small
group of merchants about to leave their night camp, and
fell in with them as far as the main road. Unfortunately
they were travelling east, and he took the familiar road
towards the Lake of Reeds knowing that he and
Karakachan were now at risk.

All the traffic that morning seemed to be going east,
and he almost turned round at one point when an elderly
merchant told him they'd been attacked by bandits the
night before and lost their valuables.

"Have you passed any groups of travellers going west,
Efendi?"

"There is a big group several hours ahead of you, but
I doubt you'll catch them up before dark on your donkey. Pity he's not a horse. Good luck, boy. Take care."

"Now, Karakachan, what's the best thing to do? Hurry like hell to catch them up or hide until we see the bandits pass by tonight, and then go as fast as we can? But maybe the bandits are ambushing everyone from a fixed spot, and we'll never know where until they attack us."

Karakachan twitched his ears, and slowed right down to make it clear he was tired and needed a rest. He'd been going all night and it was now midday.

"Maybe we should play safe and wait. Surely we'll see a group going our way soon."

There was a spring nearby with a good patch of grass, and not far away a cave known to be full of bats. Osman let Karakachan graze, and made sure his knife was in his belt as he went to check out the cave. He peered inside – too dark to see much, but it was certainly big enough to hold the donkey as well as himself. It seemed empty, but suddenly he heard stones crunch and a large man appeared in the entrance. Heart hammering, Osman fled back to Karakachan, the man in pursuit.

"Stop, boy, nothing to fear. Stop. Why this panic?" He didn't seem to be armed, so he probably wasn't a bandit. Osman stood tensely beside Karakachan, who continued to eat. "You're a bit young to be travelling on your own. There are bandits around here, you know.

That's why I'm hiding."

"I know."

"I'm waiting for the next caravan going west."

"I too."

"Two's better than one, boy. We should together." The man smiled, but his eyes didn't leave Karakachan. "And bring your donkey in the cave, when he's finished eating, otherwise he'll draw attention to us."

Osman felt he had no choice, and as dusk fell with no group passing, settled in the cave with Karakachan, still saddled up, in one corner, and the man in the other. He seemed friendly enough, but Osman was uneasy because he knew that a man on foot would always prefer to be riding. When the man settled down to sleep, Osman eased his father's big knife out of the saddlebag and put it under his own body. He then forced himself to stay awake while feigning sleep, terrified he would drop off for real he was so tired. But the knife digging painfully into his back was enough to keep him awake, and when the man started to creep across the cave he was up and ready for him.

"Now, now, don't do anything silly, boy. Give me your donkey and you won't get hurt." He put one hand on Karakachan's neck, feeling for the end of the tether.

In the other was a scimitar, pointing at Osman. "Be sensible —"

Osman lifted Ali's knife in both hands and flung himself forward in a dive, using his body weight to drive the knife into the man's side. The man dropped his great blade with a clatter and clutched himself, his expression blank with surprise at the suddenness of Osman's attack. He then sank to his knees and rolled over gasping as Osman dragged the sleepy donkey out of the cave and leapt on his back. Karakachan dug his hooves in and refused to budge.

"Go, Karakachan, go. Please be a good fellow. GO." Osman had to give him a hard kick before Karakachan would get going, and it was only as the donkey picked up speed on the road he realized he'd left his father's knife behind. Nothing would make him go back for it. If the man lived, he was welcome to it. If he died — Osman's brain froze at the possibility he might be a murderer. His hands were shaking and he felt sick. He longed for the night to end.

Karakachan trotted morosely down the empty moonlit road, and slowly the *clip-clop* of his hooves calmed Osman. They met nothing that night and, as dawn broke, found themselves near the hot springs and the Cave of the Seven Sleepers. Karakachan turned that way automatically and Osman was too tired to stop him. They both needed a break, there was grass and water for the donkey, and a bathe would refresh Osman more than anything else.

He heard shouts and voices as he drew near, and there beside the springs was a large group of travellers, with at least half their number splashing about in the water while others tended fires. Camels, mules and donkeys were grazing under the trees, and when Karakachan brayed a greeting several donkeys brayed back. As Osman slid off Karakachan's back he realized that he was so tired he could hardly stand.

The cavalcade was heading for Konya to trade their goods, and the leading merchant said he was happy for Osman to join them as long as he didn't mind a day's wait. They had a lame horse that needed a rest. Osman explained he and his donkey had been travelling without a break for two nights and a day, and would be glad of a proper rest themselves.

"And why are you in such hurry, boy?"

"Efendi, I have to give news of my father's death to relatives."

The man touched his shoulder in sympathy and told him to give Karakachan to the drovers to feed while he offered him some breakfast. And so Osman found himself with the sort of group he'd dreamed of, and spent several happy days with them until they reached a large karavansarai on the outskirts of Konya.

As they clip-clopped through the huge gates, amongst the crowds he thought he saw Yacut talking to another man across the courtyard. Osman ducked down behind a camel and when he dared to look back, his uncle – if it was his uncle – was riding out through the gates, clearly leaving to go on his way. The man looked even more like Yacut from the back view, and the horse was very familiar. Osman found he was shaking all over after this narrow escape, but at least he knew he was safe for a while because Yacut would hurry on ahead to Constantinople.

Osman could only afford to sleep in the large hall used for the animals, where he parked himself with Karakachan near the drovers, and asked the crowds coming and going if any were travelling as far as Constantinople. He drew a blank for several days, and knew he'd have to move on soon because he was running out of money. He needed to earn some for the next stage of his journey, and decided to do his contortion act.

He found a basket of the right size in the kitchens, and was allowed to borrow it for an hour or two during the serving of the evening meal. He put it on a wide shelf and stood beside it. Then he raised his arms, and with a rhythmic clatter of little wooden castanets he'd made himself, drew the attention of the men nearest him, did a handspring into the basket and folded himself away so quickly their jaws dropped. Soon the whole hall was watching him and, when he went round with his bowl, many of them gave him money. Small coins worth little, but he already had more than he'd started out with. He decided he'd stop there, but at that moment a large red-haired man came up with an empty wooden box. He banged it down on the platform and challenged Osman to fit into it. It was smaller than the basket, and at once there was a murmur round the hall.

"He'll never be able to get into that, it's too small." Men stood up to see better and crowded round Osman.

Osman looked at the red-haired man, who stared back, daring him.

"What will you give me if I manage to do it?"

"I'll double what you've got in your bowl." The red-haired man smiled, showing blackened, uneven teeth between fang-like eyeteeth.

Osman knew he'd been able to fit into boxes that size last year, but wondered whether he'd grown too much over the winter to do it now. He decided he had nothing to lose by giving it a try. He stood inside the box and folded himself down into a squatting position. Yes, he'd just about get in but his head might stop the lid closing properly. He exhaled, wriggled, and compressed himself down further while the watchers all shouted encouragement. He squeezed his face hard into his knees as the red-haired man brought the box-lid down smartly. It hit the back of Osman's skull, which prevented it closing completely. He came out of the box as gracefully as he could, and resisted rubbing the sore part. He suspected the man had meant to hurt him.

"Not quite closed. You've lost the bet."

There was a roar of protest from the other men.

"Don't cheat him, Kizilbash. The box was only open a tiny chink," shouted one. "Come on, pay up."

Kizilbash let the shouts die down and then looked slyly at Osman. "All right, young man, I'll pay you what I promised. But on one condition."

Osman stared at him and waited. The men around all went silent.

"The condition is this: that you join my troupe. I need a contortionist like you."

"Your troupe?"

"Yes, I run a troupe of entertainers. Dancers, acrobats, that sort of thing. Have no fear, it's a professional, well-organized troupe."

The audience lost interest and moved away, and Osman didn't know what to do. He didn't like the look of Kizilbash at all. He was about to say he didn't want his money and turn down the offer, when the man added that the troupe was on its way to Constantinople in the hope of finding fame and fortune.

With an outward show of reluctance, but inwardly a heart beating with joy, Osman pushed his bowl towards the man, took the money, shrugged and agreed to join him.

"Fetch your things and follow me. My troupe is camped not far away. I'll wait for you outside."

When Osman appeared riding Karakachan, the man's sly look returned. "So we are a young fellow with means, are we? Or did we steal the donkey?"

"He's my own donkey."

"If I ask no questions I'll be told no lies, eh?" Kizilbash grinned his unpleasant grin. "Follow me." And he got on a well-kept horse and led the way further out of town.

THE TROUPE

THE GROVE OF TREES ahead was dark and full of sounds, and Osman began to regret losing his father's big knife. Kizilbash rode ahead and gave a sharp whistle. Immediately a small odd-looking man came running up, and it was then Osman noticed the extensive encampment further on through the trees.

"Ahmed, take this new boy and show him where he's going to sleep."

"And who have we here?"

"He's a contortionist. I picked him up in the kara-vansarai."

"Name of?"

"Never asked him." Kizilbash slid off his horse and handed the reins to Ahmed. "He'll probably have to change it anyway." He walked away.

"My name is Osman, and I'm not changing it."

Osman remained sitting on Karakachan, wondering whether he should obey his instinct and gallop off. He didn't like the look of Ahmed, with his yellowish oily face and long hair, any more than his master.

"Come with me, boy, and don't worry – you're the only Osman in the troupe so you can keep your name. Come and meet the other kids. They're all about to eat and I'm sure you're hungry if you're anything like them. Eat, eat, eat is all they do given half the chance."

Ahmed vaulted into the saddle of Kizilbash's horse with such ease and grace Osman was impressed, and, despite himself, he followed. Besides, he was famished and could smell food. Round a big fire was a large group of boys and girls, tucking into a good stew. Osman's stomach was so empty he felt giddy. He hadn't eaten all day because he'd run out of money, and since making some hadn't had a chance to buy a meal.

Karakachan was hungry too, and gave a loud bray when he saw the other donkeys. Osman made sure he was given a full nosebag, and then sat at the edge of a group of boys, took his spoon and bowl out of his saddlebag and began to stuff himself with the meat and chickpea stew. The boys chattered together, ignoring him after their first stare, but seeming to accept his sudden arrival as normal. Osman noticed a group of girls on

the other side of the fire. They were laughing and making more noise than the boys.

"Just be quiet the lot of you. You're worse than a tree
full of starlings." Ahmed didn't seem very perturbed
when the noise continued, but later his shout of, "Right,
off to bed," made the crowd all move at once.

"Osman, you go to the boys' tent over there."

"I have to make sure my donkey's all right."

"He's fed, he's watered, he's tethered. What more
does he want?"

Osman ignored Ahmed and ran through the trees,
finding a happy Karakachan having his nose stroked by
a dark-haired girl with intensely blue eyes. She smiled as
she pulled at one of the donkey's ears. She obviously
knew exactly what donkeys liked.

"My donkey had white eye-patches in a black face
just like yours. I adore donkeys. What's your donkey's
name?"

"Karakachan. I'm Osman. What's your name?"

"Yildiz. Well, it isn't really Yildiz, I was born Ioanna.
I'm Greek, like most of the girls in the troupe —"

"GO TO BED!" shouted Ahmed as he came up.
"Stop fussing over that donkey and get some sleep. We
leave at dawn tomorrow."

The girl ran off as Ahmed pushed Osman towards the

boys' tent. Osman wrapped himself in his blanket and squashed himself into a corner. Exhausted, he fell asleep at once.

On the move, the troupe formed a lengthy cavalcade of twenty young performers, plus some older boys who were musicians, three adults – Kizilbash, Ahmed and Omar, the keeper of the animals, who also did the troupe's cooking – and several horses, mules and donkeys. Karakachan tried to run away when he saw he was to be given a big load. He'd got used to being ridden by Osman, and kicked Omar when he came near. Omar called Osman over, and he soon found himself helping Omar every day. This suited him. He preferred to be near his means of a quick getaway should it be necessary.

He had kept a sharp look out for Yacut, but since the first possible sighting, there'd been no sign of him. Osman had hoped he was now far ahead on the road to Constantinople. So he was horrified to arrive at a small town and see Yacut bargaining with a horse dealer in the market square. He ducked down behind a camel, and prayed that Kizilbash wasn't going to make a stop here. He could hear his uncle's loud, unpleasant voice trying to beat down the dealer, who was getting angry. Yacut's own horse had collapsed on the ground, with whip marks on its flanks. A crowd was gathering, enjoying the row.

As Osman went past out of sight behind his camel, Yacut shouted, "It's a ridiculous price for a horse! And you've got mine in exchange—"

"Your bag of bones is nearly dead!" The dealer shook his fist, and Osman hoped he'd hit Yacut. Then the troupe moved out of earshot, and headed out of town.

Osman felt weak with relief after the close shave.

The troupe soon turned off down a side road, and by nightfall reached a good camping spot near a hot spring, where they were going to base themselves for a week or two to rehearse their performance. The hot spring had only two pools and no waterfall, but the troupe still found it wonderfully refreshing. There was also a good flat area where they could practise, Kizilbash rehearsing the acrobats and contortionists, and Ahmed the dancers. Osman was given the practice uniform of simple cotton trousers and loose top with rope girdle that both sexes wore, and told to follow what was going on as best he could.

They were all far more skilled than he was, and he had to concentrate very hard to keep up. He was poor at juggling, and only had a limited repertoire of contortions – the amazing range of things these boys and girls could do made him feel very clumsy. He'd also prided himself on his forward and back flips, until he saw how many they could do at speed in one go.

Yildiz was one of the acrobats as well as a dancer, and shone at tightrope walking. She ran lightly along the rope Kizilbash had strung between two trees at shoulder height and did a cartwheel in the middle before running on. She was working on doing forward and back flips on the rope, she told Osman, but so far only did these on a rope close to the ground. She'd done the cartwheels high up without anything to break her fall.

"Kizilbash is pleased he's found you," she whispered when they were waiting their turn to climb a pole. "His star contortionist grew too fast and couldn't do his act properly."

"What happened to him?"

"Kizilbash threw him out."

"What do I have to do on this pole?"

"Watch me and try to copy."

Yildiz shinned up it like a lizard, and then came down twirling round it with her body parallel, but Osman failed miserably to do the downward part.

"Don't worry. It's just a knack – you'll pick it up. Three of us come down the pole together when we're performing, one after another. It looks good."

Osman was convinced Kizilbash would throw him out for not being good enough, but at the end of that first day, he redeemed himself. He disappeared into an earthenware jar so tall and narrow that everyone cheered and applauded. No one else had managed to squeeze into it. What they didn't know yet was that this jar was not the smallest he could fit into. He also knew it was only a matter of time before he'd be too big for any of them. He prayed that he'd grow slowly, and that he'd still be the star contortionist when the troupe reached Constantinople.

But he also had to be an acrobat, and there were so many things he couldn't do yet, from walking the tightrope on his hands to somersaulting onto his partner's shoulders. But Kizilbash made no allowances for Osman, forcing him to practise endlessly despite many painful falls.

"You catch up with the others or you're out."

Osman knew he meant it.

The boy dancers being trained by Ahmed had long hair like the girls, and were taught to move and use castanets the way the girls did. Osman was puzzled. He thought of the fierce sword dances traditional for nomad boys, and, when Yildiz came to help him feed and groom

Karakachan, he asked her why these boys were being trained to dance like girls.

"They're chengi dancers, that's why. Don't you know what a chengi is?"

"I wouldn't have asked you if I did."

"They have to try and look like girls when they perform – you know, long hair, make-up, girls' clothes – and they can go where the girls can't. Like dancing for the janissaries in the inns, or for the pashas in their palaces. All men like to watch the chengis dance, and the boys look so pretty they sometimes forget they're not girls. And of course the chengis all have to choose a girl's name – so for instance Orhan, the chief dancer, is known as Yasmin." She laughed. "Don't look so disgusted!"

"Why can't you girls pretend you're boys pretending to be girls? Then you could go into the same places."

"We wouldn't get away with it. Anyway we have to dance for the women in the harems. Boys can't go in there just like we can't go in the selamlik. Where do you come from, Osman, if you don't know this?" Yildiz was still laughing at him, but she had such twinkling eyes he didn't take offence.

"I'm a nomad, and we have different customs in our tribes."

"Well, as you know, I'm a Greek and we have different customs too, but not so different." Her face suddenly lost all its light, and she sighed. "Why did you agree to join this troupe if you're a nomad? They don't usually want to go and work in towns and cities."

"I have to get to Constantinople and it seemed a good way."

"Why would a nomad boy need to go to the city?" Her eyes glinted as if she didn't believe him. He stared at her, and suddenly longed to talk to someone about Iskander.

"My twin brother is a slave in the sultan's palace." He said this so softly she had to lean in close. "I want to find him and set him free."

She stared back at him, her blue eyes alert but expressionless. "Was he stolen?"

"His freedom was stolen. He was collected in the youth-levy." Osman stopped, feeling he'd said enough. He couldn't say Iskander's name and she didn't ask. There was a silence, then he asked her how she'd come to join the troupe.

She didn't answer, but instead turned and hugged Karakachan. "My donkey was called Nanos. It means midget in Greek. He was the smallest donkey in the village, but with a mind of his own – like Karakachan."

Then she slipped away, as usual doing a few cartwheels en route, to join the other girls.

Osman wondered if Yildiz had been stolen or maybe even sold by her father to Kizilbash for money, or if she'd been left an orphan by the plague like some of the others in the troupe. Well, she might decide to tell him one day, or she might not. She was very independent, and kept herself apart from the other girls. There was something about Yildiz that made you look at her twice. She wasn't pretty – her nose was too big and her mouth was crooked – yet when she performed her face became so alive it made all the pretty girls around her look insipid.

Osman had got to know her best of the whole troupe because she so loved Karakachan, and he had to admit he looked forward to her visits as much as his donkey did. The other girls took no notice of him and all the boys were rather unfriendly. The eight chengi dancers formed a tight clique of their own, as did the group of musicians, and the acrobats seemed to resent him because he'd come into the troupe and very quickly been billed as the best contortionist. But he didn't mind being ignored by them; one friend in the troupe was enough, even if she was a girl.

❀　❀　❀

When they were about to strike camp and move on, the chief chengi dancer, Orhan, alias Yasmin, developed a fever and became too ill to travel. After a couple of days waiting in vain to see if he'd improve, Kizilbash decided to leave him behind at the nearby village, much to Ahmed's utter dismay.

"Never be ill," whispered Yildiz. "Kizilbash just ditches you. He doesn't care. That evil man has no heart. Ahmed has a heart but he spends too much time with his boss for it to show very often."

"Shush. Here comes Ahmed." Osman turned and continued his packing until a tug from behind pulled off the piece of cloth he usually wore turban-style round his head.

"Your hair's quite long now I see, boy."

"I'm going to get it cut at the next hamam."

"Oh, no, you're not. You're going to grow it longer. You, Osman, are going to train as my new chengi. Congratulations." Ahmed's tone was so ironic for a moment Osman wasn't sure if he was serious. Ahmed laughed and clapped him on the shoulder. "Right, that's settled. Now you must choose a girl's name – I find new chengis do better if they have a girl's name right from the start. What'll it be? What about Shireen? We've never had a Shireen before."

Osman stared aghast at Ahmed's yellow face and leering eyes.

"I refuse to be a chengi, Ahmed. Ask one of the other boys."

"Don't be cheeky. Everyone wants to be a chengi."

"Not me. I'm happy as I am."

Ahmed gave him a hard clip on the ear. "Too bad. I need you as a chengi, and the boss agrees. Tell me what name you've chosen when you come to the practice tomorrow."

Yildiz was hiding behind Karakachan, and bobbed up the moment Ahmed left. "You must do it, Osman."

"NO! Never! I'd die rather than wear make-up and girls' clothes. Ugh. I'm going off now to tell Kizilbash I refuse point-blank to be a chengi."

"Wait." She crept close to him and whispered. "Don't forget your twin brother."

"What do you mean?"

"Everyone knows the sultan loves watching chengi dancers. They're always welcome at Topkapi Palace. And a chengi who's also a good contortionist … might be especially welcome."

"I can't be a chengi, Yildiz. Just the thought of it makes me feel sick."

"It's only because you're a nomad and chengis aren't

part of your way of life." She went up closer, looking at his face and picking up a lock of his hair. He pulled his head away impatiently and she gave a wicked grin. "I think you'll make a stunning girl. And I promise I'll help you with all the steps so you catch up with the others."

Someone yelled her name at that moment and she ran off, still grinning as she turned some cartwheels. Osman went over to Karakachan and put his arms round his donkey's neck.

"What shall I do, Karakachan? Even if it gets me into the palace, what on earth will Iskander think if he sees me pretending to be a dancing girl? I can't do it, Karakachan, I can't do it."

AN UNWELCOME VISITOR

IT WAS RIFAT WHO FOUND ISKANDER. The old gardener was walking back from dawn prayers gazing dreamily at the sword-like streaks of light formed by the rising sun above the Asian shore when he heard groaning. At first he couldn't work out where it came from, and then realized it was from his precious broadbean bed. Something had knocked a patch of plants flat, and he hurried angrily towards the noise. He stopped dead when he saw a boy's prone body, and rolled him over carefully.

"Iskander! What are you doing down here – did you fall off the wall?" Iskander groaned again, eyes shut. "And you've broken your arm! How did you manage that falling onto soft earth such a short distance! It's a bad break too."

"I didn't fall … I was pushed…" Iskander felt faint with pain.

"It's a bad break, but clean by the look of it. Now listen, boy, I'm going to get some of my canes and twine and splint your arm with them. You'll feel more comfortable. Then I'll take you to the pages' hospital."

He hurried off and came back with some clean canes, rope and soft leaves to serve as padding round the arm.

"Here's a piece of wood to bite on when I move your broken bones. This is going to hurt like hell for a moment."

It hurt so much Iskander passed out, much to Rifat's relief. He quickly joined the break and bound the arm securely between the canes. He then found a length of fencing to use as a stretcher, called another bostanji, and between them they carried Iskander to the pages' hospital, which was situated beyond the great kitchens near the main palace gate. Iskander regained consciousness on the way, and smiled up at Rifat. "Thanks, Rifat. My arm feels a bit easier."

"The doctors will check what I've done, but I've set many bones in my time and they've all come out well. Who did this to you? Don't tell me it broke by accident because I won't believe you. Somebody smashed that bone on purpose."

Iskander said nothing.

"I'd bet my pay it was that page Jelal. He's so jealous

of you I'm surprised he didn't kill you."

Iskander remained silent, but despite himself his face said it all.

The prince was annoyed to find his team short of a promising player, particularly as he was told by Jelal that Iskander had been showing off when he fell off the wall.

"Showing off about what?"

"Saying he was going to score more hits than you, Sire."

"He's always so quiet. How surprising."

"You only see him on his best behaviour, Sire. Like many nomad boys, he's two-faced." Jelal smirked.

"Tell the reserve he's playing. Well, I had high hopes of Iskander, but he's let me down."

Naturally, this conversation was overheard by a member of the palace staff on duty at the jerid pitch, and eventually it got back to Rifat. The old man was furious, and decided to do something about it if he had the chance. He'd been working in the palace for so long he could say what he liked to the royal family, as long as he picked the right moment. A few days later he was part of the crew rowing Prince Murad, whom he'd known since he was a little boy, up the Bosphorus to the Sweet

Waters of Asia for a picnic with his mother, and as the prince boarded he passed close to Rifat.

"Sire, I need to inform you of something."

The prince paused.

Rifat didn't care that he was breaking the rules of protocol addressing the prince like this, and didn't mince his words when he described what had happened, accusing Jelal not only of breaking Iskander's arm, but also of spreading lies about him. The prince listened, nodded, thanked him for the information, and went calmly to sit as usual in the little carved and gilded cabin on the stern of the long wooden boat. Rifat was satisfied. If his information hadn't been accepted, he'd at best have been ignored, at worst banished from the boat and punished.

Doctor Reuben, one of the royal physicians, crossed the large first courtyard as he headed for the pages' hospital. He very rarely treated patients here because he was attached to the royal household with its own hospital, but Prince Murad had asked him to report on the condition of a particular page and offer any treatment necessary. He pushed his way through the chattering crowd of courtiers, traders, carters and woodcutters. Since the silence rule didn't apply to this outermost area it felt more like a bazaar than a royal palace. Doctor

Reuben found Iskander sitting at one of the Hospital windows watching the crowds.

"Prince Murad has sent me. He wishes me to examine your arm to see how it is healing. Please remove the sling. Stretch your arm straight. Don't be nervous, it won't drop off. Excellent. It's been well set – there's no distortion. Have you been using it at all?"

"No, sir."

"Then you must start doing some special exercises from today. Let me demonstrate. Stretch out the arm, then press against the wall, like this. You mustn't be timid, boy. My methods work. Increase the frequency until you feel confident enough to leave off the sling. You'll be writing with this hand very soon, and playing jerid again before you know where you are."

Iskander had been assuming his arm wouldn't be much good in future, and stared in amazement at this imposing figure who was taking such an interest in him. The regular doctors, once they saw the splint had been well done, had more or less ignored him.

"I will return in a week and if you have made good progress, the prince has asked me to take you to see him."

"Thank you, sir."

"It's the prince you should thank, not me," said

Doctor Reuben. He stared at Iskander disapprovingly before sweeping out. There seemed nothing special about this page to warrant such royal interest.

"Well, well, who's the royal favourite?" teased Omar, a page who'd come in a couple of days before with a high fever, but was now so much better he was being discharged next day.

"Sending a doctor doesn't make me a favourite. It's the last thing I want to be anyway." Iskander felt very uneasy. This boy was in Jelal's class and would no doubt tell him about the doctor's visit. He could imagine Jelal taking great delight in breaking his arm again the moment he was back in the pages' hall. Or the other arm. Or both.

"Actually, I believe you, Iskander, though the others might not."

"I'd be grateful if you didn't tell Jelal about it."

"Why should I? Jelal's no friend of mine. He doesn't approve of me because I'm Russian. He says Russia is the Ottoman Empire's enemy and I'm not to be trusted." Omar laughed. "I keep telling him I'd rather be Omar here than Dimitri in Russia, but he doesn't believe me."

"How did you get here from Russia?" Iskander stared in curiosity at the page – he'd never met a Russian before.

"Oh, I ran away from home, stowed away on a cargo

boat going across the Black Sea, nearly starved to death when I got to the city, was picked up by janissaries and then hit it lucky because they brought me to the palace. Lots of pages had suddenly died from some disease so they were short on numbers. That was five years ago." He grinned. "Now tell me your story."

Iskander gave him an edited version, with no mention of a twin brother. He was relieved when Omar was sent back to the pages' hall, because he'd realized being in the hospital gave him the best chance yet of escape. This was where the outside world intermingled most closely with the palace and, in the noise and confusion of wagons entering and people buying palace produce, he hoped he could slip out of the window and join a team of carters. His main disadvantage, apart from the broken arm, was that he was so obviously a page, with his shaven head, little cap and special uniform. Rifat had brought his bag of personal stuff over, including his precious coat, but it would be too small now. He needed some different clothes and something to cover his shaved head. He'd have a look in the hospital's little hamam next time he went there to bathe.

He spent all day at the window, watching everything. The detachment of janissaries on duty at the main gate checked everyone arriving and leaving. The black eunuchs in charge of running the hospital left him alone, but he noticed there were always at least two on guard nearby. Omar had told him that the oldest pages had a system for getting out: they pretended to be ill and, once they were admitted to the hospital, bribed the eunuchs to let them out through a special postern gate to go for some fun in the city. But this cost a lot, and besides, the eunuchs wouldn't let anyone out who hadn't been in the palace school for years and could be trusted to be back by dawn. Iskander hadn't a hope – he was too new and too young.

So he watched and waited, just in case some unforeseen opportunity suddenly arrived. He did his exercises standing at the window, but kept his sling on even though he didn't need it, hoping that would lengthen his stay in the hospital. Each day he expected to be sent back, but everyone seemed to have forgotten about him, including the prince's doctor. If only the eunuchs didn't guard the hospital so closely.

One morning he noticed a boy he hadn't seen before darting round a large wagon and climbing nimbly up onto the logs. The boy looked very familiar. Surely it was Osman? The quick movements, the way he tied his head-cloth. Yes, it was Osman! Trust him to find a way into the palace on a carter's wagon. Heart pounding,

Iskander leant out of the window and hissed "Osman" as penetratingly as he could without shouting.

No reaction. There were janissaries nearby and he didn't dare shout, so he hissed again a little louder and started waving as the boy turned round.

The boy jumped down from the wagon without even looking in Iskander's direction. Iskander stared at his fat ugly face. Of course it wasn't Osman. How could he have mistaken this squat, heavy boy for Osman? Iskander felt stinging tears of disappointment collecting, and forced them back because one of the black eunuchs came up at that moment and told him not to hang out of the window. Then the window was banged shut and barred on the outside.

Iskander slumped against the wall. He couldn't believe he'd mistaken a complete stranger for his twin. But perhaps when they next met they might both have changed so much, they'd find it difficult to recognize each other. The months were passing, he was changing fast, and so, no doubt, was Osman.

He had a sudden overwhelming desire to look at his half of the talisman and slipped it out of its hiding place in his old coat. Oh, what intelligent eager little eyes the bird had today. Surprised, almost cheerful.

"What do you know, little bird? Where's your twin,

because where he is, there Osman will be. Where is he? Tell me, tell me." As Iskander stroked the talisman the hairs on his neck rose in response to an unseen presence. Then a voice seemed to fill his head.

Don't look for answers, my son. The answer will find you...

He looked round, puzzled. Rifat? It sounded like an ancient voice, and the only old man he knew was Rifat. Did he hear the voice or did he dream it? It seemed to be linked to the talisman. Then the sound of real footsteps approached and he tucked the talisman away just before a janissary entered and told him brusquely that he had a visitor. Expecting the doctor, Iskander looked at the door. To his complete surprise, there stood Uncle Yacut with a very uneasy-looking Jelal in tow. The janissary pushed them in and stood on guard in the open doorway.

For a moment Iskander thought he was hallucinating again, and blinked to dispel it. No, it was his uncle in the flesh, giving him a big smile that didn't quite reach his close-set eyes, and opening his arms to embrace his nephew.

"I was paying a visit to my son and of course I insisted on seeing you too! They said it was irregular, however your Amja Yacut succeeded in persuading the authorities. But I didn't expect to find you in hospital! Poor Iskander, how did you break your arm?"

"An accident, Amja." Iskander didn't look at his cousin. "I'm fine, and I'll be out of here soon."

"Well, you're looking splendid – and how you've grown. It must be all the sultan's good food, eh?" Yacut laughed, winking at the janissary who totally ignored him. A silence fell, and Yacut shuffled his feet and shifted his gaze about. Jelal stood with his eyes fixed on the floor, unusually quiet. Then Yacut cleared his throat.

"I have come with some terrible news, Iskander. My brother – your father – has also met with an accident, only his was more serious. He fell down a ravine and, alas, did not survive." Yacut put his hands together and fell silent. Iskander stared at him, clearly not quite following. "Ali is dead, Iskander."

Iskander slumped onto a stone ledge as his legs gave way. He felt giddy and fixed his eyes on his uncle's thick black beard as if it would steady him while his uncle went on talking, talking, talking. Some of the words went in – ewe, ledge, dead for some days, funeral. Then a silence fell, and the janissary moved his feet and made signs the visit should end soon.

"Please go, Amja."

"Iskander, I know this is a very difficult time for you. I fully understand you need to be on your own after this tragic news, but I have an important question to ask you. I wouldn't ask you now but I won't have another chance. Your mother told me you are the only person who knows a secret hiding place of your father's. You need to tell us where it is."

"Did Ana send you?" Iskander felt as if part of his brain was frozen, and only questions of no importance could come out.

"Yes, in a manner of speaking. Don't forget, as my brother's widow she's my responsibility now. You see, some gold" – Yacut cleared his throat – "some gold has disappeared which belongs to the family—"

"My family."

"We're all one family now, Iskander. So you must tell me where Ali hid it." His voice grew sharper.

"I think it should go to Osman and my mother and Gul. They're going to need it. So I'll only tell Osman."

"Ah." Yacut put his hands up as if forced to say something he did not want to. "Forgive me, forgive me, I was hoping I would not have to tell you – Osman lost his life trying to save his father."

Jelal took a swift intake of breath as he turned to Yacut. "Baba—"

Yacut took no notice of his son. "I was trying to keep it secret from both of you – after all you boys were never going to find out, shut up as you are in here…" He tailed off. "I thought it would be too upsetting." He rubbed his cheeks. "As indeed it is."

Iskander stood up to his full height. He was slightly taller now than both his uncle and his cousin. His eyes and face were frozen. "Please go away, both of you."

"The secret, Iskander."

"The gold is hidden in the pommel of my father's saddle. It belongs rightfully to my mother." Somehow he kept control of himself.

"You're wrong, Iskander — your mother will soon become my wife, and that is the reason why the gold is mine. And I found the tomb it came from first—"

Iskander turned to the janissary. "Please take my visitors away." The janissary, who'd been greatly intrigued by the unexpected end to the conversation, did so with alacrity, and then gave orders that the poor young page weeping his heart out behind the door was not to be disturbed.

FATIMA

"COME HERE, OSMAN. Oops, sorry, sorry, I must call you Fatima." Ahmed beckoned, an evil grin on his face. "Your turn now. Let's make you look beee-oootiful."

The other chengis tittered as Ahmed waved his rouge pot. Osman eyed the doorway to see if he could escape, but Kizilbash stood there solidly blocking it. He always came to watch the chengis being transformed into pretty girls. Osman/Fatima was the last to be made up, and fidgeted in misery while Ahmed kohled his eyes and defined his brows and reddened his cheeks and lips.

"Hair's still a bit short, but what fine curls we have here." He pulled at one and laughed, while Kizilbash leered at his new chengi. "And look how well his outfit suits him."

"Not bad." Kizilbash grinned and picked his teeth as

he watched the final stages of Fatima's transformation.

Then Ahmed forced Osman to twirl and show off his new clothes. His outer garment was like a long waistcoat with splits in the sides, made of pink brocade and liberally covered with embroidery. Underneath it he wore a pale green silk top and matching baggy trousers tightly bound round his ankles. On his feet were pointed embroidered shoes. He had never felt so ridiculous in his life and was ready to die of shame and embarrassment. He wanted to rip the whole outfit off.

"I can't dance in these stupid shoes."

"You don't have to. They're for show. You take them off once you start dancing."

"This is crazy, Ahmed. I haven't had enough training, I'll mess it up for the other dancers."

"Just do what I told you, stay at the back and copy the others. Keep still and play your clackers if you're lost. At least you're good at those." He gave Osman a pair of wooden clackers to thread on the fingers of one hand and a castanet for the other hand, and led him outside to join the others. The whole troupe, boys and girls, promptly made exaggerated "ooh-aahs", waggled their hips and cried, "Oh, what a beauty Fatima is!"

Osman was ready to hit them all, but Yildiz came up and whispered, "Take no notice. They're trying to put you off. They love it when boys make a hash of their first chengi dance." She glared at Osman, her blue eyes fierce. "And don't you dare let me down, Osman, not after all that extra work we've put in."

It was true – Yildiz's coaching had consolidated much that he'd learned. Osman could now twirl for minutes on end without feeling giddy, could bend himself backwards until his forehead touched the ground while still keeping a rhythm going on the clackers, and could do all the complicated dance steps without falling over himself. He didn't like some of them, particularly those in which he had to wiggle his hips round in a circle, but Yildiz had been adamant.

"You've got to be as good as the others by the time we get to the city or Kizilbash will look for someone else to take your place. There are plenty of good chengi dancers there, and money will buy anyone he wants. If our troupe isn't the best it won't be invited to the palace. So come on, Fatima, when you're dancing you've got to think 'I am a girl' and enjoy it! It's only play-acting after all."

"I just wish I was making my debut in a small village rather than here in Bursa."

The troupe had been in the royal city of Bursa for

several weeks now, and since it was the last stop before Constantinople, Kizilbash and Ahmed had worked everyone hard. That evening the boys were performing for a local pasha and his male guests in the selamlik, with the girls entertaining his wives in the harem. Kizilbash obviously knew the pasha well, and had dressed up splendidly for the occasion. He sat with the guests, leaving Ahmed to deal with the chengis.

Osman lurked at the back of the troupe, aware that the boys around him were giggling excitedly and had started behaving like girls, calling each other by their girl's names – Nilufer, Fayruz, Nasrin, Leila. One of them turned to him and said, "So why did you choose the name Fatima?"

"Why not?" Osman was not going to admit he'd named himself after his mother so that he wouldn't forget what he was called.

"Too much noise, girls," called Ahmed. His eyes gleamed; he'd been a chengi himself until he grew too old and there was nothing he liked better than running a private performance in a pasha's luxurious selamlik. "Come here, Fatima, you naughty thing, your rouge is a bit smudged."

Luckily at that moment the chengis were summoned, and Ahmed didn't have a chance to tinker with Osman's make-up. Osman slunk in last, hoping no one was looking at him. He felt utterly ludicrous and wanted the floor to swallow him up. The musicians started playing a catchy dance tune, and he followed the others and kept his clackers and castanet going more or less in time with them. He noticed how sharply the mens' eyes assessed all the chengis, often turning to each other with a remark about them as they sat smoking their nargiles and nodding to the beat. Kizilbash was near the front, watching Osman closely, and the man's hard eyes were deliberately trying to put him off his beat. He tried to calm himself – he mustn't make any mistakes. His hands were sweating with tension. So far so good.

There was a pause as the musicians and chengis took a short break, and then the band launched into the final number, fast and rhythmic so that the whole audience started to sway and clap their hands to the rhythm. On cue, the dancers started to join the beat and twirl, Osman included. He was so pleased he hadn't missed this entry he began to enjoy the dance more. *I am Fatima*, he said to himself as he twirled, *I am Fatima*. He caught the fever of the beat, and found himself as carried away as the other dancers. He forgot Kizilbash, he forgot Ahmed, he was aware only of the dance and the dancers around him all doing exactly the same steps in unison, and then disaster struck. His castanet slipped from his hand and he skidded on it, falling flat onto his back. He knew the other chengis were now working up to the finale and bending backwards until their foreheads touched the floor behind them while their hands and heels still tapped to the beat, so he lay still until the dance was over. Then he leapt to his feet and bowed with the other chengis hoping his fall hadn't been too obvious. The audience applauded wildly but Kizilbash sat quite still, his cold eyes fixed on Osman and his mouth turned down.

"So how did you get on?" Yildiz caught up with Osman as they walked back to the encampment on the edge of Bursa.

"Don't talk about it."

"What happened?"

Osman described his fall and how he'd dealt with it.

"Sounds as if no one noticed."

"Oh, yes, they did. Kizilbash gave me a filthy look."

"Where is he?"

"He's stayed on at the pasha's, but no doubt he'll kill me in the morning. I'm sorry I let you down, Yildiz."

"It doesn't matter." She looked depressed.

"But in a way I didn't let you down." Osman felt shy

describing his experience, yet felt he owed it to her. "I ... sort of lost myself in the dance." He stared down at his fancy slippers. "Even though I mucked it up at the end, it was all much better than I expected. I understood what you were trying to explain." He looked quickly at her to see if she was laughing at him, but Yildiz wasn't even smiling. "It was magic, a bit like I imagine flying to be—" He stopped because he couldn't put into words that sense of exhilaration. Yildiz still said nothing. "Anyway, all the chengis were given gold coins by the pasha, even me, so it wasn't too much of a disaster."

"Lucky chengis. The wives weren't so generous." Yildiz forced a smile. "Being a girl is a real pain sometimes. Chengis have much more fun. And they're always paid double the money."

"I want you to have my gold coin."

"Don't be silly. That's not what I meant."

"Well, I mean it. I couldn't have done it without you, Yildiz. Next time I'll keep the money, but this time you must have it." He put the little gold coin in her hand. She tried to hand it back, but Osman refused to take it. They walked along the dark lane behind the others in silence for a while, and then Yildiz suddenly said with a catch in her voice, "This is the first gold coin I've ever had."

"You did me a favour. You deserve it."

"When my uncle sold my donkey he never gave me any of the money. I'm sure he got several gold coins for Nanos."

"Poor you." Osman was inwardly praying that at last she'd tell him the story of her life. After a silence she went on.

"I was living with my uncle and aunt because..." She paused and Osman was afraid she'd stop. But she didn't. "You see, I lost my parents and my brothers when they all died of plague. The pilgrims brought plague to our village when they returned home from Mecca. Almost everyone in the village, both Muslims and Greeks, died that year. I don't know why I didn't, but somehow I got better. I was alone except for Nanos, so I decided to go and find my uncle and aunt down the coast not too far away. I rode there on Nanos. I really loved that donkey. He was the most intelligent donkey in the world – yes, even more intelligent than Karakachan – and he used to twitch his ears if he heard me crying, as if he was saying, 'Cheer up, it'll all be better soon.' He kept me warm at night. He was such a comfort to me." She said nothing for a while. Osman waited, hoping none of the others would come and interrupt them.

"At first my uncle was kind to me, but he had some

bad luck with the harvest and needed money and that's how Nanos was sold. I was out in the fields helping my aunt, and I came back and found my donkey gone. It was like losing the last bit of my family, Osman. That sounds stupid but it's true. I cried and cried. Then I ran away to see if I could find him, and of course I couldn't. Then I came upon Kizilbash's troupe on the road, and here I am."

"It's such a sad story, Yildiz." He put his arm over her shoulders and hugged her, near tears. He saw she had tears on her cheeks too. She rubbed them away roughly.

"No sadder than some of the others I've heard."

"But you lost all your family."

"The plague that comes back with the pilgrims is a terrible thing." She gave a big sigh and moved away from his arm but smiled at him as she did so. "I'm glad I've told you my story. I've never been able to talk to anyone about it before."

"I'm glad I know it."

She had her hand in her pocket, and Osman knew she was fingering the gold coin. He felt very happy he'd given it to her, even happier to realize how easily he could earn more. And in that moment he decided he'd make sure Fatima became the best chengi in Constantinople. He'd practise till he dropped. He'd stop being so worried about being dressed up as a girl when he danced, and he'd let Ahmed have his way over make-up and clothes. He had to make sure he became good enough to dance in the palace. He needed to earn lots of gold, so that when he and Iskander found each other and escaped together they'd have plenty of money to live on, and there'd be enough over for Yildiz.

Ahmed shouted for him at that moment and he had to join the other chengis. After the boys had all hung their costumes up, cleaned off their make-up and changed back into rough ordinary clothes, Ahmed took him aside.

"Well, you didn't do too badly for someone who doesn't want to be a chengi. Pity about the fall, but I expect you did it on purpose. Anyway, this'll cheer you up. Kizilbash has decided you're too inexperienced to stay in the chengi troupe. It would take too long to train you and there's no time anyway. He's decided to look for someone already famous in the city to hire as our lead dancer. He's riding on ahead of us to find one by the time we arrive. So you can relax, Osman, and go back to acrobatics and contortions. I'm sure that's made your day."

YILDIZ AND THE GOLD COIN

"WHAT'S THE MATTER, OSMAN?"

"Nothing."

"Is Karakachan sick?"

"Don't be silly. Does he look sick? If anything, he's getting too fat stuck here in Bursa."

"Well, something's the matter. Would you like the gold coin back?"

"Yildiz, I gave it to you. When I give someone something, it's theirs to keep."

"All right, all right. If you're going to be so touchy I'll take myself off." She stroked Karakachan's nose in farewell and cartwheeled away. Osman felt mean, but he couldn't bring himself to talk to anyone right now about his disappointment. Instead he rubbed his donkey down so hard and so long Karakachan grew restless and gave him a sharp nip.

"Sorry, Karakachan, sorry. I'm just fed up and taking it out on your skin. I don't know what to do next. Everyone says the acrobats and contortionists don't get asked to perform in the palace because the sultan has his own troupe. It's only the chengis and girl dancers who get asked. And I've mucked that up. How on earth am I going to get in there to help Iskander? But perhaps he's already escaped and is now looking for me." Osman stared into Karakachan's long-suffering black eyes. "If he has got away we'll never find each other. I had no idea Turkey was so big, Karakachan. It's scary. It makes me feel I'm no more than a flea on your back and Iskander's a flea on another donkey's back a hundred miles away. How are we ever going to meet up? It's nearly summer and soon it will be winter again and it's all hopeless."

Feeling desperate, Osman went to sit on a bale in the corner of the stables. He hugged his knees and, putting his face down on them, rocked himself. Then a hand tapped gently on his shoulder. He could smell sesame seeds and when he opened his eyes he saw why. Yildiz was holding a simit – a ring of sesame-coated bread – under his nose.

"Come on, Osman. Snap out of your gloom and eat this. I've just been talking to Ahmed, so I know why you're upset."

"I was expecting too much to be a proper chengi after so little training."

"It was my fault too. I thought we could do it. But listen to me, Osman, because I've thought of a way we can still make it happen. We've got a bit of time before Kizilbash rejoins us. Ahmed said we've got another week here in Bursa, and then we have to make our way to the sea where we'll meet up with him again. We'll be based in a port called Uskudar on the opposite side of the Bosphorus from the city. Ahmed says that's where Kizilbash always stays with his troupe because there's a big karavansarai there run by his brother, so he gets a special deal for all the animals as well as us."

Osman stared at her, puzzled. "And how are we to perform in the city if we are over the sea from it?"

"We go over by ferry. Ahmed says it's a short journey."

"I've never seen the sea."

"Really? I love the sea. I miss not seeing it every day."

"But I don't see what all this has got to do with me getting back to being a chengi."

"You really are being thick today, Osman. Time is what you need and you've got some time. You can train like mad. Ahmed'll help you."

"Why should he? He knows Kizilbash doesn't want me.

Ahmed won't waste his time on me."

"Yes, he will." Yildiz sat silent for a moment and then added in a rush, "I told him I'd pay him a gold coin if he gave you extra teaching."

"No, Yildiz."

"Yes."

"I won't accept it. That money's yours."

"I know it's mine. So I can do what I like with it, right?" She stared at him, her eyes bright with frustration. Then suddenly she laughed and prodded him. "Come on, Osman, don't be so boring. It's the only way out, and you know it. You can give me another gold coin when you're Fatima the Famous!"

"But Ahmed thinks I don't want to be a chengi."

"I told him you'd changed your mind. He was pleased. He thinks you could be good."

"But Kizilbash is going to hire some star chengi to lead our troupe and he won't want me in it as well."

"You're getting on my nerves, Osman, you really are. I didn't know you could be such a moaner." Yildiz bent over backwards and walked around like a crab. She reached Karakachan who looked distinctly puzzled to find her face upside-down beside his. "Don't you agree, Karakachan? What's happened to the get-up-and-go-for-it Osman?"

"I've been feeling really low. It all suddenly seemed so hopeless. I don't know for sure where Iskander is. I don't know if he's alive. Even if he is, and he's at the palace, it's full of people who are going to stop him getting out. The more I think about it, the more hopeless it seems."

She stood up straight again in a quick, graceful movement and grinned at him. "Then don't think about it. We're going to get you into that palace, never fear. I've got this feeling Iskander's there, and when I get one of my feelings I'm usually right. Think how thrilled he'll be to see you!"

"Even dressed as a chengi?" Osman was smiling at last. "I can just imagine his face!"

"He won't care what you are when he sees it's really you. He'll be so pleased. You'll both have to be very careful not to give the game away."

"I know." He hesitated and looked away. The thought of seeing Iskander again brought him suddenly close to tears. When he turned back to go on talking to her, her mood had changed completely. Her blue eyes were dark with pain. Osman was sure she was thinking about her own dead family, and waited for her to say something. When she did she took him by surprise. "What's it really, really like being a twin?"

He opened his mouth and then shut it again. He wanted to say that you had a bond that was like a bridge between two brains, and that since he'd been parted from Iskander he'd felt incomplete. He wanted to say it was the closest two human beings could get, being together before birth and then being born almost at the same moment. He wanted to say many things, but didn't want to upset her any more than she was already. She'd suffered enough in her short life. In the end all he said was, "He's just a brother. I suppose we're extra close because we were born together."

"Oh. I thought you'd feel close in a different way — even know what the other was thinking. I had brothers, I loved them, but I didn't feel close to them, maybe because they were older than me. To tell you the truth I was closer to my donkey!" She laughed, but Osman could see the pain hadn't left her eyes. He gave her hand a quick squeeze just as Ahmed gave his loud familiar shout summoning everyone to supper.

Since Osman was now serious about his chengi training, Ahmed began to work him hard both with the chengi troupe during the day and on his own each evening. The other chengis began to accept him too, now that they saw he didn't despise them.

"They say it takes years to become a good chengi but that's nonsense if you're already an acrobat – which you are. But it can take months and you don't have months." Ahmed and Osman were sitting resting one evening, with Yildiz nearby. She came to every evening practice session to make sure she was getting her money's worth. "Let's see you do that series of steps again, this time without following me."

Osman leapt and twirled, bending his body as sinuously and gracefully as he could. He'd noticed how boys tended to be angular in their movements in a way that girls weren't. It wasn't just that girls had softer skins, and more rounded limbs, it was something much deeper. He watched Yildiz dancing and copied her faithfully, but was afraid he'd never get the special quality he was after. Maybe it was impossible. Maybe you had to be a girl to get it.

"Well done, Osman. Not a single mistake that time." Ahmed yawned. "That's enough. End on a good note. Time for bed, both of you." He yawned again and left them. They didn't move – while Kizilbash was away, they could ignore some of the rules without getting punished.

"What did you think?"

Yildiz pursed her lips and closed one eye as she often

did while thinking. "Well, the steps themselves were perfect. But—"

"But?"

"You need a bit of fire in them. Or something."

"It's hard to feel fire dancing in a field on your own, Yildiz. Anyway, isn't that something that can only happen when you're actually in front of an audience?"

"Yes, you're right – audiences always make us spark. And the music helps too – I agree it's hard to dance well without music, just me clapping the beat. I've got an idea – let's ask Ahmed if you can dance again with the other chengis. They've got a show tomorrow night before we leave for Uskudar."

Osman stared at her and sighed. "I'm sure he won't mind. But I do hate having my face covered in make-up by Ahmed – I must learn to do it myself like the others."

"I can help you."

"No." The thought of Yildiz touching his face made him feel quite strange. "No, I'll have to learn anyway. But I'm certainly not going to rub on jasmine oil or wear that awful women's jewellery like the others."

"The audience won't notice if you don't, I'm sure." Yildiz was trying not to laugh, but Osman didn't care. He sighed again.

"But the really big problem is one we can't do anything

about. I'm trying to be a girl, I'm not a girl, and I don't want to be a girl. That's the real trouble!" Then they both started to laugh, and the sound of their laughter made Ahmed stick his head crossly out of his tent to see what was going on. Before he could shout at them to get to bed, they quickly slipped away to their separate tents.

Yacut treated himself to a comfortable bed when he stopped in Bursa on the way home – he reckoned he deserved it after his successful visit to the palace. And he'd just learned that a troupe of chengis were performing in his inn that evening. Perfect. He was very fond of chengi dancing.

After a good meal, he settled back to watch the entertainment, smoking his nargile and nodding happily to the music. Then the dancers came on, and, after a while, he noticed that one of the chengis at the back of the group, whose make-up was decidedly slap-dash, kept looking in his direction. The chengi reminded him strongly of his niece Leila, with the same mischievous bright eyes and slightly tipped-up nose. But it couldn't be Leila, because this wasn't a girl. And surely it couldn't be Osman – he'd never be a chengi. No self-respecting nomad boy would stoop so low. On the other hand, this chengi was quite remarkably familiar.

He leaned over to ask a neighbour about the troupe, and was told the owner was a certain Kizilbash.

"Can you point him out to me?"

"He's not here tonight, Efendi."

"Who's in charge of them?" As he talked his eyes never left the chengi who looked more and more like Leila, and at that point the performance ended.

"You'd have to ask the innkeeper. Or catch them outside."

By the time Yacut fought his way through the crowd, the troupe had disappeared into the night. He rushed back to the innkeeper.

"Where are they based?"

The man shrugged. "Oh, they have a camp outside the town somewhere – but I wouldn't try and find them now. It's not safe after dark. Go in the morning."

"I can't. I have to leave at dawn." Feeling confused and uneasy, Yacut went to his sleeping quarters, telling himself that anyway if the dancer really was Osman, what did it matter now? Iskander had passed him the secret, and even if Osman reached his twin and Yacut's lie was out in the open, it was too late to save the gold. But just in case, he'd better travel back to Fatima and get that saddle off her as fast as possible.

✽   ✽   ✽

Osman ran back to the camp ahead of the others, still in a state of shock over seeing his uncle. Why was Yacut in Bursa? Was he on his way back already? Yes, that was the most likely explanation. He seemed to have recognized him, but Osman knew his uncle hadn't been sure. Thank goodness the troupe was moving on tomorrow.

He was usually so tired after each day he fell asleep the moment his head touched his blanket, but tonight his brain was full of jagged, tumbling thoughts. Had his uncle been to the palace and got the secret hiding place out of Iskander? Surely Iskander wouldn't have told him – he never broke a promise. He would have told him a false place and fooled him. But then Yacut would soon find out he'd been tricked and head back again in a rage. Osman tossed and turned.

And then there was his shame at being a chengi. But he had to be a chengi, because he could think of no other way to reach Iskander. His twin would understand. He knew he couldn't simply turn up and ask to see him, because only parents could do that – just once a year. And the advantage of being a chengi lay in the fact that if their troupe caught the eye of the sultan, they'd be returning again and again to perform.

The talisman – the talisman usually calmed him. He quietly took it out and held it above his head close to his face. The bird's eyes were just visible in the darkness and he stared up at them expecting to find the familiar eager expression. But tonight the bird looked blank and unhelpful.

THE NEW PAGE

PRINCE MURAD SAT LISTENING to Doctor Reuben in one of the many airy pavilions dotted about the palace grounds. Iskander stood in front of them, eyes to the floor, and waited. Doctor Reuben gave the all clear on Iskander's arm, and said he thought the page was ready to play jerid.

"He could use an armguard if he prefers, but the bone is as good as new."

"What do you feel about that, Iskander?"

"I am very grateful for your doctor's care, Sire."

"No, I mean about playing jerid."

"I'm happy to play again."

"Get some practice in, and then you can come back in my team."

"Thank you, Sire." Iskander bowed to the inevitable. He had absolutely no desire to be back in the prince's team with Jelal still in it. He hadn't spoken to Jelal since Yacut's visit, and got the impression his cousin was avoiding him. Good. Iskander was surviving each day as it came by keeping his heart and mind numb. He only allowed tiny amounts of grief to penetrate the numbness each day – any more and he would collapse completely. He couldn't tell Ismail about what had happened, and knew his friend was hurt by his silences. For this reason he'd also been avoiding Rifat – though he loved Rifat almost like a father, he wasn't ready to open his heart to him and talk about his tragedy.

But Rifat had other ideas. As Iskander was walking back to the pages' hall, the bostanji managed to waylay him, grab his arm and lead him down through the vegetable garden to a little shed he used just inside the tall palace walls.

"How are you, boy? I heard the bad news. I've been very worried about you." He put his hands on Iskander's shoulders, seeing them begin to shake. "I am so very, very sorry. My poor, poor Iskander."

Iskander looked into the old man's dark eyes and felt as if he was going to dissolve. Sobs began to rack his body and Rifat helped him sit down on a pile of sacks.

"Cry, my son, cry. You need to cry. Let it all come out. I've seen you walking about keeping it all in and I knew you'd never come to me of your own accord so I planned that ambush." The word "son" had slipped out because he'd often thought if he'd had a son, Iskander was the sort of son he'd have been proud of. Iskander sobbed and sobbed.

Rifat pottered round the shed, content to watch the tears flood out of the boy. He boiled up a kettle and made him a drink of crushed mint leaves and sugar, and slowly Iskander's storm of grief subsided as he sipped it.

"I feel as if my future's been taken away." Iskander stared into his greenish drink. "It's as if I was standing on a mountainside and half the mountain suddenly slipped away and I'm now on an edge with the abyss below."

"I'm not surprised. It's bad enough to lose your father, but your twin as well – the Fates have not been kind. To me, your twin has been part of you even though he's not here. That won't change, you know. He'll always be part of you, always. Tell me his name. You've never told me."

"Osman."

"Well, that's a strange thing. I had a little brother called Osman. He wasn't my twin, but he was only a year younger, and we were very close. He died of fever when he was five, and there's been an Osman-shaped hole in my life ever since." He sat beside Iskander. "It's much worse for you, Iskander, I know. Much, much worse."

They sat in silence for a while, and then Rifat sighed and stood up. "Well, I've work to do and you'll be missed if you don't hurry back now. If you run all the way, you'll get hot and red-faced and no one will guess you've been crying." He opened the shed door. "Courage, Iskander. Life has to go on. Come and talk when you can't bear it any more."

"Thank you for everything, Rifat. I don't know what I'd do without you."

Iskander's group had now reached the stage when they were assessed again and moved, if necessary, to different places for further training. Ibrahim was told he was to join the janissaries, and grew very upset when he learned this meant he would be parted from his friends, crying openly because he had to move straight to his new life. It seemed to be a palace rule that changes took place as soon as they had been announced.

The boys stood at the door of the pages' hall as Ibrahim was marched away by one of the sultan's own janissaries, whose tall hat crowned with even taller nodding plumes made him a giant beside Ibrahim in his page's cap. Ibrahim looked round once at his friends, his tearful face pale with misery, before disappearing round a corner. They all wondered whether they'd ever meet again.

Much to their relief, Ismail and the two Greeks were told they'd be staying on to complete their studies at the palace school before being transferred to the chancery. They were good at mathematics, languages and history, and had just the sort of minds the sultan needed for his civil service.

"Well done, Ismail. I'll take a bet you'll be grand vizir one day!" Iskander grinned at his friend and Ismail's face lit up – perhaps Iskander's strange cold moods were over.

At that moment Iskander was told he'd been appointed to the prince's own entourage of pages. Since he'd be a junior page, he'd be staying on in the pages' hall and would continue to have lessons with his friends in the school, but he'd spend part of each day in the prince's quarters learning the duties of a royal page.

Iskander didn't want to be a royal page, and was horrified to find out that his cousin Jelal had been also appointed to the prince's entourage, as a senior page in full-time service. Though that meant Jelal would be moving permanently from the pages' hall, Iskander would still have to endure him every day in Prince Murad's quarters. As he walked back despondently to the hall, to his surprise Jelal caught him up and congratulated him on being made a junior page.

"Congratulations to you, too."

"Our family has done very well. Very well indeed." He cleared his throat. He didn't sound entirely happy about his promotion. Something was clearly bothering him.

Suddenly he burst out, "Thank you for not telling my father it was me who broke your arm."

Iskander didn't answer. He had no desire to talk any more to his cousin and wished he'd go away, but Jelal stood there shifting from foot to foot and blocking his way while looking at anything but Iskander.

"I wanted to talk about Osman—"

"I don't." Iskander turned to leave but Jelal grabbed his arm.

"No, you must listen. I think Baba was lying to you about Osman's death."

"What on earth do you mean?" Iskander swung round so fiercely that Jelal flinched. They stood facing each other, both breathing heavily. Jelal opened his mouth twice before he found his voice.

"Before we came to see you in the hospital, he told me

all about poor Amja Ali's death, and I know for sure he'd have said then if Osman had died at the same time. It's not like my father to keep something so important back. It doesn't make sense unless – unless he was lying to you. You refused to tell him the secret, so on the spur of the moment he pretended Osman was dead too. He wanted to get that secret out of you without delay and it was the only way that was foolproof. That's what makes me almost sure he told you a lie, Iskander. And he rushed away afterwards, as if he was feeling guilty about something."

Iskander stared at his cousin, stunned.

"I've been losing sleep over this, because of course I might be wrong. I even decided it was better not to tell you because I didn't want to give you false hope, but I can't keep it to myself any longer. Osman is still alive. That's what I truly think."

"If you're lying to me about this, Jelal, I'll kill you."

"I'm not lying." The two cousins stared at each other for a long moment, then Jelal turned away. "I'm deeply ashamed of what my father's done," he muttered, before straightening his shoulders and hurrying off.

Iskander ran as fast as he could to share all this with Rifat, but the bostanji was nowhere to be seen. On hot summer days like this one, the sultan liked to be rowed up the Bosphorus to the Sweet Waters of Asia, and no doubt that was what Rifat was doing. Iskander went to Rifat's little shed, and flung himself down inside to think about this amazing new development. Jelal believed Osman was alive and that Yacut had lied. His reaction made sense, it really made sense. Deep inside himself, Iskander had been puzzled by the abruptness with which his uncle had told him of Osman's death. It wasn't the way even someone as horrid as Amja Yacut would break terrible news like that to a twin brother. Iskander was almost sure Jelal was right, and he hugged himself and laughed in his joy and relief. There was no way of being certain his brother was alive until Osman himself proved it, but at least now Iskander could live with some hope in his heart again.

Iskander, Ismail and the Greeks were transferred to a platform nearer the big fireplace in the pages' hall, with more space. Iskander made sure Ismail was next to him and laughed with him when they saw the latest batch of new recruits arrive one morning and nervously settle on that platform in the far corner they knew so well.

"They all look so terrified and young. Did we look like that?" Ismail himself still looked young for his years, but he'd filled out a lot and had, at last, started growing.

"Worse – in addition to being terrified and young, we were pea green and stank of puke! Ibrahim was the only one who looked human."

"I'm really going to miss Ibrahim."

"I miss him already. It would've been great if he'd been made a page as well. Or you. I hate being in the prince's apartments, Ismail. It's deadly boring. All the other people ignore me, except when they give me orders. I've never felt so alone. Much more than I ever felt when I was completely alone on the mountainside."

Ismail frowned, not really understanding. They sat watching the new boys for a while before he broke the silence. "Anyway, how's Jelal behaving now he's a senior page?"

"He ignores me, which suits. Luckily as a junior page, I'm less than pigeon shit in his eyes."

At that moment the muezzin started the call for the last prayers of the day, and the boys all filed out. Iskander had never spoken to Ismail about Osman, and knew he never would. It was safer that way, when or if he ever managed to escape.

Iskander lay awake for a long time after Ismail and the other boys on his platform had gone to sleep. He thought about Ibrahim on his own, facing the unknown. Then his thoughts turned to Osman, as they nearly always did before he slept. Having been given hope again, hanging onto it was now his problem. Every night the thought crossed his mind: what if his uncle hadn't been lying? Then he'd go through what his cousin had said, and his own reactions, to reassure himself, and usually fell asleep comforted. But not tonight.

Iskander decided he needed the talisman. He needed to hold it and look at it. Moving as quietly as possible, he crawled to the edge of the platform and pulled his tattered old coat out of the cupboard he shared with the others. Lying down on his mattress again, he withdrew the talisman from the lining and stared at it. Just holding it in his hands was a comfort, and the almost cheeky expression in the bird's eyes added a little dose of hope. Dear little bird, how he loved it.

He was about to slip the talisman back into its hiding place when he became aware of someone watching him. A boy in the corner by the big stove was staring at him. He could feel the gaze almost as if it was a touch, and it came from the direction of the big platform where the oldest pages slept. Iskander didn't look that way or give any sign he was aware he was under scrutiny, but as he put his coat back he kept the talisman in his hand. Then he lay down again and slowly and silently worked a hole in his mattress cover with a finger until it was big enough to slide the talisman into the straw stuffing.

When he looked in the cupboard the following evening, his coat was gone and so was his knife.

A KNIFE IN THE BACK

"I WANT YOU TO BE TRAINED AS MY MANICURIST," announced Prince Murad.

Iskander bowed and retired, horrified. He'd hoped he might be posted to the stables to help look after the prince's horses, or take care of their harnesses, or attend him when he did archery and look after his bow and arrows. Why did the prince need a manicurist anyway, with his bitten-down nails? Iskander felt he was having his leg pulled.

"Cheer up, it's an honour," said Ismail when he told him that evening. "It means he wants you near him. You probably won't have to do anything, just talk to him when he's bored."

"I don't know about him, but I'm bored out of my mind! I have to stand in a corner watching what's going on – not much – and try to keep awake. And at the moment that's quite hard." He glanced at Ismail, wondering if he'd noticed how badly he was sleeping at the moment. He'd told Ismail about the theft, but asked him to keep quiet about it. The loss of his knife as well as his coat frightened Iskander, particularly as nothing had turned up and nothing more had happened. He knew someone in the pages' hall was watching him, but he had no idea which of the five senior pages it was. There was one with bushy dark eyebrows and a sinister expression he suspected for a day or two, but Ismail said he was only interested in mathematics; he was already working part-time in the sultan's treasury and had no time for stupid tricks like stealing a coat.

After one particularly dull afternoon, Iskander was returning to the pages' hall with all the other pages whom he'd joined for afternoon prayers in the palace mosque. He and Ismail were walking at the back when the column of boys slowed down and started pointing upwards, exclaiming about something ahead. It looked as if someone had climbed up a tree and was stuck.

Iskander went cold when he saw it was his coat up there, fixed to the tree trunk by a knife pushed through the fabric between the shoulders. His knife. He started to run towards the tree.

"Hey, Iskander, look! Isn't that your old coat?"

Ismail tried to follow him through the press of boys. "Is this a joke or something?"

Iskander got to the tree and realized his coat was far out of reach, but there was a lower branch at the back of the tree he could use to climb up and get it. He turned to the crowd of noisy laughing pages and began to laugh too. Everyone had forgotten the rule of silence.

"Looks very real up there, doesn't it? I hoped you'd think it was me inside the coat!"

"Did you do it?"

"Life was a bit boring – I decided to liven it up."

He gave them all as wicked a grin as he could manage, and then shinned up the tree and retrieved his property. While he was up in the branches, breathless, with hands still shaking from the shock, he paused for a minute to watch the boys below. There was a tall, thin senior page at the back frowning uneasily as if this wasn't quite the result he'd expected. Iskander quickly climbed down and made everyone laugh again by trying to put his coat on and finding it was so small for him now, he couldn't get his arms into the sleeves properly.

Two janissaries came running up at that moment, angry at all the noise. The boys shut up at once and hurried back to their quarters.

"Did you really do it?" whispered Ismail later.

"What do you think?"

"I'm confused, Iskander. You told me your coat and your knife were stolen, and I believed you. But now... You seemed to find it such a good joke. I think you must have pretended to steal the coat and knife and put them up there yourself."

"My father used to say the best way to upset an enemy is to laugh at him." Ali had never said anything of the kind, but Iskander found the words coming unexpectedly out of his mouth and decided they were very true.

"I don't understand you, Iskander." Ismail turned away, clearly hurt.

Iskander shrugged. He didn't want to upset Ismail, but was afraid if he told him the truth, his friend might let it out. Confusing his enemy and keeping him guessing was more important than his friendship with Ismail. He couldn't take any risks. That coat in the tree said very clearly, "I'm going to put a knife into your back."

He must use all his wits to stay alive, because as time passed he grew more certain that Osman was alive, would come to help him escape, and maybe come soon. The summer was ending, and today he felt full of hope, particularly after he'd been so quick-witted and Osman-like in his reaction to the coat in the tree.

He put his coat back in the cupboard in the pages'

hall, and his knife he took to bed. He'd keep it on him in future. He felt cheerful for the first time in days, and slept very well that night. Next day he found out that the tall boy's name was also Iskander, that he'd been born in Athens and originally was called Alexander.

Apart from the fact they had the same name, Iskander could discover nothing more about him. He was rather arrogant, kept to himself, and took care to give the impression he was destined for high office. So it didn't seem at all likely he'd have any reason to pin the coat up, and since everyone now believed Iskander himself had done it, there wasn't much more he could do to find out who actually had.

"You don't come with Ismail any more." Rifat's gnarled face did not let on what he was thinking. Iskander shrugged. "Well, you'd better take him his pomegranate."

Rifat took the two goldish-pink fruits out of his pockets and cradled one in each hand as he looked fondly at them. "God was in a happy mood when he first made a pomegranate. To my mind they are the most beautiful of all fruit." He held up the two globes with their tough leathery coats. "One for you, one for Ismail, remember. Don't eat both yourself."

"Of course I won't, Rifat."

"Is he jealous of the favour the prince has shown you?"

"Not a bit. He knows how boring it is being a royal page."

"Ismail told me you'd lied to him about your coat. First you said it had been stolen with the knife – and then you went and stuck them both up in a tree. What game are you playing, Iskander?"

"It's not a game." He met Rifat's wise old eyes, and noticed how the irises were ringed with cloudy white. He took a deep breath. "I didn't lie to him – someone did steal them and then put them in the tree like that, with the knife in the back. It's not Jelal for sure – not only has he moved out, but he's lost interest in me. He's got where he wants to be. But whoever put the coat in the tree was giving me a clear signal. He wants to kill me." He looked away. "I pretended it was me to make him give the game away. Only one page – who happens to be called Iskander, like me – looked shifty, but it can't be him – he has no reason to get rid of me."

Rifat was silent. He was still holding the pomegranates, staring at them as he revolved them in each hand. He was silent for so long Iskander wondered whether he'd forgotten what they were talking about, but suddenly the old man said, "Come and see me tomorrow. Alone. Now go."

Then he passed the pomegranates over and walked away.

The next day Rifat wasn't in any of his usual working areas. Iskander finally found him putting fruit canes into a new field beside the sea wall near his shed. The sea was rough that day and Iskander could hear the crash of waves beyond the big gates nearby. Rifat saw him coming and immediately beckoned him into the shed.

"Put this on, Iskander. It could save your life." Rifat held up a leather waistcoat sewn all over with little metal rings. "Wear it inside out, the rings on the inside. No one will realize what it is."

"Where did you get it?" Iskander had to whisper as a janissary patrol was passing the gates.

"I made it myself a long time ago. It's home-made chainmail. I once had an unknown enemy like yours, and I wore it to protect myself until…"

"Until?"

"The danger was over."

"What happened?"

"I had to kill him. He tried to put a knife in my heart, so I grabbed his knife as it slipped on the chain mail. We fought until I managed to turn it back on him. It was him or me." He pushed the waistcoat at Iskander. "Take it. You need it."

"Thank you, Rifat." Iskander put it on under his

page's jacket. "I won't be so frightened now of a knife in the back."

"If he aims at your neck or your guts you'll be in trouble. But it's better than nothing."

Iskander wriggled his shoulders. "I feel safer already."

Rifat picked up a bundle of canes and went out of the shed. "Don't relax your guard. You laughed at him and turned his trick to your advantage. It won't be long before he tries again."

"I know, Rifat. He could attack at any time. When I'm asleep, or walking to and from the royal apartments or from the games field. He could put poison in my food or drink—"

"Stop it, Iskander. Stop thinking about what might happen. Just keep alert, hold your head up, keep smiling as if nothing's happened. And never take off that waistcoat."

It took several days for Iskander to realize just how much easier he felt both night and day with this snug new protection, and wondered what he could do to thank the old man. He decided to carve him something, and looked around for a good piece of mature wood in the many heaps stacked ready for use in the palace stoves as winter drew near. He found a chunk of wild cherry that neither looked nor smelt green.

It wasn't a suitable length for a spoon, so he started to carve a bird-bowl for Rifat. Though he hadn't carved anything since he and Osman had hidden together in the Cave of the Seven Sleepers, his old skill soon came back. He roughed the wood out in the shape of a dove, beak one end and tail the other, and began the long business of hollowing out the body into a bowl whenever he had a spare moment. Osman seemed right beside him as he worked, and sometimes he felt Osman had helped him make the bowl, when he saw what a perfect balance there was between the head and the tail. The hollowed dove-bowl looked as if it might fly away, yet sat firm and steady on a table. Iskander was thrilled with it and longed to see Rifat's reaction. He sanded it until it was silky smooth and then oiled it. It was ready to give to Rifat.

As he left the workshop admiring the bird-bowl in his hands, he was suddenly knocked over by a vicious blow to both his head and his back. Winded, he rolled on the cobbles as he fought for breath and tried to look up at his adversary. But all he heard were running footsteps, and by the time he'd staggered to his feet and got his breath back, his attacker had disappeared behind the long row of palace workshops.

Someone had hit him a heavy blow on the head and simultaneously tried to force a dagger through his ribs. He could now begin to feel where it had broken through the skin below his left shoulder blade, but because of Rifat's waistcoat the actual wound was superficial. He looked round. Whoever had attacked him had not dropped his weapons. Iskander leant against a wall feeling giddy. The bird-bowl, where was the bird-bowl?

There it was on the path some distance away, undamaged. Hugging it to his chest, he hurried off to find Rifat, but hadn't run very far before the mild soreness in his back increased into an agonizing sting. He stopped, stood stock-still and began to concentrate on what was happening to his back. The sting was quickly turning into a red-hot coal, sending waves of heat and pain through his body.

This pain wasn't normal. He at once changed course and headed for the palace apothecary. Iskander was sure he'd been poisoned.

ZUBAIDA

THE TROUPE was now on the last leg of the trek to Uskudar, and as the road curved round a shoulder of the mountain, people ahead shouted, "The sea! The city!"

Osman's heart started to beat harder. In his mind's eye was a magical sight of towers and domes gilded and shining in the sun, but when he turned the corner all he could see through the murk and drizzle was some rough grey water with an indistinct, darker grey lump behind. He looked at Yildiz over Karakachan's loaded back and rolled his eyes.

"What a let-down."

"Bad weather." Yildiz shrugged and then twitched her nose. "But I can smell the lovely, lovely sea."

"It doesn't look a bit lovely at the moment."

"It's always lovely to me."

Osman looked at the empty road behind them, and sighed. "I think I can stop worrying about Amja Yacut at last. He'd have caught us up by now if he was going to. I'm sure he was on his way home when I spotted him in Bursa. He looked so pleased with himself, as if he'd got what he came for." Osman had told Yildiz everything with a sense of great relief. She patted his arm.

"Relax, Osman. I'm sure you're right. And look!"

A slanting beam of sunlight suddenly lit up a section of domes and minarets like a heavenly vision, before thick cloud swirled up and extinguished it. Then rain started to beat down and the troupe increased its pace, desperate to be done with the march. In weather as bad as this Ahmed would normally have looked for shelter, but he knew they would reach the karavansarai belonging to Kizilbash's brother in less than an hour, and decided it was better to keep going since everyone was already drenched. Kizilbash's brother, Bulent, would treat them well, and indeed when they finally arrived extra fires were lit and hot food was given out with a minimum of delay. Never had lentil soup and lamb wrapped in flat bread tasted so good, thought Osman, and gobbled down several helpings of both.

He then helped unload and feed the animals, and rubbed Karakachan down before going off to find the boys' quarters – a long room upstairs with a couple of windows giving onto the street. The boys were all crowding round the windows, fascinated by the hubbub below. Shouts, bangs, creaking wheels, yells of warning, cries of food and drink sellers – everyone seemed to do everything at top volume.

Osman had only just stowed his baggage in his corner of the cupboard when the call to prayer from a nearby mosque was added to the noise. The muezzin had the most powerful and resonant voice Osman had ever heard, rising easily above the city's din. The boys ran down the steep stone stairs. Apparently Kizilbash had just arrived from the city, and would lead them all to the mosque to give thanks for their safe arrival. As they waited in the main courtyard, Osman gave a quick look at the men filing past to the mosque, automatically checking to see if Uncle Yacut was there. It was the sort of place he'd stay in, but there was no sign of him.

And there was Kizilbash, wearing his best city clothes, his red beard unmistakable in the crowded courtyard. He barely acknowledged his troupe before leading them out of the door into the throng of men pushing through the streets towards the mosque. Walking just behind him was a stranger, an older boy with blond hair, pale skin, and an insufferably smug expression. He looked down his nose just like a camel would, and gave the impression he might be just as bad-tempered and unreliable.

"Osman, you do realize who that is?" whispered Yildiz, weaving through the crowd to his side.

"The Camel?"

She gave him a quick grin. "Yes, him. He's Regip, the new lead chengi, but he likes everyone to call him Zubaida, his performing name." Then she slipped back again with the girls and disappeared into the women's section of the mosque.

Osman was so busy watching the Camel out of the corner of his eye he paid virtually no attention to his prayers. Regip/Zubaida didn't look at all like the sort of boy who could excite an audience – far too haughty and pale – but Kizilbash wouldn't have gone to the trouble of travelling ahead to the city to find a star and then hire a dud, so he must be better than he looked. Osman couldn't wait to see him dance.

The opportunity came much sooner than he anticipated. Part of the rent Kizilbash paid his brother was in kind: he had to entertain the karavansarai's other guests with performances. On the second day the troupe gave a show. First of all the acrobats performed in the centre of the courtyard, including a special session of Osman the

Amazing Contortionist, who was announced as "able to fit into smaller spaces than any other performer".

Osman was carried in already folded into a basket, and jumped out to bow to applause. Then Kizilbash invited the spectators to challenge Osman with smaller containers, having already planted his stooges round the audience with suitable baskets. So the progression down the sizes began, as each man jumped up with a smaller one and handed it up for Osman to squeeze into accompanied by shouts of appreciation and applause. The moment he'd fitted into the smallest basket of the series, the acrobats came bounding on to continue the show and by doing so stopped anyone handing up something far too small.

After a break, the chengi troupe came on, without Osman now. They'd had very little time to rehearse with Zubaida, but Osman could see from the moment the new dancer came in and ran to the front, he was in a class of his own. He no longer looked like a camel. It was a breathtaking transformation. His make-up was vivid but tasteful, his golden hair was full of twinkling chains, and his clothes were of the finest silks and muslins. He made the other chengis look exactly what they were: provincial boys doing their best. As he stood waiting to begin his solo, the whole audience went completely silent in anticipation. He did not move, yet no one could take their eyes off him. At the point when his stillness had lasted almost too long he made a sudden preliminary leap and started to spin in such a way that his clothes and hair flew round him, then the musicians began and he was in the dance.

Osman, who was watching from one of the upper balconies, felt something inside himself shrivel up and die. How could he ever match this quality of dancing? Zubaida was a star. Even the other chengis, who were doing their very best, looked clumsy by comparison. He joined in the wild applause at the end of the performance, but remained sitting on the balcony when the others went down to the courtyard to mingle.

The girls never performed in the karavansarai, but had been allowed to come in from the women's quarters to watch from a screened-off window. Yildiz waved at Osman and made signals through the screen with her hands, but he didn't respond. He didn't want to talk to anyone tonight.

Zubaida managed to upset the whole of Kizilbash's troupe in the course of his first week in Uskudar. He despised the other chengis and refused to rehearse properly with them because he said they made him lower his standards; he watched the acrobats practising and made sneering comments that completely put them off their stride and caused a boy to fall off the tightrope; he said there were contortionists better than Osman all over the city. The close camaraderie of the troupe, built up over months of travel and hard work together, melted away in bickering, blame and constant punishments. Even Ahmed was losing confidence, and Kizilbash grew increasingly violent, lashing out with his whip at the slightest mistake. He forced Osman to crush himself into a money chest which was too small and stood on the lid in an effort to shut it, beating Osman afterwards for failing to fit in. Kizilbash's temper was like a bubbling volcano and each day the troupe waited in trepidation for the really big eruption.

Osman escaped at some point most days to the stables, and usually Yildiz managed to join him. They'd sit together near Karakachan, and whisper gloomily. Osman noticed that Yildiz had stopped doing her usual cartwheels.

"That Camel is poison, Osman. Real poison. He doesn't miss a chance to pick on us." Yildiz pointed to a red spot she'd developed on her forehead. "He came up and told me I was going to become one of those poor spotty girls who have to wear a veil all the time because they look so disgusting. I told him it was only an insect bite and he just laughed mockingly. I hate him. I really hate him. He seems to go out of his way to upset us."

"But he's a brilliant dancer. Every time I see him dance, I'm amazed."

"So what?"

"He is, Yildiz."

"All right, he's a brilliant dancer. Some of us were pretty good too until he came along and rubbished us. I begin to wonder if he's been planted on us by some top city troupe to make sure we fall apart before we get there to compete with them!"

"What makes you think that?" Osman stared at her. No one had come up with this idea before.

"It just came into my head right now. It's an obvious trick though, isn't it? He makes us think we're rubbish and we believe it. Kizilbash gives up on the idea of trying to launch his troupe in the city, and we go round the towns in the countryside instead. Mission accomplished!" She started to look excited. "I bet Kizilbash hasn't thought of this charming plot."

"It sounds a bit far-fetched to me, Yildiz. You don't have any proof it's true."

"There's plenty of proof only we haven't seen it. Just think about it. Why did he come over and upset the acrobats? I wondered why he bothered to come to our practice sessions at the time. The other chengis never have, so why should he? But there he was, lurking and mocking us. The more I think about it, Osman, the surer I am he came along on purpose to undermine us. And he totally succeeded. It was lucky more of us didn't lose our balance on that rope and get hurt." Her eyes were flashing now, her cheeks pink. She jumped to her feet. "It's obvious. He's deliberately undermining the whole troupe. There's no other explanation."

Osman stood up too. He was beginning to think she might be right, but wasn't going to admit it yet. "What are you going to do?"

"I'm off to see Kizilbash myself."

"He won't listen to a girl. He'll whip you instead. Go and see Ahmed first."

She stood staring at Osman. "Ahmed doesn't make the decisions. I'm not afraid to tell Kizilbash. Aren't you going to come with me?"

"I haven't fed Karakachan yet."

"Coward. Karakachan can wait. Let's go!"

By the time she'd done three cartwheels towards the stable doors, Osman had caught her up. But they couldn't find Kizilbash anywhere, and since Ahmed was sitting talking to Zubaida, they didn't want to ask him where Kizilbash was.

"We could ask Kizilbash's brother," whispered Osman.

"Not now. Zubaida's watching – I don't want him to suspect us. You go back to Karakachan and I'll go to the girls' quarters. We must wait for a better moment." She ran off up the steep stone stairs, and Osman wandered uneasily back to the stables. Yildiz was full of mad ideas and by the time he'd reached the stables he'd begun to lose faith in her theory.

He was also growing very uneasy about Yildiz's future. What would she do when he left her behind and went to find Iskander? He was her only good friend in the troupe, as she was his. What would Kizilbash do to her? And how would he, Osman, feel when he abandoned her? What would he do without her? It hurt him to think about it. And there was the question of Karakachan – he didn't want to leave him behind either, but how could he not?

He pushed these painful questions to the back of his mind. He couldn't face them now. And maybe they'd answer themselves somehow.

"Don't look for answers," he whispered to his donkey as he fed him. "The answer will find you."

So far it had. He fondled Karakachan's ears. "*Inshallah*, Karakachan, *inshallah*."

VIOLENT KIZILBASH

"**H**AVE YOU SPOKEN TO KIZILBASH YET?**"** whispered Osman to Yildiz through the screens of the women's area above the courtyard. He'd noticed her waving to attract his attention as he was about to go downstairs.

"No. Haven't seen him anywhere. Someone said he's gone to the city again."

"Shall I tell him your idea if I see him this evening? I know we're performing and he usually turns up for that."

"But you don't really believe it's true, Osman. Admit it."

"I don't know what to think." Osman stared at her miserably. Life was suddenly full of problems he wasn't sure he could handle.

Suddenly they heard an unearthly, high-pitched

scream from the courtyard below, followed by furious shouts.

"What's that noise, Osman? Quick go and see – it sounds like Kizilbash."

Osman was already on his way downstairs, but stopped halfway when he saw what was going on. Kizilbash was beating the bent-over figure of the new lead chengi using a heavy wooden stave. The thuds sounded horribly hard, and Zubaida's screams were piercing.

"You miserable little worm, take that. You thought you could destroy my troupe and slip back to your old job with a nice little bag of gold for your labours, didn't you?" He grabbed a hank of blond hair and pulled back Zubaida's head. Osman could see the stark terror in the dancer's eyes. "Well, you're free to go back, but not till I've finished with you. I'll make sure that pretty face isn't pretty any more." Blood suddenly poured from a slash down one of the boy's cheeks, and then on the other. Zubaida tried to protect himself with one arm – the other appeared to be broken. "And what about a smashed up leg to finish your career—"

Kizilbash lifted the stave high as the dancer screamed for help, and got it from an unexpected source. Bulent caught the stave and held it. Bulent was larger and stronger than his brother, but Kizilbash was in such a manic rage it looked for a moment as if he'd win.

"Calm down, calm down, brother. You've done the boy enough damage."

"I want to kill the little bastard!"

"Not under my roof. That's enough, now. Give me the stave. Come on, brother." Suddenly Kizilbash crumpled and handed the weapon over as Zubaida crawled away to a dark corner of the karavansarai.

Osman felt quite sick as he looked at the trail of fresh blood across the courtyard. Other members of the troupe were beside him watching from the stairs, frozen with shock. Kizilbash would have killed Zubaida if he hadn't been stopped.

Ahmed came rushing into the courtyard at that moment, and quickly sized up the situation. His master's violence was only too famliar, and he was obviously relieved to see Kizilbash being led away by Bulent. Ahmed waited until they'd left the courtyard, and then scuttled over to help Zubaida. Osman took a big breath and went down too. He'd bandaged up Iskander often enough to know what he could do to help.

There was no performance that night. Next day no one could find Zubaida – he had disappeared completely, despite his injuries. Ahmed was very distressed, but

Kizilbash simply muttered "good riddance".

"At last," said Yildiz as she arrived in a rush to join Osman in the stables. "I've been dying to talk to you. So I was right about Zubaida. And I bet he had an accomplice nearby because otherwise how could he just vanish?"

"Either that or Kizilbash has shoved him down a well."

"That's horrible."

"Could be true though, from what we've seen of Kizilbash. But I wonder what's going to happen now."

Yildiz didn't speak for a while, though Osman could see she wasn't thinking about the chengis. There was something else on her mind. Finally she whispered, "I'm frightened of Kizilbash, Osman. Perhaps we should try and escape now in case things get worse."

"But I can't lose the chance of getting into the palace..." Osman stopped. Yildiz had tears running down her cheeks. He'd never seen her cry openly like this before and didn't know what to say or do.

"Your twin is the most important person in the world to you." She gave a sob as she tried to wipe away her tears.

"Yes. He always has been." It was the truth, but he could see how much it hurt her. "I'm sorry—"

"Have you ever thought what might happen – happen to me – if you manage to get him out of the palace and escape with him? Kizilbash knows we're friends. He'll go mad if he sees you've gone. He could do to me what he's done to Zubaida."

Osman stared in silence at her blue eyes, still full of tears. He realized in that moment that he couldn't abandon her. How could he run away and leave her, his only true friend and ally, after all she'd done to help him?

"You'll have to come with us, Yildiz." As the words came out, he felt a huge burden dropping away. "We'll pretend you're our sister." He laughed in his relief and she tried to smile back.

"I'd much rather disguise myself as a boy." She gave a gulp, but she wasn't crying any more. He gave her an encouraging hug.

"That's a much better idea. You'll make a good boy. Besides, you're the clever one – I couldn't do without you."

"But what'll your brother say when he sees me?"

"He'll understand, he always does." But Osman's smile faded and he gave a little rueful shrug. "He'll have no choice anyway, will he? Besides, we're going to need your help, Yildiz. Your job … your job could be to meet us with Karakachan over this side of the Marmara Sea once I've picked Iskander up from outside the sea walls of the palace. I've been chatting to the merchants here, finding out how the palace works. They've told me about the gates all round the sea walls, and the most suitable one for the escape seems to be the one used by the palace fishermen. If Iskander can get out of that one, I'll take a boat round to meet him." Even as he said this, Osman could see how weak his plan was. But he couldn't think of a better one.

"Have you ever rowed a boat?" Yildiz's blue eyes narrowed. She wanted to say the plan was rubbish, but stopped herself.

"No."

"You'll need a boatman to do it. Someone who knows the currents."

"I can't risk bringing someone else in. It's risky enough already."

"Then I'll row it. I'm good at rowing – my father taught me. But I need to find out about the currents from the fishermen – I'll go down to the harbour disguised as a boy—"

At that moment Omar the groom came in, and they moved away from the stables. As they walked back to their own quarters, Yildiz leant close to his ear and whispered, "Shall I tell you something? I was so afraid you'd leave me behind I was comforting myself that at least I might've had your donkey when you'd gone!"

"Fat chance! Wherever I go, Karakachan goes too!"

They both laughed. Just for that moment, the future was full of hope.

When Osman went to the next practice he found he was to be taken on in the chengi troupe again. As the troupe was one short, Ahmed had persuaded Kizilbash that with a little more practice, Osman could be as good as the others. And indeed the first rehearsal went well – Osman knew he'd gained a lot from watching Zubaida perform.

Then next morning Osman discovered Zubaida's bagful of clothes and possessions still in a cupboard and, without telling Ahmed, took them down to the stables. He wanted to try them on alone and ask Yildiz, who was good with a needle, to alter anything if necessary. He opened the bag behind Karakachan's manger, and took out the sweetly scented silk and brocade garments, looking round rather nervously as if Zubaida himself would appear any minute. Instead, Yildiz came in.

"Look what I found left behind." He held up a pink damask entary, a sort of long waistcoat. Yildiz didn't need telling whose it was. She pulled diaphanous silk blouses and baggy trousers out of the bag.

"Fabulous stuff." Yildiz held up an embroidered waistband and put it round herself. "Really fabulous. I wonder who paid for all this? Zubaida must've had a rich backer. Watch out though, Osman, he might come back for his kit."

"If he's alive, he'll be too scared to come back. If he's dead..." Osman chucked the entary on the straw, and Karakachan brayed in his ear, reminding him he needed attention and food. "All right, all right. First you, Karakachan, and then I'll try this stuff on."

Yildiz measured the entary against herself. "He wasn't much taller than you. In fact, most of this will fit you." She rummaged in the bag and found a leather pouch. "Ah, here's his jewellery. Here are those fine chains he put in his hair. And rings, and bangles. My, what a lot."

"I'm not wearing any of that jewellery," said Osman from behind Karakachan. "Never. You take it."

"I don't want it either." She slid him a wily look. "But I'll keep it safe for you – we might be able to sell it later." She tucked the pouch away.

"Good idea." He did the chores for his donkey, washed his hands and then held the clothes against himself. "I'm hoping they'll help me dance as well as Zubaida did." He disappeared behind Karakachan's stall and came out, standing nervously in Zubaida's full chengi gear. "What do you think?"

"Great. Everything looks great. But Ahmed will probably take them all away from you and share them out with the others."

"I won't give him a chance. I'll put them on at the last minute when I'm performing in the city. But somehow, Yildiz, I've got to become the lead chengi. Then he'll let me do what I want."

"Ekrem thinks he's going to be the lead chengi."

"Let him think that for the moment. I need to find a new angle, something original. Our chengis have no imagination – they always do exactly the same thing every time."

"Maybe it's what the clients want."

"Everyone likes something new once in a while."

"What are you cooking up, Osman?"

"Wait and see."

"Oh, go on, tell me."

"*No*, Yildiz. Not now."

Osman would say no more, but in his mind he'd already started working on an idea. He wanted to incorporate a bit of contortion as part of the chengi performance: a mysterious chest could be carried in and put in front of the other chengis while they did the first dance, and then he could fling back the lid, jump out and join the dancing, or even do a solo. He'd have to practise folding himself up in this new chengi costume to make sure he didn't tear it as he jumped out. He could also try and see if he could end his dance by stepping into the chest and disappearing again. It would take a lot of practice, and he wasn't sure how he'd get it done without the troupe guessing what he was up to. He'd have to work somewhere out of sight.

Nor did he want to involve Yildiz this time. He wanted to do it on his own and surprise them all.

POISON

THE HEAD APOTHECARY had a long white beard and very white skin, and was so old he'd served under six sultans – as he was fond of telling anyone who stopped to talk to him. He was alone in his little kingdom of jars, bottles and dried herbs when Iskander came in. Most of his assistants were out of the city, travelling in the sultan's entourage. He stared at Iskander's frightened face and sighed.

"Show me the wound, boy."

Iskander took Rifat's jerkin off and turned round as he lifted his shirt. The head apothecary leaned forward.

"Come closer. Keep still. Hmm. Hmm." He seemed to be sniffing Iskander's skin. "You have indeed been poisoned. Luckily for you it's only a scratch. If that knife had gone in deeper you'd be dying now. Or dead."

As Iskander started to panic, the old man moved

maddeningly slowly towards a wooden cabinet of little drawers, muttering to himself. "Balsamina. Haven't seen a case of balsamina poisoning for a few years. Someone knows what they're doing."

"Please hurry, it's hurting me." Iskander felt as if the knife was still there, burning a hole in his body. The old man's hands shook as he measured a potion into a cup.

"Drink this. It's a very strong emetic, so go and lean over that sink to be ready."

It tasted and smelt so disgusting that Iskander started retching up the contents of his stomach almost at once.

"Now for the opium – it will work quicker on a empty belly."

"Opium—"

"Opium is the best antidote to balsamina. Come here, boy. Swallow this and then lie down over there while it takes effect."

Iskander swallowed what he was given, then put his jerkin back on before stretching out on a padded seat under the window. He shut his eyes, aware of the head apothecary gently clattering about in the background. All the tension in his body melted away, and then his mind began to fill with a waking dream. A beautiful dream in which he was flying over the familiar mountains and plains of his homeland under piercing blue skies, until he was lying snugly in their nomad tent, back to back against Osman. Then somehow without moving they were swimming in steamy hot springs, they were running, running through green meadows after the sheep and goats, and then an eagle dropped through the blue sky and landed on his arm with its claws…

"Sit up, boy."

"Jus' leave me alone…" His voice was slurred as he tried to shake his arm free of the eagle and keep running through those meadows.

"Sit up; you must sit up and drink this now. It's a stimulant, part of the antidote. Drink!" He forced it down Iskander's throat, who couldn't wait to lie back again for the delicious dreams to go on. But the colours slowly faded, Osman ran out of sight, the mountains shimmered and disappeared and only the eagle returned to his arm and gripped it.

"Another dose, boy. Come on. Drink!"

Iskander shivered as he sat up again to swallow the unwelcome second dose. He felt cold and miserable, and remained sitting, bent over with his head in his hands. He could hear the head apothecary moving about muttering to himself, then the door opened and someone came in.

"Ah good, Iskander, it's you. Very timely – you've

come just when I need you. I seem to be out of honey –
will you fetch me a supply from the kitchens please? I
need to give this boy a demulcent."

Raising his head up in surprise at hearing his own
name, Iskander instinctively kept his face covered with
his hands as he peeped through them. A familiar page
stood near the door – the tall, thin senior page he'd
noticed at the back of the crowd when he'd climbed the
tree to rescue his coat. Iskander the Greek.

"A demulcent, Efendi?" The other Iskander had
close-set, bulging eyes, and the heavy black shadow of a
shaved beard on his chin. Like all pages, he wasn't
allowed to grow his beard until he'd left the rank of
page.

"Yes. I've given this boy the antidote for balsamina
poisoning, and we need to balance his body fluids."

"Very good, Efendi."

As soon as the page had gone out, Iskander straight-
ened up. "Does Iskander work here with you?"

"He has been studying with me for two years – he
shows great aptitude. I hope I can persuade him to join
my staff when his education finishes."

"I didn't know any pages were learning to be apothe-
caries."

"Not many do, boy. But Iskander's father was a

doctor, a Greek doctor, so I imagine it's in his blood. Stand up. How do you feel now?"

"Shaky, but much better, thank you."

"Good. Good. Lie down again while we wait for Iskander."

He lay down and shut his eyes, uneasily recalling the page's expression when he'd seen who it was sitting on the bench. Those bulging eyes had shown not only surprise and annoyance at finding him there unexpectedly, but something more. Iskander couldn't understand why a page he'd never spoken to before and had no dealings with, should stare at him with a look of such focused hatred. It made no sense.

The head apothecary was pottering about, muttering to himself as usual, when the door swung open and Iskander the Greek hurried back in with a large piece of honeycomb on a plate.

"Excellent, excellent. Now I'll mix a sweet drink of honey and hot water and you'll be back to normal, boy."

"Let me do it for you, Efendi."

Iskander the Greek did not wait for the old man's answer as he went to a shelf and took down a cup. Iskander tried to watch him through his lashes, but the Greek page was busily mixing and stirring with his back turned all the time so that Iskander couldn't see what he was doing. He seemed to be making rather heavy weather of preparing a drink of honey and water, but when he turned round with the cup in his hand Iskander saw his expression and suddenly understood why he'd taken so long. This Greek was his enemy, his attacker and his poisoner. And there was more poison in that honey drink.

The head apothecary took the drink from his apprentice and held it out. "Now for the nice part of the antidote. Drink it up, boy, drink it up." His old hand quivered and Iskander was forced to take the drink from him. The Greek page's eyes were fixed on him, hard and cold as stones.

What would Osman do? He'd pretend to drink it and then drop the cup or get rid of it somehow. Iskander lifted the cup to his lips and as he tilted it saw a faint smile on the Greek's lips. Then he jumped up making retching sounds, ran to the sink he'd used previously and appeared to vomit violently as he poured the honey drink into the sink.

"Hey, what do you think you're doing?!" shouted the Greek page, rushing towards him past the head apothecary. Iskander darted to one side, putting the old man between them as he headed for the door. He ran and dodged and wove his way through the palace grounds, forcing his shaky legs to keep going until he reached Rifat's little shed down against the sea walls. To his relief he found the gardener inside smoking his water pipe. Iskander's legs gave way and he sank to his knees in front of him, dropping the bird-bowl which was tucked into his jerkin as he did so. It rolled away into a corner.

"Have you any honey, Rifat? Quick, quick." He knew Rifat usually kept a supply of honeycomb in a box in the shed, and gratefully sucked a piece of comb before he told him the full story. Rifat was pleased his chainmail jerkin had come in useful, but shook his head over Iskander's certainty that the Greek page was guilty.

"You must have imagined things. Opium can have strange effects on the brain. Why in the name of Allah should this Iskander fellow want to poison you?"

"I agree, Rifat. It's crazy. But I'm sure I'm right."

"It doesn't add up, and I like things to add up." Rifat finished his tobacco, and put his water pipe away. "Let me think about it, Iskander, and ask around." He went and picked up the bird-bowl as he spoke. "What's this?"

"I made it for you. I was just bringing it when I was attacked—"

Rifat held it in his hands, stroking the smooth wood. He didn't say anything, but Iskander could see he was delighted and touched. At that moment they heard footsteps approaching and froze, but a familiar voice called Rifat's name.

"Hullo, Ismail. Come in, stranger, come in, don't just stand in the doorway. Nice to see you again."

"Excuse me, Rifat, but I was looking for Iskander —"

"He's right here."

Ismail stood in the doorway and looked across at Iskander. "I came to warn you, Iskander. The other Iskander is on the rampage looking for you. He's furious about something." Ismail shuffled his feet, obviously still hurt by his former friend's behaviour.

"Thanks, Ismail." Iskander stood up and held out his hand. "I'll stay here and hide. Why don't you stay too? Come on, let's be friends." Ismail frowned and did not move.

"Oh, come on in, Ismail," said Rifat taking his arm and pulling him inside. "I can't be doing with you two behaving like this. Iskander, you tell him about the coat and the knife and the poison, and be friends again. And don't you dare move from my shed." He went out and banged the shed door shut, leaving the two boys staring at each other in the half dark until they started to laugh.

"Shut up," hissed Rifat from outside. "I can see the Greek looking down here. How timely – I'm going to have a good chat with that young man."

Rifat walked right up to the wall and stared at the Greek page. "Can I help? You look as if you've lost something."

"I was looking for one of the young pages – I think he ran down here somewhere." The Greek had a deep, hoarse voice, and met Rifat's gaze squarely.

"They like running about down here." Rifat started tying back an unruly creeper. "They come and talk to me, but I haven't seen any today." He smiled at the Greek. "Now, you've never stopped to talk to me before. Since you have, tell me your name."

"Iskander." The Greek page tried to look bored and busy, and Rifat could see he had the proud, bruised eyes of a person who never lets his guard down.

"Iskander. That's a fine name."

"I am of Greek origin. I was baptized Alexander. When I was brought here, I was told that I could keep my real name as long as I used the Turkish version." He spoke stiffly as he stared at the view, as if unused to talking to someone like Rifat.

"Many Muslim boys called Iskander have no idea about the famous Greek they're named after."

"Oh, so you know about Alexander the Great?"

"I may be a bostanji, but I too was educated at the palace school."

"My sincere apologies. I didn't realize pages became bostanjis."

"Well, they didn't want me to be a janissary, and I wasn't suitable for the civil service. I was a loner, so this life has suited me. What's your hope when you finish training?" Rifat deliberately kept his eyes down and his hands busy, and spoke as lightly as possible as if he was just making small talk. There was a long silence, and he risked a look upwards half expecting to find the Greek had gone. He was very surprised to see him biting his lips and scowling, with his eyes unfocused but full of tears, seemingly of rage. What on earth could young Iskander have done to cause this fury?

"Why don't you come down here, lad? Sit on this step and tell me what's the matter?" Again to his surprise, the Greek page stumbled down the little flight of steps and collapsed onto the bottom one with his head in his hands. Rifat worked quietly while he waited for the boy to compose himself. He knew only too well the intense loneliness of a page's life if one was the sort of person who didn't like joining in with group activities.

"I'm more intelligent than all the others and I've always worked hard. I want to get to the top. And everyone knows the way to succeed in the palace is to be asked to be a royal page." The words came out in a rush followed by a silence.

"Sultan Suleyman the Great had a Greek slave called Iskander who got the top job – grand vizir. Are you modelling yourself on him?" Rifat's quiet comment obviously took the page completely by surprise.

"Of course I am! But I never tell people that."

"Wiser not to." Rifat prayed that Iskander and Ismail would stay put in his shed and not suddenly assume the coast was clear. "And from what you're saying, you might do as well as him one day."

"No. Something terrible happened." The boy couldn't go on for a minute, then took a deep breath. "Not long ago I heard at last that Iskander had been appointed a royal page. I went along to the prince's apartment absolutely sure it was me. They threw me out. They'd appointed that little peasant, that nomad idiot Iskander!" His disgust was intense. "He needs to be taught a lesson." The Greek page stood up, clearly about to go on with his search.

"Trying to poison him was a lesson too far."

"Who says I poisoned him?" The Greek hissed. "You've got no evidence."

Rifat's eyes were icy. "Leave that boy alone or I'll tell the authorities what I know. And if they learn you poisoned him then you can wave goodbye to any chance of promotion."

"You know nothing, you stupid old man. There's nothing to know."

Rifat watched the page turn on his heel and stalk off, and wondered whether he'd helped or hindered the situation. But at least he'd found out why Iskander the Greek was so angry.

GETTING CLOSER

I SKANDER FELT SURPRISINGLY WEAK for a few days after the poisoning, and was relieved Prince Murad was away with his father on a summer excursion, so he had no duties or games of jerid. He told his tutor he'd had a stomach bug to explain his poor form in class. And he kept a sharp eye on the corner where Iskander the Greek was based, but hardly saw him. The Greek page was obviously avoiding him.

"I can't help feeling a bit sorry for him."

"You're mad. He wanted to kill you." Ismail was not impressed by his friend's reaction. "I bet he still does. Don't let your guard down."

"He must have felt such an idiot, turning up to be the prince's page, only to find it wasn't him they wanted."

"Iskander, you have to take this seriously. He'll try to attack you again."

"Don't worry, Ismail. I do take it seriously. I wear my chainmail jerkin night and day, I keep my eyes open – and it's a great comfort that you're watching too." Iskander meant it – having Ismail in the know made all the difference. They went back to playing their chess game.

Prince Murad returned from his trip full of energy and plans for his jerid team. Iskander now found himself practising until he dropped for matches against the sultan's team. In addition he was also needed to serve the prince for a new range of social engagements. The sultan had decided that his son was now old enough to be seen more in public, and be involved in government matters and meetings with dignitaries. Iskander found these very tedious because he had to stand still for hours, so far in the background he had no idea what was going on. Jelal on the other hand stood nearest the prince and, to Iskander's great relief, this promotion seemed to have cured him of his former jealousy. Having told Iskander about his suspicions of his father, he had washed his hands of his cousin and now totally ignored him.

"I'm going to die of boredom, Ismail. I don't think I'm cut out for this palace life. All I do is stand around in fine clothes, waiting for something to happen. Luckily the manicurist idea seems to have died. The only good bit of the week is archery, or playing jerid."

One morning Prince Murad announced to his pages that they were to attend a prestigious banquet given by the sultan, to be followed by some entertainment – jugglers, acrobats and chengi dancers. The pages were excited at the prospect of a lavish party to break the monotony of palace life.

Iskander knew roughly what chengi dancers were, but he'd never seen any perform. He found there was such a crowd at the banquet he couldn't see very well, and when he did catch sight of them, he was horrified to find they really did look like girls. He could hardly believe they were boys, and couldn't bear watching them dance. To blot them out, he shut his eyes and recalled the exciting sword dances the nomad boys did back at home, flashing their swords perilously near their audience, stamping their feet so that the dust rose from the kilims on the floor of the tent, and pouring with sweat from their efforts. Real man's dancing, not this effeminate twirling about.

He was glad when the sultan sent the prince and his pages away after the first half of the entertainment, and returned thankfully to his bed in the pages' hall, hoping he wouldn't have to endure too many evenings of chengi dancing.

Osman managed to catch Yildiz on her way back from a performance in a local pasha's harem.

"Come to the stables as soon as you can. I've got something to show you."

When she arrived, all she saw near Karakachan was a small studded trunk of tooled leather.

"Osman?" She looked round the stables. "So where is he, Karakachan?" She stroked the donkey's muzzle. At that moment she jumped in surprise because the trunk suddenly sprang open and out of it, like a genie, came a beautifully dressed chengi beating a castanet. For a moment she didn't recognize Osman, he looked so different made up properly and dressed in Zubaida's clothes. He took no notice of her at all, concentrating instead on dancing as best he could on the stable floor. Yildiz watched him in silence until he did a final twirl, stepped back into the chest, folded himself down giving a final roll on his castanet, and then pulled the lid on himself. A small piece of muslin hung out, the only evidence he was inside. She tapped on the lid and this time Osman came out grinning at her in sheer triumph.

"What do you think?"

"Absolutely brilliant, Osman!" She was laughing in delighted surprise. "Even Kizilbash is going to like it.

But where did you get the chest and how have you managed to practise in secret?"

"One of the merchants lent it to me and even made me some space in his warehouse area to rehearse. He says he'll sell the chest to Kizilbash if he can get the right price for it. It's crucial I get Kizilbash to approve my act. What do you think I should do? Let's make a plan."

"First you've got to dance for Ahmed and see what he thinks. You need him on your side before Kizilbash sees this act. Hey, I saw Ahmed talking to Omar just round the corner as I came down here – shall I fetch him now?"

Osman's eyes lit up. "Get him. I'll go back in the chest." Yildiz ran off and came back a couple of minutes later with a very unwilling Ahmed.

"What's all this?" Ahmed looked round suspiciously. "What trick are you playing on me?"

"It's not a trick. Just watch, Ahmed." She clapped her hands and Osman repeated his performance, this time playing very much to Ahmed as he whirled in the dance. And this time when he folded himself back out of sight, there wasn't a trace of him left.

Ahmed stood there in dazed delight, wordless for once. Osman climbed out of the chest and stood in front of him waiting, and finally Ahmed cleared his throat and said, "I think we have our star chengi."

"I'm wearing Zubaida's clothes – he left them behind and I found them."

"Good, good, keep them. You deserve them, Osman. I'm very impressed with your progress. Now, we have to be very crafty with my master. Somehow we must make him feel he's thought up this act himself. Let's think. When we're playing in the karavansarai tonight I suppose we could try to slip your act in and see his reaction. Hmm. How best to do it, Osman?"

"What about you and Omar carrying the chest in first without explaining anything to Kizilbash, then the other dancers could come on – and then I do my dance and you make sure the praise goes to Kizilbash for putting on this new act?" Osman pretended he was searching for a solution when in fact he had planned exactly what should happen.

"Yes, first they could dance around the chest without you and then you could surprise everyone – but the other chengis must know about it or they'll falter and the dance will be a mess. We must all rehearse. I'll fetch them here, so there's no chance of Kizilbash seeing." Ahmed scurried away, and within half an hour had his troupe briefed about what they had to do.

And so it was that the troupe introduced their new act that evening to huge applause. Kizilbash received so much praise from the audience that he basked in it all, and by the end of the evening believed the new act was his own bright idea. Encouraged by Ahmed, he announced his troupe was ready to take on the city, with Fatima as the star dancer.

Prince Murad told his pages that the sultan had invited a new troupe of chengi dancers to perform privately for the royal family and of course their entourages. Iskander's heart sank but Ismail was very envious when he heard about it.

"You're so lucky, Iskander – I'd love to watch a chengi troupe."

"If only you could go instead of me."

"Why don't you like them? Everyone else does. The janissaries never stop talking about them."

"It bothers me to see boys pretending to be girls."

"Don't be so stuffy, Iskander. It's only an act. They have to earn their living like everyone else. Actually, I've always fancied myself as one." Ismail made Iskander laugh by pirouetting and tossing back imaginary locks from his shaved head with a silly smirk on his face.

"Since they shave our heads I've almost forgotten what colour your hair really is."

"Red. Carroty red. I bet that would go down well in a

chengi troupe!" Ismail turned to get his bedding out of the cupboard, but then remembered something else. "I heard one of the janissaries say that there's a new chengi troupe in the city, with a star dancer called Fatima who's taken everyone by storm. Perhaps that's the new troupe that will be performing at the sultan's banquet. Promise you won't go to sleep this time, because I want to hear *all* about it."

ON WITH THE DANCE

SMAN, his heart beating with excitement, sat with the troupe on the ferry, crossing over to the city for the first time. As usual he checked the crowd on board in case he saw his uncle, though he was certain by now Yacut was on his way home with false information about the gold from Iskander. No sign of his nasty weasel-face. Osman relaxed.

It was a beautiful, calm, late-August day with a few puffs of white cloud in the bright blue sky. The dramatic skyline of the city rose and fell in domes and spires and red-tiled roofs on its seven hills, but Osman wasn't interested in the view. He was staring fixedly at Topkapi Palace in its commanding position on the promontory.

The sea walls circling the palace grounds were tall, and the huge forbidding gates set in them were tight shut. The Sea of Marmara lapped on the shoreline on one side, and the waters of the Golden Horn and the Bosphorus channel on the other. Osman counted three or four gates on the Marmara side, a large main gate with guns outside it on the tip of the promontory facing the Bosphorus, and half a dozen other gates in the stretch of wall that lay alongside the Golden Horn. Inside the walls he could see the roofs and towers of dozens of buildings, small and large, surrounded by trees. His throat tightened and he felt near tears. At last he was sailing right under the walls of the sultan's palace where his twin was living. He felt for his piece of the talisman deep in his pocket. He didn't have a moment's doubt that Iskander was inside the palace somewhere, tantalizingly close, but locked away.

The ferry docked beyond the palace walls on the busy waterfront that lay at the bottom of the hill leading up to the heart of the city. Crowds milled about and shouted under the wheeling seagulls as Osman stepped onto the quay hugging the bag containing his costume. A huge grin spread across his face. Here he was, Osman the nomad from central Anatolia, right beside the palace walls.

Kizilbash and Ahmed had brought over only the chengis and the band for this first engagement in a janissary soldiers' club. Kizilbash had played his cards with care. He wanted word about the excellence of his dancers to reach the sultan's ears from reliable sources, and had booked a series of performances both in the old city and in Pera on the opposite side of the Golden Horn, the area where all the foreign embassies were situated. He chose taverns and hostelries where he knew janissaries, politicians and government officials dined and drank. He'd spent evenings in all of them to see the standard of entertainment offered by other performers and knew that Osman's act was unique.

Kizilbash looked across at him. This boy had surprised him with his amazing progress and enterprise. Thin and scruffy, his long hair hidden away in the striped cloth wrapped round his head, he gave no sign of the vibrant being he became when he danced. He was like that wretch Zubaida. Nothing much to look at, but get him in front of an audience and he transformed himself. Ahmed had called both Osman and Zubaida true performers. Ahmed didn't say that very often.

"Right, boys. Follow me, keep together and no messing about or you'll get a clip on the ear and my clips hurt. Ahmed, you bring up the rear. Off we go."

Osman felt sick with nerves as he waited folded inside the chest. So much depended on this first performance.

He heard the musicians start playing, then he was swung into the air and put down in a room humming with men's voices and laughter. Then the chengis entered, beating their castanets and clackers as they danced round the chest, and he waited for his cue: the musicians were to stop playing for a moment so that he could fling open the chest as the dancers stepped aside. The lid always made a good bang to catch the audience's attention. Then he would unfold himself to a drum-roll as the musicians launched into more music. At least, that was the plan.

But the musicians forgot to pause, so Osman had to come out anyway as he couldn't stand another second of confinement. No one noticed the lid when it banged open because the other chengis were still dancing and beating castanets to music between Osman and the audience, and he hissed at them to move so that he could begin his own act. It was a bad start, and though he did his best to retrieve the situation, it wasn't until he folded himself back into the chest, shut it and disappeared that the roars of real appreciation started to build. The rest of the chengi performance went to plan, and the audience seemed satisfied. But Osman was worried and miserable.

"I'm not blaming you, Osman," said Ahmed as they sat in a corner of the ferry waiting for it to sail. "It was those stupid musicians and the dancers. They should have stopped – they knew you were waiting."

"They've got to understand I can't stay folded up very long. I have to get out. Two minutes is maximum and they left me longer."

"Kizilbash will give them hell at the rehearsal tomorrow. It's lucky for them he has stayed behind to chat up the janissaries."

"I'd rather there wasn't a big fuss, Ahmed. It won't do any good."

Osman was sure he'd been made to wait in the chest and then enter at the wrong moment on purpose. The other chengis were jealous of his sudden rise to lead dancer, and had plotted with the musicians. And he didn't like they way they'd stared at Zubaida's clothing – he'd have to keep a sharp eye on it or he'd lose it.

The sun began to set as the ferry sailed, and Osman suddenly saw how the Golden Horn had got its name. It slowly became a long sheet of rippling gold full of the dark silhouettes of boats. The sky was vivid orange, with the minarets and domes of the city black against it. Distant music and laughter came from the shore. Osman had never seen anything so beautiful in his life, and couldn't tear his eyes away from the magic skyline as the ferry returned to Uskudar.

Not very far away, his twin was also watching the sunset from a high vantage point directly above the ferry landing. Prince Murad liked to go and sit in the little pavilion called the Sunset Bower, while his musicians played as the sun went down. This was one duty Iskander loved. All his life he'd seen the sun go down at night and rise again each morning, and he'd sorely missed being close to this natural rhythm now he was living inside stone walls.

As he stood near the prince, watching the sky darken from blood orange to purple to deepest blue, he remembered how often he used to sit in the doorway of their tent with Osman, playing a game with knucklebones as the glowing sun disappeared and it was too dark to see any more. He swayed on his feet in pain at the memory.

"What's the matter, Iskander? Don't you like the sunset?"

"Of course I like it, Sire. And tonight it's especially good."

"You think all the time about Anatolia, that's what it is. Listen, Iskander, you must try and forget it. Surely you have a good life here?"

"Yes, Sire."

"Put your homeland out of your mind. When I go

travelling with my father I never think about the palace once! Seeing new things all the time makes me happy. Why doesn't it make you happy?"

Iskander knew the other pages were listening and exchanging mocking glances. He took a deep breath.

"I am happy, Sire. I must have one of those faces that doesn't show it." He smiled as warmly as he could at his master, hoping they'd all believe him. But nobody did, because Iskander couldn't hide what was in his heart.

Kizilbash's chengi troupe quickly began to improve and match the standard Osman was setting. Each chengi was now given his own solo moment and so was more supportive of Osman's star turn. Then Kizilbash had all the musicians, dancers and acrobats kitted out in new clothes, and this too raised morale. Zubaida's clothes were still the finest, but it wasn't so blindingly obvious.

When the summons to perform at Topkapi Palace arrived there was general jubilation. The girls were to perform in the royal harem, and the boys – the chengis – in the selamlik for the sultan, male members of his family and chosen palace officials. On the ferry going over the whole troupe was bubbling with excitement, and Ahmed didn't even try to keep order.

"I'm so excited," whispered Yildiz to Osman during

the hubbub. "I didn't sleep a wink last night."

"Nor did I."

"What'll you do if you see your brother? He might not recognize you all dressed up."

"I've thought of that, Yildiz. I'll try and use the family sign language we invented for my sister – you remember I told you she's deaf. As soon as he sees that, he'll know at once it's me." He didn't mention the talisman that he'd also brought with him in case he needed it. He'd never shown that to Yildiz.

"I suppose he might not be there in the audience at all."

Osman ignored her and stared ahead, biting his lips.

Yildiz couldn't stop herself stressing the negative things today. She was in a strange mood, and as they drew nearer to the moment Osman might see his twin again, she was slowly facing the fact that the return of Iskander into Osman's life could ruin a friendship that meant everything to her. She'd been so desperately alone and unhappy when she'd met Osman and his donkey, and they'd given her hope again. Not that she would ever have admitted it to Osman.

She stared up at the sea walls as the ferry drew near to the end of the promontory, and was afraid. She could see the same fear in Osman's eyes.

"Your brother's going to find it very hard to get out. Look at those walls, and those big solid gates." They both stared glumly upwards as the ferry glided by. "Even if you do manage to contact him, how is he going to escape?"

"Shut up, Yildiz."

"And I don't like the look of the currents here—"

"I said shut up." He got up and moved away. Why didn't she understand that it was better to say nothing than make things worse?

The troupe were taken through a small side gate on the city side of the palace walls, and immediately the girls were led away by a huge black man with the most imposing turban Osman had ever seen.

"The Chief Black Eunuch," whispered Ahmed. "He runs the royal harem."

Kizilbash was bowing to another imposing figure with an equally tall turban, who warned the troupe they must not speak until they entered the building where the performance was to take place. He then led them forward at a stately pace through the palace complex. Osman found the total silence in the big courtyards very intimidating and was glad to reach a small chamber where they were to get ready for the performance.

"You may talk now. I will come and fetch you when the sultan is ready for you," said the imposing man, who turned out to be the Chief White Eunuch in charge of the selamlik. But no one felt like chattering; even Ahmed was subdued. They changed into their costumes and made up their faces almost in silence, and Osman noticed his hands were shaking as he put kohl on his eyebrows. He was the first to finish getting ready, and sat on the stone ledge running down one side of the room to wait, comforted by the fact he had his talisman in a secure inner pocket.

The other boys joined him on the bench, all looking as nervous as him.

"What's happened to you lot?" said Kizilbash when he rejoined them. "You look as if you're going to a funeral!"

"We're scared!" piped up the smallest chengi, and everyone laughed.

"There's no need to worry, boys. The sultan loves chengis – and you're miles better than the ones he's used to watching! Relax, all of you – you're going to enjoy yourselves. Dance as well as you can and I promise they'll shower you with gold coins. Ahmed – a sweetmeat for everyone." The palace staff had provided a tray of little honey cakes – baklava and halva – which Ahmed had told them they could have after the performance. Rather reluctantly he began to dole out a small cake to each of them. Osman didn't take one. Contortions were best done on an empty stomach.

They'd never known Kizilbash so amiable, and though they suspected that his good mood had only one aim – to make his troupe relax and do well – they all cheered up. After a while the Chief White Eunuch returned and led the troupe out. At the end of a long corridor just outside the royal quarters, Osman folded himself into the chest and was then carried in front of the sultan and put down. He heard the band start up, and the castanets of the other chengis beating as they danced, and could sense they were in a large tall chamber by the way the sound reverberated.

Then the music and dancing stopped, followed by an expectant hush. Osman flung back the chest lid and out he leapt.

A NEAR MISS

ISKANDER GALLOPED DOWN THE PITCH following Prince Murad, who was leaning over in the saddle about to launch his javelin through the ring and score. As the prince lifted his arm, a runaway rider-less horse from the opposing team barged into him. Horrified, Iskander watched him sail into the air knowing there was nothing he could do to break the prince's fall. Both teams began to rein in their mounts as Prince Murad landed on his shoulder and rolled over on his back.

Iskander saw that the runaway horse was milling round in the confusion, and backing right into the prince's body. He dismounted and flung himself at the reins of the loose horse, pulling it away from the centre of the pitch. Other pages rushed to the prince's side and, to their relief, saw he was not only conscious, but doing his best to stand up.

"Put me on my horse again. I was about to score!" Then he pulled a face as the pain began to bite.

"The Prince is hurt – fetch a stretcher –"

"It's not serious – look, I can walk. On with the game, everyone. Where's my horse?" Prince Murad looked wildly around as palace officials now rushed onto the pitch, and he was carried off on a stretcher – protesting loudly – to be thoroughly checked over. Iskander watched him go, feeling proud of him. He'd grown fond of Prince Murad, and was sure if they'd been born equals, they'd have become very good friends by now.

Luckily the prince had no broken bones, but he was badly bruised and told by his doctors to stay in bed for a day or two. To his immense disappointment this meant he wasn't allowed to attend the reception his father was hosting that evening. He had been agog to see the new chengi troupe everyone was talking about, but made the sultan promise to invite them again very soon.

Iskander was the only member of the prince's entourage to be delighted about missing the debut of the chengis and their star, Fatima.

As Osman unfolded himself from the chest and straight-ened up with a roll of his clackers, he was blinded by the amount of light in the large royal chamber. Everything glittered: the gold leaf, the shiny patterned tiles on the walls, the polished marble pillars. It took him some moments to adjust to the brightness, so it was fortunate that before he started dancing he had to bow deeply towards the sultan sitting cross-legged on his throne, the diamonds on his turban and his clothes catching the light with piercing blue flashes. There were finely dressed men behind him, and round the four walls of the chamber, all sitting on divans. Osman then gave a roll of his castanet above his head, as a sign for the music to start, and launched into his dance. As instructed by Kizilbash, he directed his entire performance exclusively at the sultan, never letting his eyes leave the throne except when he had to spin.

"Doesn't matter how much the others applaud, you fix on His Highness and don't let anything distract you. If he doesn't like us we're all out on our ears. Permanently." Kizilbash glared at Osman, his eyes like flints. Osman knew he'd be utterly merciless to the troupe if they failed to please the sultan and his court.

Osman finished his solo performance to loud applause and then folded himself swiftly into his chest, a moment which always made the audience go silent with surprise before they renewed their shouts of approbation. Then the chest was carried out, and Osman ran straight back to dance as part of the troupe. At last he had a chance to look round the large crowd in the chamber.

The first he thing he noticed was that, except for uniformed men with shaved heads and faces standing at the back, whom he rightly guessed to be senior pages, everyone was bearded. There was no one young in the whole audience. No young princes, no young pages. Perhaps they never came to events like this. His heart froze a little as he whirled and beat his castanet along with the others in a spirited finale. Perhaps Iskander wasn't a page, wasn't even in the palace at all. No, he mustn't think like that. Surely all his efforts to become a chengi weren't in vain.

The dance ended and, as the exhausted chengis bowed in front of the throne, they were showered with a rain of small gold coins. Startled, they looked up and saw that the sultan himself was throwing the money. When he stopped, others did the same, and the floor glittered with gold. The chengis gathered up every single coin in their upturned castanets, and poured the money into Kizilbash's collection bag as each passed him in the corridor. He would redistribute some of the coins later, keeping a major percentage for himself and Ahmed. Everyone was buzzing with the amount of gold that had been thrown – they'd never seen so much.

"Of course the sultan will be more generous than his subjects." Kizilbash tried to sound blasé about the haul, but all the chengis could see the satisfied gleam in his eyes.

Ahmed didn't even try to hide his delight. "Well done, my chengis. That was brilliant. And to think that Zubaida told us we'd never be good enough to please the sultan!"

"His Highness may be pleased with us today, but forget us tomorrow. Let's see how long it is before we're invited back." Kizilbash spoke sharply, and the elation around him slowly subsided.

Osman hadn't felt any of the elation because the realization he might never see Iskander was sinking in. Dejectedly he removed his make-up and fine clothes, and changed back in his scruffy day gear, hiding his long hair in his simple turban as usual so that if he met Iskander by chance, he'd be recognizable. He followed the Chief White Eunuch out of the palace making sure he was at the back of the line of chengis so that he could look round unobserved. They were led the same way they had arrived, but this time Osman tried to take in every detail of the route. As he crossed the first courtyard, he looked across at the buildings on the far side.

There was no one in sight, no sign of life, except for some janissaries marching across the open space, their plumes nodding. Osman shivered. There were too many janissaries guarding the palace – they lurked in every corner. Even if Iskander was in here somewhere, how would he ever manage to escape all these guards? And the silence everywhere was increasingly creepy. He couldn't wait to leave the place.

One of the buildings Osman had stared at was the pages' hall, where his twin was happily playing chess with Ismail.

"Summer's nearly over." Rifat stared out over the Marmara Sea at the grey waves under an even greyer sky. "But it will warm up again – there's a final heat wave on the way."

"How do you know?" Iskander found all his mountain-based weather knowledge was not much use here. There were too many factors playing on the city: three big waterways, and a different balance of winds.

"Instinct." He sniffed. "There's heat on the wind coming across from Anatolia." He turned to Iskander. "How's the prince getting on, by the way?"

"His aches and pains seem to be worse today."

"I'm not surprised, with all those doctors fussing over

him. If they let him mend on his own, he'd be playing jerid again in no time."

"But he says no one's going to stop him getting up for the reception tomorrow. The new chengis and this dancer Fatima have been invited back – they say Fatima comes out of a tiny box like a genie out of a bottle." Iskander grinned at his old friend. "Pity you can't creep in and see the show. Sounds a bit more interesting than all the usual boring chengi dancing."

"Oh, don't worry – the sultan always gets the popular chengi troupes to perform for all his staff at festivals."

"I must go now, Rifat. I'm on duty soon."

As Iskander hurried down an alley between two buildings leading to one of the big courtyards, he suddenly noticed two feet sticking out of a doorway, as if someone was pressing himself flat against the door so as not to be seen. He froze. He had a nasty feeling Iskander the Greek was lying in wait. And if he was, he'd be armed.

Iskander hesitated. He could run back towards the gardens; he could run forwards and meet his attacker at speed, perhaps catching him off guard. In the seconds he stood poised, two janissaries crossed the far end of the passage, obviously patrolling the courtyard. In that moment he made his decision, and ran as fast as he could towards the courtyard with the same bloodcurdling howl of warning he'd have used in the mountains to announce immediate danger.

It brought the Greek out of his hiding place, and Iskander could see his knife glittering in his hand. With only twenty paces between them Iskander reacted instinctively, doing what he'd have done in the mountains if a wild boar or a bear had rushed at him. He ran for the Greek's right side and only swerved to the left at the very last moment. He flung his right leg out to trip him and the Greek went over with a thud, his knife spinning across the cobbles. Iskander kept running, straight into the arms of the janissaries who promptly arrested him for breaking the law of silence.

Iskander began to explain why he'd shouted, but when he turned round the alleyway was empty. The Greek page and his knife were gone.

"I tell you, I was being attacked—"

"Shut up and come with us."

Iskander stared at his captors and realized he would get nowhere by arguing. If he spoke he'd be breaking the law again. He turned his head to look down the alley again, and saw a welcome figure coming down it. Rifat. Relief poured through him. He was sure Rifat would follow him when he saw he'd been arrested, and was comforted by the hope that the old bostanji would be believed where he himself wouldn't. Rifat was loved throughout the palace.

He was taken to the Chief White Eunuch's office where, as bad luck would have it, the Chief himself was present.

"Yelling his head off in a silent zone, sir. You said clamp down on the pages for rowdiness."

"Explain yourself, Iskander."

Iskander looked into the ice-grey eyes of the Chief White Eunuch and said nothing because it would all sound too far-fetched to be credible. He'd never reported being poisoned by the Greek, or the episode of the coat. Explanations had never worked with his father, and he was sure they wouldn't work here.

"Well?"

At that moment there was a tap on the door and Rifat came straight in. The Chief Eunuch turned with a glare but his gaze softened when he saw the old man. "Could you wait a little, Rifat? I won't be long. Just let me deal with this unruly young oaf."

"I've come about him, sir. I heard him shouting for help, and then I saw his attacker run out of the alleyway. Would-be attacker it turns out, which I'm very glad to see. But it's not the first time he's tried to kill this boy—"

"Stop, Rifat, stop. What is all this about?"

"Well, sir, it's a long story and you need to hear it all to understand that his attacker is an extremely dangerous young man."

"It seems I have no alternative."

So the Chief White Eunuch heard the full story, and sent Iskander back to the pages' hall without punishing him for shouting. But his solution for the Greek page was unexpected: he arranged that his promotion into the sultan's chancery department should take place immediately. "I believe in removing the thorn that caused the problem in the first place. That Greek is clever and diligent. He has not transgressed before. The sultan cannot afford to lose someone of his calibre."

By nightfall the Greek and his possessions were gone for good from the pages' hall, never to be seen again.

THE MEETING

THE BIG HALL WAS PACKED. People had managed to push themselves in with all sorts of excuses, and the prince himself had engaged a far bigger entourage of pages than he needed to come and see the new chengis. As a result, Iskander found he was squashed into a corner where he could hardly see. Not that he cared very much, for at first sight these new chengis seemed no different from any others – boys dressed as girls dancing about in the usual boring way banging castanets. Suddenly they paused and there was a distinct hush of expectation. He craned forward to see a chest being carried on and laid down in front of the dancers. Men who'd seen the show before whispered the name Fatima, and Iskander realized this must be the chest he'd been told the chengi came out of.

It was about the size of the baskets Osman used to

hide himself in, to surprise the family or entertain Ali's friends. Iskander remembered the night when he'd last seen his brother play that trick – in the merchant's camp on the trek down to the summer pastures. The memory was so painfully vivid he felt he had to get closer to see what was happening here. He wriggled through a wall of pages and men, and knelt in front of them. Plenty of people were still between him and the performers but at least they were all sitting cross-legged.

Suddenly the chest lid flew open and Fatima appeared in a single sinewy movement, to roars of appreciation. Iskander stared at her (she looked so like a girl he couldn't believe she was really a boy), with her lively eyes ringed with black, her red lips and cheeks, her long wavy hair full of twinkling chains, and began to feel alarmed. She looked exactly like his sister Leila, and she was called Fatima, his mother's name. Fatima was a very common name so that coincidence didn't mean much, but the chengi's likeness to Leila was extraordinary. Leila. He'd missed his sister's wedding, and he'd most likely never see her again. Or Gul, his feisty little sister Gul. And maybe never see Osman either, if his uncle hadn't been lying after all.

He shut his eyes, full of fresh pain at the loss of his whole family. He also felt a pang of guilt that he hardly thought about his sisters these days, or even his mother. He'd recall Ali's death at bad moments, but it was only his twin he thought about every day. Osman. How he missed him. Seeing this Leila lookalike made him want to weep.

He could hear the chengi, Fatima, beating his castanet and the *pad-pad* of his feet as he danced, but he kept his eyes tight shut because he couldn't bear to look at this travesty of his sister. Then an odd thing happened. Iskander distinctly felt a sort of pull on his brain, as if someone was urgently trying to capture his attention.

His eyes flew open and he looked round to see if it was one of the pages near him, but everyone was goggling at Fatima, who at that moment had turned away and was dancing towards the royal dais. Then the chengi swung round and came towards Iskander again, skirts and hair flying, eyes now looking in his direction. The chengi's gaze was fixed on Iskander as he beat the castanet at him, his eyes seeming to speak Iskander's name as his left hand quickly made the little sign he and Osman had always used to signify "look out", before he turned and danced away again. Iskander put his hands to his head, almost dislodging his page's cap as he struggled to make sense of what he was seeing. Could Fatima look like Leila because she – he – was really Osman? No, it couldn't be true. It didn't make sense. But how did the chengi know their private sign language?

Back came Fatima, again looking in his direction. He seemed to be making another sign but was moving so fast in the dance Iskander couldn't be sure. Iskander was now feeling totally confused. He simply couldn't take in that this chengi dancer appeared to be his twin, suddenly there in front of him in the flesh. He watched as Fatima, with an extra burst of energy, tossed his castanet to another chengi, did a series of back-flips and then disappeared into the chest as the audience exploded with shouts of delight. The chest was then carried out.

The shouting and clapping gave Iskander a chance to try and control the storm of emotions raging inside him. Uppermost was disbelief. Surely he was imagining the whole thing because the chengi looked like his sister? And inventing the private signs because he so longed to believe his brother was alive? He stared, unseeing, at the remaining chengis as they continued their dance, while the crowd called for Fatima and roared a welcome when she ran in again to join the others. At the renewed sight, Iskander was sure he'd fooled himself. This pretty chengi flirting wildly with the audience simply couldn't be Osman. Osman would never lower himself to become a chengi. As for the sign language, Iskander must have imagined it.

Yet he couldn't take his eyes off Fatima, and closely watched every move. The chengi didn't look at him or come near him because the complicated pattern of the dance kept all the dancers in a tight group. Only when the dance was over, and the sultan threw the first gold coins for the chengis, followed by a shower of gold from the whole audience, did Fatima come near Iskander and hold up something quickly in one hand as he collected coins with the other. It was Osman's half of the talisman.

Iskander stared in shock and disbelief at his twin, then his eyes filled with tears and his heart with something he hadn't been able to feel since he arrived in Topkapi Palace. It was hope. He made the little sign for "good" and saw Fatima break into the most Osman-like grin. There were tears in Osman's eyes too.

Luckily no one noticed anything because of the applause and the glee of the other chengis as they gathered the money lying all over the floor into their upturned castanets. Then with a final twirl and flourish, the troupe ran out of the chamber. Osman was gone. Iskander immediately wriggled his way through the excited crowd and slipped out of the hall into a corridor. The chengis must be changing somewhere nearby. He ran down several passages until he heard the unmistakable sounds of a roomful of boys. Iskander slowed down and then in a stately official manner stood in the doorway. The boys were eating sweetmeats and drinking sherbet, and a skinny greasy-haired man seemed to be in charge. Iskander announced to him he his was a page of Prince Murad's and that the prince wished to meet Fatima.

"Now? He's still in his make-up and costume."

"Yes, now." Iskander stared stonily ahead as Osman, his face also giving nothing away, rolled an eye at the troupe and followed Iskander out. They walked round two corners in silence before they reached a convenient alcove. There they hugged each other tightly without saying anything for a long minute, before they started to talk in almost silent whispers.

"I can't believe it's you."

"I can't believe it's you."

"Baba—"

"I know about Bàba, Osman. Amja Yacut told me."

"I wanted to be the first to tell you, but it took me longer to get here. He was in a rush to ask you about a secret hiding place of some gold – Ana told him you knew it."

Iskander was on the point of telling his twin the full extent of Yacut's betrayal, but decided it was better to wait. He pulled away and stood half in, half out of the alcove so that he could keep a watch.

"We haven't got much time, Osman. I'm bound to be missed and they'll start looking for me."

"Here's my plan. If you can get out of that big gate in the sea walls — I think it's called the Fisherman's Gate — I'll be outside it with a boat."

"When?" Iskander swallowed. He had no idea how he'd manage to get out.

"The next time we come here. I think it's in a couple of days' time. It'll be the same night as the performance."

"I'll do my best. But if I'm not there —"

"You've got to be there, Iskander. Or think of a better plan. We're going to get you out somehow."

"Iskander!" The voice was cousin Jelal's. Osman recognized it at once, but the warning in his twin's eyes made him stay out of sight. "You're meant to be on duty — what the devil do you think you're doing?"

"Coming." Without a backward glance, Iskander ran down the passage towards Jelal.

"The prince is furious!"

"Sorry —"

"It's the prince you have to apologize to, not me…"

The voices died away, and Osman waited, reflecting that cousin Jelal hadn't changed. Still the same arrogant know-all. After a minute he stuck his head out of the alcove. All clear. He nipped back to the changing room, and told his troupe that he hadn't seen the prince after all – by the time the page had led him to the hall, the prince had left.

Iskander did catch another glimpse of Osman a little later. By chance, he was standing near one of the big glass windows in the prince's quarters, holding a tray of sweetmeats in one hand and a flask of sherbet in the other, ready to serve his master. The window gave onto an inner courtyard, where he saw a gang of boys in rough clothing being led across by the Chief White Eunuch. Right at the back of the line was Osman, looking like himself again, long hair tucked out of sight in his turban, eager face turned up as he scoured the windows just in case his twin was there. Sweetmeats slipped off the tray onto the carpet as Iskander tried to catch Osman's eye, but the distance between them was too great, and a moment later Osman turned a corner and was gone.

Yildiz sat waiting uneasily in the ferry for the chengis to arrive from the palace. She was still feeling edgy, and hadn't performed very well in the royal harem. She kept thinking about this unknown brother of Osman's, whom the two of them were going to risk their lives to rescue. Was she mad to involve herself? On a day like this when everything had annoyed her – from a torn nail to the fat women in the harem audience who were more interested in eating and gossiping than watching the dancing – she was sure she was.

Then the chengis came running along the quay to catch the ferry and Yildiz saw the expression on Osman's face. She guessed at once he'd made contact with his twin, and a rush of excitement pushed out her bad mood. She went to sit in a dark corner of the ferry, curled up against the cold, and Osman joined her. They began to whisper excitedly.

"He must have been so surprised!"

"He was. He just didn't believe his eyes."

"Was he upset to see you as a chengi?"

"He didn't say anything, but I'm sure he was. Think of how I look when I'm all dressed up."

"You look prettier than most of us girls!"

Osman pretended to push her over the side of the boat. "You just shut up!"

"Well, you do."

"Oh, Yildiz, we managed to meet afterwards and I told him our plan of bringing a boat round to the Fisherman's Gate!"

"The trouble is, how is he actually going to get out? It looks impossible. Sorry, but we need to be realistic."

"You don't know Iskander when he's determined. Somehow he'll get out of the Fisherman's Gate—"

"What are you two whispering about?" Kizilbash had crept up close to them without them noticing. "What's this about fishermen?"

Yildiz simpered up at him, pretending to be coy, while her brain raced to find a convincing explanation. Osman got in first.

"Yildiz is going to ask the fishermen for a live octopus. Keep it secret; we want to play a trick on Ahmed."

"An octopus?" Kizilbash glared at him in disbelief.

"He's frightened of them. It's just for a joke, Kizilbash."

"Why don't you fetch the octopus yourself?" Kizilbash was still suspicious.

"I'm scared of them too, and she isn't."

"Remember I was brought up by the sea, sir."

"Why should I remember where all you kids came from? Drop this stupid idea, anyway. I don't want you wandering about on your own down at the harbour, any of you. It's out of bounds, get that?" He turned away, then turned back again. "And you, Osman, are not to leave the karavansarai at all — you hear me, *at all* —

unless we're going over to perform in the city. Got that?" He glared at Osman before going off.

"You fooled him," whispered Yildiz. "It was such stupid reason I didn't think he'd fall for it."

"I'm not sure he did. Otherwise why would he gate me? How will I get out now? He'll be watching us like a hawk."

"He gated you because he's realized he can't risk losing you. You're bringing him riches and fame beyond anything he's had before, so of course he's going to gate you. And he's not going to like it when you disappear, Fatima. He's not going to like it at all!"

INSHALLAH

OSMAN WOKE UP IN A BAD MOOD. If he was permanently gated how was he going to rescue Iskander? He and Yildiz had to get over to the city to buy a boat as soon as possible, so that it was ready and waiting. It would take at least a couple of hours to do that. He lay wrapped up in his bedding going over and over the problems in his mind, with a loose corner of his blanket over his head to stop anyone talking to him. All the other boys got up, dressed, and hurried off downstairs for breakfast. Osman lay so still in his corner they forgot he was there, and he heard one of the boys say that Osman must have got up early and gone down ahead of them. This gave him an idea.

He hurried straight to the stables to feed Karakachan, hoping Yildiz would turn up as usual. But she didn't, and it was only at the evening feed she crept up beside him.

"Let's get out of sight of the door, Osman." They sat on a bale of hay behind the donkey. "Kizilbash is watching me. I didn't want to lead him to you here so I waited until the coast was clear. And I had a bit of luck while I hung about. The woman who runs the women's section of the karavansarai is married to a fisherman, and she knows all about the waters round here. She says there's a strong current coming out of the Bosphorus, and so when you're crossing from the city to here, you have to make sure you row diagonally across." She picked up a piece of straw. "Imagine this is the boat, that's where we want to land and this is the palace. You have to aim the boat like this, to get here. That way the current helps you across."

"What about the currents round the point by the palace?"

"Oh, they're a bit tricky too, but you just have to keep as close in as you can and keep rowing." She stared eagerly at him, proud of what she'd found out.

Osman said nothing.

"What's the matter?"

"Perhaps we're mad to try doing it by boat."

"So that's all the gratitude I get." She turned away, offended.

"Don't be annoyed, Yildiz. I'm really grateful for what you've found out, but you can see why I'm worried.

Those currents sound scary."

"They are, but we'll manage. We're both very strong, and don't forget that unlike you, I do know a bit about the sea." She frowned at him. "What you need is a bit of rowing practice, but now you're gated how are we going to organize that?"

They heard Kizilbash's voice shouting in the distance.

"If we got up really early I think I could safely get away for a couple of hours without anyone noticing I was out. I'll just make my bedding look as if it's occupied."

"I'll see if my friend, the fisherman's wife, can lend us a dinghy to row around in the harbour."

Kizilbash's voice was coming closer.

"You'd better go, Yildiz. The last thing we want is Kizilbash to catch you here."

At that moment, Karakachan pushed his nose between them as if to remind them of his existence. Yildiz promptly stroked and kissed it. "He doesn't want to be left out of things, the poor darling. I'm sure he senses we're up to something. It's all right, Karakachan, we won't ever leave you behind in that horrible man's clutches." She flashed a wicked look at Osman. "Just imagine Kizilbash's rage when he finds out not only has his money-making Fatima run off, but his useful little donkey's gone too!"

"And you as well."

"Oh, I don't matter – he can easily replace me."

"Well, you matter a lot to me, Yildiz. I couldn't do this boat thing at all without you."

Yildiz froze as she blushed. "Are you joking?"

"No, I'm not. I've never had a friend like you before." The donkey gave a little bray. "There, Karakachan agrees!"

"He's just hungry," whispered Yildiz, pink with pleasure, and then ran out, so overcome she forgot to do her usual series of cartwheels. When she reached the women's quarters, she curled up in a corner and hugged herself. Not since her mother died had anyone said she mattered to them and meant it.

Rifat kept breaking into chuckles as he dug over a bed that he'd cleared of weeds. "That's a good one. Disguised as a chengi. He's got a cheek, your brother."

"He's always been full of good ideas."

"So does he want to dress you as a chengi as well and get you out that way?" Rifat thought this was very funny, and continued to chuckle at his joke for so long Iskander started to fume, and would have left then and there had he not needed Rifat's help so badly. After a couple of minutes the old gardener stopped digging and turned round, at last serious again. "Come on then, boy. Let's go to my shed. I need a break."

Rifat shut the door when they were inside.

"Now tell me what your brother's plan really is."

"He wants to bring a boat round to rescue me and told me to try and find a way out of the sea walls through the Fisherman's Gate. But the gates are locked most of the time and there are janissaries on guard when they're open." Iskander looked miserably at Rifat. "How am I going to get out – can you help me think of something, Rifat?"

"I don't see how you'll manage it if I don't." There was a long silence, in which Rifat stared at his muddy boots and pondered. Iskander waited. "When is the fair Fatima coming back to perform?" Rifat grinned to himself, but at least he didn't start chuckling uncontrollably again.

"In two days' time. He's bringing the boat late that night, he said. But how am I going to get out of the Fisherman's Gate?"

"Stop bleating and go away, boy. Leave me to think. Come here tomorrow and with God's help I might have a plan. *Inshallah*."

"*Inshallah*."

"Now hop it."

Osman stared out of the boys' dormitory window at the street below. He heard distant music and shouts of appreciation from the courtyard where the rest of the chengi troupe were performing, but was glad for once he wasn't down there. He had too much to think about.

Osman sighed. Apart from his fears concerning the boat, the sea and the currents, he was uneasy about Iskander. He'd looked so different, with his shaved head and smart page's uniform, all shiny and clean. He lived cut off from the mess and dirt of everyday life; his hands were white and soft and his skin was pale from not having to do hard manual work out of doors. Osman looked at his own hands: though they were certainly no longer rough shepherd's hands, they were still used to mucking out donkeys and camels and putting up tents and chopping wood. Iskander's hands looked like the prince's own.

And then there were the things Iskander didn't know yet. He didn't know his mother planned to sell most of their herd, and was going to live with Gul in her family's village. And he didn't know about Yildiz. This was where Osman's thoughts came to a halt, as if they'd been moving along a path and met a rock-fall blocking it completely. He left the window and started pacing round the room. He knew he could never give up Yildiz.

Osman also knew that Iskander wouldn't have seen or met a female all the time he'd been in the palace. All the women who lived there were secluded in the harem and were never seen by any men except those in the close family. Nomads were much more free – women and girls mixed freely with men and boys. But even though they'd been brought up in this open way, Osman remembered how in the old days he and his brother had thought nomad girls were a complete waste of time. Except for their sisters, they'd ignored them. And now Osman's only true friend was this Greek girl. Not only that, Yildiz would be bound into their lives come what may when – if – they managed to escape together. And it wouldn't take very long for Iskander to guess she was a girl. What would he say then?

Osman went back to the window, and made himself calm down. Perhaps he needn't worry too much about what Iskander would make of Yildiz. She was a remarkable girl – he'd surely see that at once. No one could help liking her when they got to know her. And she was wonderful with Karakachan.

At that moment he had a sudden horrible shock: there in the street below was his uncle riding up on an exhausted-looking horse. No, surely it wasn't. Osman shut his eyes and opened them again. But it was indeed

Amja Yacut, clearly in a foul temper as he dismounted and led his horse through the gate underneath Osman, passing out of sight into the karavansarai.

Osman banged the window shut and sank onto a ledge, feeling sick. He was pretty sure he knew why his uncle was here again. Though Iskander hadn't had time to tell him during their brief meeting in the passage, he must have lied to Yacut about the secret hiding place of the gold, and now Yacut was back with a vengeance.

Hands shaking, Osman wrapped his turban cloth round his head and face again making sure only his eyes showed, and crept out to stare down at the courtyard. His uncle was directly below him, his voice rising clearly as he talked to Kizilbash's brother, Bulent.

"Yes, lodging and food for several days, and could you tell me whether a gentleman called Kizilbash is still here with his troupe. I was informed in the town he'd been here for some time." Amja Yacut's abrupt autocratic manner didn't seem to impress Bulent, who said he'd go and check. Osman watched him go across the courtyard to find Kizilbash. After a few minutes Bulent returned.

"Sorry, Efendi, Kizilbash has moved on, but if you tell me why you want him, I'll make sure he gets the message if he happens to return."

"I'm searching for my nephew, Osman. I saw a boy

very much like him performing some weeks ago in Bursa, and was told he was with Kizilbash's troupe. I need to find Osman urgently. Whose troupe is that then, performing over there?"

"Ahmed's. Go and watch them. See if you can spot this Osman of yours." As Yacut strode off, Bulent went to find his brother again, grinning to himself because he knew Osman wasn't dancing. Osman grinned too, blessing the fact he'd become so valuable to Kizilbash that he'd do anything to hide him from people who wanted him. Within minutes Kizilbash skulked round the courtyard with his red hair and beard covered, and ran lightly upstairs to Osman.

"Get back in your room at once, boy, and stay there."

"I just saw my uncle arrive. Please don't tell him I'm here, Kizilbash – I don't want him to find me."

"Strangely enough nor do I, so for once we're thinking along the same lines. Keep out of his sight, and make sure when we go to the palace tomorrow your face is covered. Now beat it. In fact, in case you change your mind about your uncle, I think I'll lock you in until the other boys join you and can keep an eye on you."

Kizilbash pushed Osman roughly back into the room before turning the big rusty key on the outside of the door.

THE ESCAPE BEGINS

HERE WAS A PERSISTENT GREY DRIZZLE just before dawn next morning when Yildiz (in her boy's disguise) and Osman met to do a bit of rowing round the harbour. He'd crept out leaving clothing stuffed in his bedroll to look as if he was still asleep. When Yildiz saw his muffled face she asked if he had toothache.

"I've got to be extra careful – my uncle arrived last night to stay at the karavansarai. He's looking for me and he's in a foul temper. Obviously my brother lied to him about the gold's hiding place and maybe he thinks I know."

"Oh, no! We could do without this." Yildiz knew Yacut was bad news.

"Luckily Bulent didn't let on he knew me, and then Kizilbash locked me in. He's afraid I'm going to run into Amja Yacut's arms."

"You wouldn't do that!"

"Of course I wouldn't. I told Kizilbash that, but he locked me in anyway."

"How did you get out just now?"

"He only does it when I'm in there on my own – he's told the others to watch me. So you've got to make sure that I can get out when he does it again."

"Of course I will. Now let's concentrate on this rowing, Osman. We haven't got long. Hold the oar like this, pull steadily and carefully – and don't tilt it over or the oar will skid out of the water and you'll lose it."

Osman was surprised at how tricky rowing was, and depressed by how badly he did it. But Yildiz was breezy about his failings – it was the first time, he'd learn quickly, it would all be fine when he got the knack.

"You make it look so easy, Yildiz. But let's stop a moment here in the middle of the harbour and go over our plans so that we're both quite sure of everything. We perform this afternoon in the palace, I tell Iskander the escape is tonight. We all come back here and then we get free time as usual after a session at the palace. You and I don't hang about – we leave the karavansarai separately as soon as we can and meet at the ferry, the last one to go over before dark. We carry as much of our stuff as we can without attracting attention. When we get to the other side, we buy the boat. I've got plenty of gold now."

"What happens if we can't buy one?"

"Then we'll have to steal one."

The fisherman shouted for his dinghy at that moment and they had to row back, Osman managing slightly better. They split up before returning, and were in the karavansarai soon after the end of morning prayers, no one having noticed their absence.

Osman felt sick with tension as he got dressed and made up his face in the usual back room in the palace. When his moment to perform came near, he squashed himself with difficulty into the chest. He was growing too big for it. Just as well today was the last time he'd use it, if all went to plan.

When he came out of the chest, Osman immediately looked for Iskander where he'd been the time before, but couldn't find him. He missed a step in his dismay, but recovered himself quickly. His twin didn't seem to be anywhere in the hall.

Osman made himself direct his performance towards the royal dais on which the sultan sat with a couple of his sons, and after a few minutes was aware that a page at the very back of the dais kept making a quick hand gesture. There was Iskander, almost hidden by the throne, making the signal they used for "be careful". But Osman was so relieved his twin was there after all he missed another step.

He could see the sultan frowning, clearly unimpressed with Fatima today. Osman did his best to retrieve the situation, but he had too many things on his mind to focus properly and was glad when his solo number ended and he was carried out in the chest. When he came back, he noticed Iskander had moved further forward to stand almost behind the prince, who sat at his father's right hand. This suited Osman, because he could keep his focus seemingly on the royal party while in fact communicating with his twin.

Osman had to make the sign for "tonight" twice, because he missed Iskander's answer. He didn't give him a time because they both knew it would be a case of wait and pray. But when Iskander signed "owl", he knew exactly what he meant: they were both good at imitating the soft high-pitched call of the local owl, and had used it before as a signal.

Then the chengis finished their final dance and the sultan and his party threw some gold coins, though far fewer than usual, followed by a small shower from the rest of the room. The chengis rapidly collected up the coins, and before running out Osman managed to meet Iskander's eyes for a second. *Inshallah. God willing.* They made the tiny gesture together. *"Inshallah,"* Osman whispered to himself as he changed quickly back into his clothes, knowing that his twin would not risk coming to meet him backstage this time.

It was lucky Kizilbash wasn't with the troupe for this performance, or they'd have been whipped for the decrease in takings. Ahmed simply bagged up the gold with a sour face. It wasn't his job to count it. There'd be a row later, and Ahmed knew he'd suffer too. It wasn't just Fatima who hadn't danced well – all the dratted chengis had let him down.

"He was there and got the message."

This short whisper was all Osman could tell Yildiz before he noticed Kizilbash rejoining the troupe, back from his business in the city. Osman immediately went to sit with the other chengis, and Yildiz sat giggling with the girls. Not that there was much more to tell her. Their plans were made and all they had to do was wait. At least Yacut wasn't on the ferry too, and there was no sign of him as they all trooped into the karavansarai. But then Kizilbash had an unwelcome surprise for the chengis.

"I've got you boys booked for an extra performance this evening at a pasha's house in Uskudar. Just as well for you all, since Ahmed tells me the palace takings are down. Now's the chance to make up the difference or you get beaten." Osman tried to hide his dismay, and was extremely relieved when Kizilbash went on, "You're not going, Fatima. I told them if they wanted you it would cost extra. They said they wouldn't pay more so you're gated as usual."

Osman shrugged and looked resigned, but in fact didn't know what he felt. This development could be good, could be bad. It turned out to be bad. When the other chengis were ready to set off again, Kizilbash locked him in the dormitory, but this time he took away the key.

Osman tried not to fret about this setback. Yildiz would be watching, she'd think of a way round it, and if she couldn't he'd make a rope to let himself out of the window. He must make his preparations as planned. He secured the small bag holding his money and the talisman by wrapping them close against his body using a long piece of cloth. He put on as many of his clothes as he could, and made a long bundle of the rest. Then he made a cocoon round the bundle with his blanket, and laid it on his mattress. It didn't look big enough for his body. He borrowed clothes from other lockers and pushed them into his blanket until it looked as much like him as possible.

Now he could turn his mind to getting out. He thought of tying several other blankets together to make a rope to lower himself out of the window, but it would alert the boys to his escape and he didn't want anyone to realize he'd gone until they all got up in the morning.

He decided to attract someone's attention and say he had a stomach upset and needed to go to the toilet. He rattled the door noisily a few times and called out with no result. There was no one around to hear. He knelt and peered into the keyhole to see if he could see out. As he did so he heard the sound of breathing on the other side, and a blue eye came briefly to the keyhole too. Yildiz whispered so softly he could hardly hear her, "I've taken the key from the hook in Bulent's office – I'm going to open the door, then go and hide. You come out and run for it. I'll relock the door and put the key back where I found it. See you at the harbour."

After the thunderous noise of the key turning the rusty old lock, Osman waited on tenterhooks to see if anyone came. No one did. He slowly opened the door. No sign of Yildiz or anyone else. He slipped out, shut the door, and walked casually down the stairs and out of the karavansarai as if going out for a stroll. He saw no one he knew, though he could hear the cooks chatting and laughing while they prepared the evening meal. He smelt frying onions and his stomach ached for them, but food was bottom priority for the moment.

He dodged down the first alley he came to, and made his way by a roundabout route towards the part of the harbour the ferries always used. He knew there was just the one evening ferry, and it wasn't there. He ran up and down the quay in dismay looking for it. It seemed they'd missed it.

He was looking round for someone to ask when a boy came running round a corner.

"Excuse me, could you tell me if the ferry's – Yildiz!"

"Shh. Don't use my name. From now on I'm Jem. The evening ferry leaves from a different jetty. Follow me, but don't show you know me." Yildiz made a most convincing boy, but as she strode on ahead Osman noticed she couldn't disguise her jaunty walk. His heart lifted. Stage one was under way.

As soon as he was free of his duties, Iskander ran down to find Rifat, praying that he hadn't been sent on some errand. At first he couldn't find him anywhere, not even in his shed, but just as he was getting desperate he noticed some curls of smoke rising behind a wall. He found Rifat smoking a pipe with another of the bostan-jis, and squatted beside them until they'd finished, doing his best to hide his impatience. Then he followed Rifat to his shed.

"I take it that your brother, the famous chengi, showed up again today."

"He told me the escape's fixed for tonight."

"He's very high-handed, I must say. Just assumed you could find a way out, no problem?"

"Yes." Iskander stared at the old man.

"I'm not sure I can help you tonight."

"I'm sorry about the rush, but there's nothing I can do about it." Silence. Iskander felt panic building up. If Rifat turned difficult he'd had it. "Please understand, Rifat. I can't let my brother down. He's been through a lot to get this far."

"And you can't do the rest without me."

"You know that."

"I don't know why I'm risking my job in order to help a pair of crazy twins." Rifat looked at Iskander's white face, and relented. He'd never doubted he'd help them, but the thought of life at the palace without Iskander was so depressing he couldn't help making the boy suffer a little too. He sighed, stood up and took what looked like rags out of a sack. "Try these on." The tattered, smelly clothing immediately made Iskander look like a local fisherman. Satisfied with the transformation, Rifat sat down again. "You're going to have to develop a bad tummy-bug as of now, and in the course of the night establish a pattern of leaving the pages' hall to go and relieve yourself. Do it a couple of times and go back, then go out again in a hurry as if your shits are much worse."

Iskander had already thought of this as the obvious way to leave the pages' hall at night, but kept quiet. "My classmates sleep like logs, but I'll still pad out my bedroll to look as if I'm in it when I leave for the last time."

"Of course. Now listen carefully. I'm going to put an empty wood-basket near the corner of the courtyard. Jump into that if you have the bad luck to see any janissaries, which you probably will. They patrol all night, don't forget."

"I know."

"If they catch you escaping, you've had it. The best thing you can hope for is imprisonment. The worst..." Rifat left it hanging.

"I know." His rags smelt of fish and he wrinkled his nose as he took them off again to hand back to Rifat. He was about to say they stank, but stopped. How fussy he'd become in his pampered palace life.

"Thank you for getting me these clothes, Rifat. They're perfect. I hadn't thought of it."

"There's a lot you haven't thought of. For instance, how is your brother going to find a boatman who'll risk bringing him right round to the Fisherman's Gate in the dead of night?"

"I don't know. Perhaps he's got a friend to help him."

"Oh, is that so? Does this friend have a boat? Or will some kind boatman say, 'Take it, my boy, take it. Never mind the fact you don't know the coast in daylight let alone at night and I'll probably never see my boat again'?" Rifat snorted. "Will he, my eye."

Iskander had been silent as his anger built up inside him, but now it boiled over. "Osman is clever, Rifat, much cleverer than me. And he's brave. He didn't have time to tell me how he was going to do it, but if he says he's coming by boat he'll get one. He'll think of a way. Perhaps he'll even buy a boat. He's earned lots of gold for his dancing – certainly enough to buy a boat. Anyway, it's not your problem, it's his and mine." He and Rifat glared at each other. "And I know that once I'm outside the walls I'm on my own. If Osman doesn't make it, I'll take the consequences."

There was another silence, and then Rifat lowered his eyes and gave another big sigh. "Let's finish making our

plans, boy, such as they are. I'll sleep in this shed tonight
– it won't be the first time – I sometimes do it in summer
before going out for a spot of illegal fishing before dawn.
There's a small door let into that big gate for the palace
fishermen, and I have a key. But I'm not supposed to
have one, understand? No one else knows about it – the
fisherman who gave it to me is long dead."

"If I'm caught, I'll never tell anyone it was you that
helped me."

"Let's hope it doesn't come to that. Now pile those
clothes properly so you can put them on quickly."

Rifat's face was sombre as he watched Iskander pile
the rags.

"Rifat—"

"You get yourself here safely and I'll let you out. Now
go."

"Thank you, Rifat." Iskander stood hovering by the
door. Just saying thanks didn't seem enough. "I – I
wanted to say that you're the best person I've ever met. I
don't know anyone else like you."

"Well, I certainly can't think of another soft-brained
idiot who'd take the risk I'm taking for you." His tone
was brusque, but when Iskander hugged him, he hugged
the boy back.

"I'm going to miss you like anything, Rifat."

"And I'm going to have a quiet life at last. Off you go now." Rifat shut the shed door very quickly to hide his tears.

Osman and Yildiz had boarded the ferry and were looking for places to sit when Osman saw Yacut already ensconced on the best seat. Osman's blood ran cold with shock as he hurried straight past his uncle, thanking his stars he had dirtied his face and pulled the end of his turban right across his mouth and the lower part of his nose. Fortunately Yacut didn't even look twice at what he thought was an anonymous scruffy boy. Osman sat as far away as he could, facing the stern and Uskudar, so that his uncle only saw the back of his head.

Yildiz, on the other hand, decided since Yacut didn't know her, she'd sit near him to see if she could pick up anything useful from his conversation with the men around him. Luckily Yacut was the sort of man who liked to bore everyone with his problems, and he began telling his neighbour how annoyed he was that he hadn't succeeded in persuading the authorities at the palace to allow him a second visit to his son so soon after the last one. He then boasted at length about how successful Jelal was as a page. Yildiz was dozing off when he changed the subject and asked his neighbour a question that woke her up sharply.

"I'm looking for a redheaded man called Kizilbash. Anyone know him? He was in the city with his chengi troupe, but I'm beginning to think they've moved on."

"No they haven't – Kizilbash is still based back in Uskudar." The man who suddenly spoke up had crossed eyes and a distinctive bent nose. Yildiz realized she'd seen him before hanging round with Bulent. "He's staying with his troupe of chengis and acrobats in his brother Bulent's karavansarai – has been for ages."

"But—" Yacut stopped, frowning at the man. "That's where I'm staying. You said Bulent's his brother?"

"Everyone knows that."

"I'm a stranger in these parts." Yacut's glare temporarily froze the conversation while he digested the implications of what he was learning. His expression grew increasingly thunderous, and he stood up and stared at the receding coastline of Uskudar as if he wanted to dive in and swim back there. "But Bulent told me the chengi troupe was Ahmed's."

"Ahmed is the manager." The cross-eyed man smiled smugly, enjoying the effect his information was having on this bad-tempered, arrogant nomad from the mountains. Yildiz looked down as if she wasn't interested, but kept a corner of her eye on Yacut. He was seething with rage, and when he asked the time of the next ferry back, he exploded with frustration when he learned there wasn't one until the morning. And no, it was too late to hire a private boat – it would be dark soon.

The ferry was now about to dock at the Golden Horn, and as soon as it touched the quay Osman and Yildiz jumped off, leaving Yacut still shouting at the captain. They ran into a crowded square where no one would know or care who they were. Osman had seen that Yildiz was laughing to herself, and joined in when he learned the full story.

"That'll teach him." But his smile faded quickly. "The trouble is, he'll go straight to Kizilbash and demand to see me and they'll find I'm not there."

"But that'll be tomorrow morning and by then we should have got to Uskudar, fetched Karakachan from the stable, and escaped into the hills." They stared at each other. "In fact, Osman, if we haven't done it by then, it's too late. We have to be away by dawn or we've had it."

The delicious smell of baked bread filled their noses at that moment as a simit seller passed them. They immediately bought a couple of the bread rings encrusted with sesame seeds and gobbled them up so hungrily Osman got two more.

"Let's forget my uncle for the moment and get on with our plans. We need to find someone who'll sell us a boat. I'm going to say I'm buying it for my master who's a rich foreigner."

"What is his name? Why does he want the boat?" Yildiz finished crunching up her simit as Osman looked blank. "They might ask you questions like that. Why don't you say he's a Greek merchant called Andreas Drosakis – that was my dad's name. Say he wants a boat because ... because..."

"Because he likes going early morning fishing on his own. You pretend you're the merchant's son enquiring about the price – say a few words in Greek to impress him – and I'll be the servant entrusted with the money and maybe bargain a bit."

"*Kala.*"

"What does that mean?"

"It's the Greek for 'good'."

They walked up and down the quayside, observing everything from a distance until they decided they'd found the right boatman. He had a few battered boats for hire and wasn't doing any business.

"We want to buy a boat, Efendi."

"I'm closing up for the day." The fat old boatman was about to turn away when he heard one boy say to the other, "We could pay him right now for a boat and he doesn't want the business."

"If you're serious, I'll consider it."

They bargained for five minutes, then the man caught a glimpse of Osman's gold and the deal was done.

"It's the worst one," whispered Yildiz as she got in the boat. "But it doesn't seem to leak and that's all that matters. Pay quickly – he doesn't look very happy about us."

Osman counted out the price, and leapt in the boat before the boatman could change his mind. Yildiz rowed expertly away as if she knew exactly where she was going, stopping as soon as she was well out of sight and mooring the boat against a small wooden jetty near a tavern. Then they sat there in silence while they recovered, shaking both from relief that they'd got themselves a boat, and hunger. Two simits each weren't enough to get them through the night, so they went to eat in the tavern.

Pretending they were going out fishing next morning, they learned a great deal of useful information about the currents round the point from the sailors and fishermen also eating and drinking in the tavern.

"But don't think of landing anywhere near the palace walls even if you're in trouble. The janissaries have a habit of chopping people's heads off and serving them to the sultan for breakfast." This came from a huge grizzled man who was drunk on raki, and the others all laughed and started inventing other horrors. Osman decided at this point he'd heard enough, so he paid the bill and dragged Yildiz outside.

"Were they joking?"

"I don't care. We're going under cover of darkness, so the janissaries won't see us." He looked at Yildiz's white face. "You must camouflage your face and hands with dirt. Come on. But first we should buy a black goat-hair blanket to cover us if we need to hide. I saw a pile of them for sale in that street."

Iskander stared down at the sleeping face of Ismail, and felt a terrible wrench at leaving his friend without a word of farewell. He was sure Ismail would see him as a traitor, leaving so heartlessly, and nearly put a hand out to wake him. But he stopped himself because it was safer for Ismail to know nothing. He hoped his friend would take his embroidered coat and other few possessions. (His knife and his talisman were safely secured round his body, under Rifat's chainmail waistcoat.) Ismail stirred in his sleep and Iskander quickly left the pages' hall for the last time, doubled up, holding his stomach and groaning.

He had to hide almost at once in the wood-basket when janissaries appeared in a far corner of the courtyard. To his horror they sat down on the basket to smoke a pipe, delaying him for a good half hour. It was well after midnight when he finally reached the lower gardens near the walls, and hurried to Rifat's shed.

"I'm afraid my brother might have come and gone, not finding me there."

"Don't be ridiculous, Iskander. It's much more likely they won't arrive at all. There are treacherous currents everywhere." Rifat was clearly in a bad mood. Iskander changed into the smelly fisherman's clothes and stood there miserably. He'd hoped to part from his friend in a better atmosphere than this, but the old man remained snappish and irritable. "Well, let's get it over with. Once I open that gate you've got to hop through it double quick, my lad, or you might be seen. A janissary patrol has been round once, but they don't keep to a regular beat so you never know when they'll be back."

"Thank you, Rifat —"

"Don't thank me until it's over."

"But then it'll be too late to thank you."

"Life's like that." He didn't meet Iskander's eye. "Now you listen carefully. I go to the Fisherman's Gate alone, I open the little door in it and duck down in the dark to one side. As soon as I'm hidden, you nip out of the shed and get through that gate like lightning, pushing it shut behind you. I won't move to lock it again until I'm sure the coast is clear. Got that?"

"Yes, Rifat."

The whole thing happened so fast that Iskander found himself outside the walls hidden under a pile of nets and sackcloth before he could think straight. When his brain finally took it in, he wept his heart out over his harsh parting from Rifat. It never occurred to him that Rifat was weeping too, wondering whether he'd done the right thing.

THE ANSWER WILL FIND YOU

SMAN AND YILDIZ ROWED towards the point of the promontory keeping well out from the shoreline, sharply aware theirs was now the only craft on the water. Osman's oars kept skidding unexpectedly on the surface or being deflected by waves, making it hard to row a straight course. As they neared the point, the going got even harder. Sudden cross-currents hit them and the boat was pummelled and pushed by these unseen forces. Osman's rowing grew very erratic, and even Yildiz was struggling. As they pulled desperately on the oars, they were both thinking the same thought, *How on earth are we going to get across the Sea of Marmara if we can't even get round this point?*

"Let's go closer in, Osman," whispered Yildiz. "The men in the tavern said it was easier if you could get in the lee of the promontory. We'll have to risk being seen."

"We've got no choice – we're getting nowhere out here."

"Try not to splash your oars."

"I can't help it."

"Then stop rowing for a bit while I turn the boat." Yildiz pulled on one oar, the boat turned towards the shore as if relieved and started to glide through calmer water almost at once. "I can manage alone now. Ship your oars."

"What does that mean?"

"Pull them right in, you idiot."

"Look, just leave off, would you?"

"Sorry."

"Digging up a field of thistles is easier than rowing." Yildiz gave a soft giggle, but Osman wasn't joking. "I mean it. At least I can be useful keeping watch."

He stared at the dark shoreline between the palace walls and the quiet surf, but saw no suspicious movements. They reached a great gate right at the point of the promontory that was flanked by cannons. There were no guards visible, but then, through the still night air, came gruff voices and the clink of weapons. So the janissaries were on duty inside, thought Osman, which meant they were likely to come out at intervals to check the shore.

As this thought crossed his mind, he saw a small door cut into the gate open slightly.

"Quick. Someone's about to come out."

Yildiz gave two powerful pulls on the oars and the boat, boosted by the current, whizzed though the water until it was far enough away to be almost invisible to watchers at the gate. Then they pulled the oars in and ducked down out of sight under the blanket just as a janissary's plumed head peered out of the gate.

"There's a boat out there." The deep voice carried clearly over the water, followed by the sounds of two men climbing through the gate.

"Where? Oh, there. A battered old dinghy and empty by the look of it."

"Probably been abandoned. Anyway, it's floating off out to sea."

More scraping sounds were followed by silence. After a few minutes Osman risked a quick peak to make sure the coast was clear, and they sat up again. The boat was now far from the actual point, and the current was fast taking it into the Sea of Marmara.

"Come on, Osman. Quick. We must row like demons."

She turned the boat as she spoke, and the agonizing pulling began again. Now they were rowing facing the dark and inhospitable open sea. The Uskudar shore was horribly far away, and curls of white cloud were beginning to hide it completely.

"I think there's a sea fog coming," whispered Yildiz.

Osman looked up and promptly missed his stroke, nearly losing an oar. His hands were raw and his arms ached. "How I hate rowing."

"Cheer up, the water's calmer already. There, we're close enough in. Let me row on my own now and you keep watch." Yildiz's hands were nearly as sore as Osman's, but at least the movement was one she found natural. "We don't want to miss this Fisherman's Gate." She pulled her sleeves down as a shield for her hands and started to row again. Osman fixed his gaze on the black shoreline under the towering walls, trying not to think of the expanse of sea behind them. Yildiz rowed quietly with small regular strokes, and the boat crept onwards.

"There's another gate ahead, quite a small one, but I can't see any fishermen's nets. And there's a funny little house. No lights."

He was looking at the outline of a royal pavilion jutting out above the walls near the gate, with big unlit glass windows like blank eyes. Osman prayed there was no one inside keeping watch, and sighed in relief when the boat passed unchallenged.

"Another gate coming up."

"Hope it's the right one. The fog's coming up thicker."

"Isn't that a good thing? It could hide us."

"Yes, but it'll hide everything else as well."

Osman stared fixedly at the big gate ahead, and as they drew nearer saw fishing nets. Some were hung from hooks in the walls, others were piled on the shore, well away from the waterline.

"It looks like the Fisherman's Gate."

"Are you sure?" Yildiz stopped rowing and craned round. With a little satisfied smile, she started to pull on one oar to turn the boat.

A few more pulls and it scraped with a deafening noise on the stony shore. They froze. Any janissaries nearby would surely have heard it. For long moments they waited in complete silence, and since nothing happened, they cautiously got out of the boat. Yildiz took the painter and crept to a post to tie it. Then they crouched down near a pile of nets so that they could whisper.

"Don't forget, I'm called Jem. I don't want your brother to know I'm a girl."

"He might guess anyway, Jem."

"Why should he? He won't be expecting a girl." She looked round through the mist. "Do you think he's hiding somewhere?"

"He won't move until he hears my signal. Let's see if he's here yet."

Osman pursed his mouth and whistled a soft *hoo-hoo, hoo-hoo*. He repeated it twice and then silence descended again. The silence seemed to last for ever, and then, from somewhere nearby, came an owl's response. Three calls, the last one after quite a gap. Osman broke into a wider smile than Yildiz had ever seen on his face before. She watched him control his mouth enough to give a final soft call, and then stand up. Where on earth was Iskander?

A large pile of nets started to heave and a white face peered from underneath, saw Yildiz and ducked out of sight again.

"Osman! There's your brother! I saw him!" She hissed excitedly pointing at the heap. "There, under there!"

Osman knelt down and helped his twin push back the nets and the two of them hugged each other in silence before standing up. Yildiz turned away, pretending to stare at the fast encroaching bank of fog as she blinked away sudden tears. She moved towards the boat, aware of Iskander's height and solidity beside his wiry twin. He was almost a foot taller, and tilted his head in a haughty way as he looked towards her, though he had nothing to be proud about – he'd changed his smart page's clothes for a heap of old rags. Yildiz sat on the side of the boat feeling miserable and wishing she hadn't come. They clearly didn't need her.

"Hullo, Jem. I'm Iskander. Thank you for coming to help us." He was right behind her, smiling at her. He wasn't haughty at all.

Yildiz smiled back just as a thick billow of fog swirled round them.

"My help's not going to be much use. This fog is getting worse."

The three of them stared at the white wall sweeping in from the sea. There was a long silence eventually broken by Osman.

"What's the best thing to do?"

"It's dangerous to wait here. We must move away to somewhere safer. There was a janissary patrol just now, and they'll be back; they always check the beach." Iskander's fisherman's clothes were damp from being under the nets, and he shivered as he looked round. "I don't think we should try to cross to Uskudar until the fog clears. We're only going to get lost."

"I agree. We must stay close to the shore." Yildiz felt despair beginning to fill her. The fog was ruining everything. "I hope you can row, Iskander."

"Never tried, but I can learn." He looked at his soft white hands, as white as his face under the black turban that hid his shaved head. He spotted the ashes of a fire nearby and went to blacken his skin as Osman and Yildiz stared at each other, fear growing in their eyes.

"Which way is best? Along the coast away from Constantinople or back to it?" Osman looked at his twin.

"Once I'm missed they'll send out a search party for sure – they'll look in both directions. We should go that way." He pointed out to sea.

"Karakachan is in Uskudar." whispered Yildiz.

"Karakachan!" Iskander's face lit up.

"Karakachan!" Osman was appalled he'd completely forgotten about the donkey in all the stress and effort of the escape.

"We've got to fetch him or we'll lose him. I know we'll never see Karakachan again if we don't get him tonight." Yildiz couldn't bear the thought of losing another beloved donkey.

"We certainly can't lose Karakachan before I've even seen him again."

"But it's dangerous to go back to the karavansarai, Iskander. Amja Yacut has come back in a rage, staying at the same place as us and telling everyone he's looking for me. He didn't realize I was there all the time, but he'll soon find out."

"Yacut? But why's he come back?" Iskander looked

extremely puzzled. "I told him where the treasure was – that's all he came for."

"You told him the real place?"

"Yes. What was the point of not telling him? He led me to believe you'd died too, in the same accident as Baba."

The brothers gazed at each other, stunned by their uncle's wickedness.

Osman suddenly collapsed against the side of the boat and put his head in his hands. "It's all too much." An extra thick billow of fog almost hid him from the others.

For a minute no one said anything.

"Where was the hiding place?" Yildiz broke the silence, hoping that Iskander wouldn't think the question cheeky, but he answered immediately.

"In my father's saddle."

Osman's head jerked up, and then slowly his shoulders started to shake. When he looked at them they saw he was laughing. Silent, almost hysterical laughter. He eventually whispered, "I've got the saddle, Iskander. Ana gave it to me for Karakachan. So we've just got to get to Uskudar before Yacut does. He's bound to gang up with our boss, and he'll see the saddle when they search the stables. Come on. We can't give up now."

With a little burst of hope, all three started to move to the boat. But the hope died as soon as it flowered, killed by the sight of the dark, heaving sea, the black sky arching above, and between the two an impenetrable bank of fog. No stars were visible. There was nothing to help them.

Yildiz shivered and turned to Osman, her shoulders crumpling in despair. "We can't do it, Osman. The fog keeps getting thicker. It's impossible." Tears were collecting in her eyes. "If we want to save ourselves, we'll have to forget Karakachan and the gold and just creep along the coastline back to the city." She thought of the donkey's confusion and misery when he found his familiar carers had deserted him, and the tears ran silently down her cheeks.

The two boys looked at her, and at the fog, and knew she was right. They had no chance of getting safely across the Sea of Marmara. Their plan was useless. Limping back to the city was the best they could do.

With heavy hearts they started to pull the boat closer in order to get into it. At that moment they all heard the quiet creak of the inner gate and froze in horror. The janissaries had arrived already.

"Quick!" Yildiz jumped into the boat and fumbled for the oars. "Hurry!"

But the figure looming through the fog was no janissary. A large old man with a long untidy beard, a stern face and the clothes of a gardener was walking towards them, his slow heavy steps crunching on the pebbles. The boys seemed to turn to stone, and Yildiz started to panic. Then she caught sight of Iskander's transfigured face. He looked as she would look if, magically through the fog, instead of this old man, her parents had suddenly appeared. On the other hand, Osman was staring at the figure as if he'd seen a ghost. She heard him whisper words that sounded like, "The answer will find you."

"Rifat! Rifat! You've come!" Iskander ran forward, his arms out.

"Be quiet, you stupid boy, you'll bring the whole platoon out." Rifat glowered at the three of them. "So you must be twin brother Osman. And you?"

"Jem. I'm here because I know about boats."

"I'm relieved to hear one of you does. And this is the boat?" The old man looked at it and gave a disgusted sigh. "If you can call that a boat. Where are you heading?"

"We hoped to go to Uskudar," whispered Osman, still staring transfixed at Rifat. He still couldn't believe a strange old man so like the one he thought he'd seen in the cave had suddenly appeared out of nowhere. And he seemed to be about to help them.

"In this fog? You'd never have done it."

"We realized that." Yildiz put her chin up, getting annoyed with all this criticism.

Rifat looked out to sea. "Well, I came out to give you a hand, and it seems you need it. Come on, boys, we must hurry. The janissary patrol will be here any minute. You can tell me the rest of your plan when we get away from the shore." He started to push the boat out. The twins still didn't move, they were so surprised at the sudden turn of events.

"But Rifat, what'll happen to you if you come?"

"Listen, Iskander, I've been a bostanji a very long time, and I can get away with breaking the rules now and again. Hop in quick, all of you."

Yildiz went first and Iskander followed, but Osman still hesitated.

"Come on, Osman. You can trust Rifat."

Iskander's smile encouraged Osman to join the others, but he couldn't help feeling confused and uneasy.

Rifat pushed the boat further away from the shore as he jumped in. "Right. You twins keep warm under that blanket and sit well down in the stern. Jem will help me row. Your hands look rather sore already, lad, for someone who messes about in boats."

"I'm a bit out of practice."

"Have these." He took a pair of leather strips out of his pocket. "Wind them round your hands or you'll be good for nothing. Now, let's get the weight balanced as best we can. I'll sit on the middle thwart with Jem forward. Don't row yet, Jem – I'll take us out. I know these waters like the back of my hand."

From the moment he dipped his oars in, Yildiz could see how skilled he was, and the terror that had been building up inside her began to melt. She didn't understand why this old man had appeared or who he was, but as she watched him row she remembered the stories her father used to tell her about the ancient sea-gods. There was one called Neptune who controlled the waves, who was strong and bearded and carried a trident. This strange man didn't have a trident, but he'd arrived from nowhere looking just like Neptune. She just hoped he wouldn't indulge in Neptune's nasty habit of conjuring up storms.

"Who are you?" Osman whispered to Rifat after a few minutes, when their world was just pure fog in all directions.

"Tell him, Iskander. It might stop him looking at me as if he'd seen a ghost."

"This is Rifat – he works in the palace gardens for the sultan. He's been my friend all through." Iskander explained how good Rifat had been to him, how he'd saved his life, and finally helped him escape through the inner gate.

"But you never said you'd row our boat for us as well, Rifat. What made you come out?"

"Madness. Utter madness." But there was a twinkle deep in Rifat's eyes, and at last Osman smiled at him. "Ah, so you've finally accepted I'm real flesh and blood, boy. I'm very relieved."

Osman was about to tell Rifat that he looked like the ghostly visitor he'd had in the Cave of the Seven Sleepers, then stopped. *The answer will find you*. The words he'd heard in the cave rang in his mind. Perhaps he'd dreamed them. And though Rifat himself was certainly the answer to what had seemed an impossible situation, the more Osman looked at his craggy face, the more he found the old man no longer reminded him of the strange apparition. Rifat was real: a kind old palace bostanji rowing them through the fog, his eyes busily darting from side to side, gauging the strength and direction of the current from the waves, missing nothing.

Osman sighed and snuggled up to Iskander. After so long without him, sitting here beside him was a real comfort. He looked up at the blackness above them and for a brief moment the fog and cloud parted, showing the stars at last, bright in a patch of clear sky.

SAVING KARAKACHAN

RIFAT'S SLOW, RHYTHMIC ROWING calmed everyone. The boat made its almost dreamlike journey through the fog in silence until at last Rifat broke it.

"Have a rest now, Jem. You've done well. This is a calm section, between currents – I'll be fine rowing on my own. We'll soon be halfway across you'll be pleased to hear. Now, boys, fill me in on the background of this great escape, and tell me what your plan is."

Osman summarized the situation at the karavansarai, and tried to make Rifat see the importance of rescuing Karakachan if they possibly could, sensing as he did so the old bostanji's reservations.

"So you hope to escape up into the mountains with that donkey before the hue and cry starts?"

"Yes."

"Tell me something, Osman. You and Iskander are nomads, so mountains are your home ground, but your uncle's a nomad too, and he'll be very quick to work out where you've gone and track you down whichever route you take. I imagine your red-headed troupe owner is pretty hot at chasing people too. And they both have horses. So my question is this: are you sure that going to the mountains is the best way to get away from them?"

Yildiz, seated behind Rifat, could see the twins lose confidence. Osman began to explain that they'd find a cave somewhere and hide in that, but Iskander interrupted and said surely it was better to keep on the move. After a few more remarks they tailed off and sat looking miserable. There was a long silence. Yildiz wished she could see Rifat's face, but she could almost feel him thinking.

"This donkey is the main problem, as I see it. It's easy to take the gold from the saddle and run away, but to get the donkey out and then hide successfully somewhere with it – that's the problem. And I'll bet it's a naughty donkey. Won't keep quiet when you want him to."

"Karakachan's full of tricks. That's why we love him." Osman's tone was defiant. "And we're not going to leave him behind." The others nodded their agreement, and Rifat sighed.

"Then we must try to work out a way of doing it safely."

The waves suddenly became rougher and bumpier, and Rifat asked Yildiz to row again to help him get the boat through the turbulence. "We're getting closer to the shore than I realized – another half hour's rowing, Jem, no more." Rifat and Yildiz rowed hard while the little boat was tossed brutally about by the waves. "Well done, boy. You're a lot stronger than you look. There, we're through the worst patch."

Iskander had gone a little green in the choppy section, but had managed not to be sick. To his relief, the water became calmer with the same suddenness as it had become rough. He swallowed several times before he trusted his voice enough to make a suggestion.

"Perhaps we could find somewhere to hide Karakachan safely, and then we could collect him later when the coast was clear."

"Now you're talking sense. Then you'll be able to disappear without giving yourselves away."

"How, Rifat?" asked Osman.

"What would your uncle and this chengi boss expect you to do?"

"Escape to the mountains with Karakachan, as we'd planned." Osman thought for a bit. "So we should do something quite different. Assuming we manage to hide Karakachan successfully without them knowing, we're free to – to take a ferry somewhere. They wouldn't expect us to do that with a donkey in tow."

"Exactly. Take a ferry. There are boats going all over the place from Uskudar – up the Bosphorus channel as well as across the Sea of Marmara to the south. There are boats to Greece, or Crete, or even Egypt." He chuckled at the twins' worried expressions. "There's a big wide world to disappear into, and it's all ruled by our sultan!"

There was a long silence, which Osman finally broke. "We don't want to go too far, because our mother and little sister will be waiting for us."

"I was teasing you, boys. My advice would be to head south towards the Dardanelles strait, and stop in a fishing village somewhere down there. It wouldn't be much more than a day's sailing. Then it's not so far to come back when the dust has settled and your enemies have left."

Suddenly they all jumped: the unmistakable sound of a muezzin calling the faithful to dawn prayers seemed as if it was only yards away through the fog.

"That'll be the mosque beside the harbour," whispered Rifat. "We're close in now. I'm going to drop you at a little jetty in front of the mosque, and the fact there'll be lots of people about on their way to pray will take attention from your arrival. Get ready to leave the boat quickly when I give the word."

The twins sat up, pushing the blanket aside. Yildiz shipped her oars and then folded the blanket and put it over her shoulder – it could come in useful.

"What are you going to do now, Rifat?" Iskander put his hand on his friend's arm. "Are you going back to the palace?"

"The boat is yours," whispered Osman. "For what that's worth."

"It'll get me home when I want to go, but not yet. I'm going to beach it somewhere, and then I'll come and find you. I've had an idea where we can hide that wretched donkey. I have relatives here who might help. One of you wait in the mosque for me while the others fetch him from the karavansarai."

"I'll wait in the mosque," said Osman. "I'd be recognized at once if I showed my face at Bulent's. Iskander and Yil– Jem will have to fetch Karakachan."

The boat touched softly against a small stone jetty. "Now go, go, children. May Allah go with you."

"And with you."

With two strokes, Rifat disappeared into the fog. The three of them stood on the quay at a loss for a moment.

Osman spoke first, seeing the slow file of sleepy men walking into the mosque.

"Kizilbash and Ahmed always go to the mosque near the karavansarai at dawn, so if you hurry you might be able to get Karakachan out before they return. I'll go into this mosque now and wait for Rifat – it's safer than hanging about in the street. We'll wait in there until you come, but if you're not back in half an hour we'll know something's gone wrong and start looking for you."

At that moment a lame simit-seller set up his stall ready for the exodus from the mosque, and Osman bought three. Wolfing theirs down, Yildiz and Iskander hurried towards the karavansarai.

"When we get to the door, follow me closely," said Yildiz. "I'll lead you straight to the stables and with a bit of luck people will just think we're stable boys."

"Won't you be recognized, Jem?"

She pulled an end of her turban over her face and tucked it in firmly. "Hope not."

Since most of the men had gone to the mosque, there were few people around as the two of them nonchalantly crossed the courtyard to the animal quarters. The camels and horses were huffing and stamping with hunger, and a couple of donkeys brayed. Yildiz darted between arches to the dark corner where Karakachan was tethered, and put her arms round his neck. But he didn't respond as usual because he'd seen Iskander. He went stiff, brayed loudly, and pulled at his tether.

"Karakachan! Look at you, so sleek and fat – what a lazy donkey you must be these days!" Iskander went on whispering sweet nothings into his ear and stroking his nose as the donkey shook his head and snorted in his delight.

"Come on, Iskander." Yildiz spoke rather sharply, jealous of Karakachan's response. "You're going to have all the time you want with that donkey later – give me a hand to saddle and load him." Yildiz slung the saddle at Iskander, who gave a soft chuckle when he saw it.

"That's Baba's saddle." He strapped it on Karakachan's back. "We'd better cover it."

"Let him eat while we're loading him." She knew Karakachan would object to being ridden before he'd had his breakfast, and tied a full nosebag on him before loading a spare bag of feed and her own and Osman's few possessions onto his back.

Noises and laughter came from the courtyard. "They're beginning to come back from the mosque. Quick. I'm going to lie on Karakachan's back – now cover me with the black goat hair blanket." She hopped onto the donkey's back and lay flat.

"With his nosebag on and that over him he doesn't look much like Karakachan." Iskander adjusted the blanket, talking quietly to the donkey to keep him calm. "What now?"

"Just lead us out of the main gate as if you do it every day."

Iskander set off briskly across the courtyard, holding Karakachan's bridle extra firmly. Just as he reached the main gate he caught sight of the back view of his uncle, talking excitedly to someone with a flaming red beard. The man frowned, pushed Yacut aside and promptly ran up some steep stone steps. Iskander tried to get through the gate, but at that moment a large group of men arrived together, effectively blocking it. A loud shout came from upstairs.

"Osman's gone! He padded his bed so no one would notice!"

"Run!" screamed the bulge under the blanket, kicking her heels into Karakachan's sides. The donkey leapt forward straight into a frightened gallop, making the men in the gate scatter. Iskander flew alongside, and they tore down the main street towards the mosque by the harbour.

As soon as she could, Yildiz pushed back the blanket and jumped off to run beside the donkey. Behind them they heard shouts.

"That sounds like Ahmed — he's the chengi trainer," panted Yildiz, looking over her shoulder. "But I can't see Kizilbash. He and Yacut are probably saddling their horses."

They flew past the simit-seller, knocking his stall over. As he shouted angrily after them, Iskander took charge. "Jem, you nip into the mosque and fetch Osman, and I'll go behind it and find somewhere to hide if I can."

Yildiz had never been in a mosque full of men and felt as if a hand would point from heaven to denounce her as a female on forbidden ground. Luckily Osman was sitting near the entrance, and he got up as soon as he spotted her.

"Rifat's not here yet. Where's Iskander?"

"Trying to hide round the back. They're following us — your uncle must have just arrived off the ferry and found Kizilbash at once. They're all looking for you. Come on, we have to get away."

"Oh, where on earth are you, Rifat?" Osman looked in all directions as he tore after Yildiz, but there was no sign of the old bostanji. They ran to the back of the mosque and couldn't see Iskander or Karakachan anywhere.

"Psst." Iskander's head came over a ruined wall just high enough to hide Karakachan, and Yildiz and Osman jumped over to join them.

"They'll find us here at once. We must find some-where better."

"Where's Rifat?"

"He hasn't come yet."

"Oh, no. Everything's going wrong."

There was a noisy clatter of horse's hooves and then they clearly heard their uncle's voice shouting a question at the simit-seller.

"Down there, past the mosque. Two boys and a don-key. They knocked over my bread—"

"Where did they go? Along the coast road or behind the mosque?"

"How do I know? I was picking up my bread—"

The horses were pawing the cobbles, and Karakachan, who'd been taking an increasing interest in the new arrivals, lifted his head at that moment to bray a greeting. Iskander clamped his arm round Karakachan's jaw and managed to silence the indignant donkey as well as keep his head below the wall.

The men were still talking loudly near the mosque.

"Are you sure they came this way, Ahmed?"

"I was just behind them. I saw them. Then they ran beyond the mosque and disappeared."

"They're most likely to go along the coast road." It was Yacut's voice. "They'll be aiming at finding a way up through the mountains as soon as they can. I suggest you and I ride along there, checking the harbour and then the coast road, and your manager has a look behind the mosque."

"Let's go. I'm almost more annoyed about the donkey than that little devil Osman – he'll be too old soon to do his tricks, but that donkey will go on for years." Kizilbash's voice faded as the horses cantered off.

Ahmed's footsteps came round the mosque and then paused nearby. Iskander handed Karakachan over to Yildiz and picked up a beam lying beside their feet. He gestured at the black blanket and mouthed to Osman to be ready with it. Yildiz quickly eased the blanket off the donkey.

There was something almost comical about the way Ahmed's head peered cautiously over the wall, to be promptly swamped by the blanket. Iskander brought the beam down with a horrible crack on Ahmed's head, and he dropped like a stone.

THE TANNERY

THE THREE OF THEM stood staring at each other in silent horror.

"You've killed him!" Osman peered over the wall in horror. Ahmed was lying completely still.

"I had to do something." Iskander's hands were shaking with panic. "Run for it." He looked frantically round. "That way." He started to run towards a dark alley.

Yildiz wanted to grab the blanket, but as she went up to Ahmed he groaned. Relieved he was still alive, she abandoned the blanket and tore after the boys and Karakachan. It was a very narrow alley and led, after many twists and turns, into a small square where shopkeepers were beginning to open up. Moderating their pace and trying to look as if they knew where they were going, they crossed the square into another long winding alley leading them always further from the seafront. It suddenly turned into a dead end. They stopped and looked at each other. Karakachan brayed and shook his head to remind them his nosebag was empty. They ignored him.

They carefully retraced their steps and, as they reached the square again, they saw a familiar figure walking quickly across it, heading for the alley that led in the direction of the mosque.

"Rifat!" they shouted in unison, but he didn't hear.

"I'll go after him. Wait round the corner out of sight." Iskander ran off and caught up with the bostanji as he reached the end of the alley near the mosque. A crowd had gathered round Ahmed. Iskander quickly explained what had happened, and Rifat looked grave.

"So is he dead?"

"Jem said he heard a groan."

"Wait here while I wander over and see what's going on. No one knows me so they won't be suspicious."

Rifat did a good impersonation of a vague old man passing the time gossiping with the simit-seller, and was back quite soon.

"He's not dead, Allah be praised. Someone's gone off to find Kizilbash, and the simit-seller will no doubt tell him which way you all ran. Hurry. We must hide your donkey and get you boys away from here as quickly as possible."

Iskander followed Rifat at a slight distance, only joining him again when they picked up the others hiding round the first corner of the blind alley.

"Now, follow me, but not too closely. And you, Iskander, always stay right back and see if anyone's following. We're going to my cousin's tannery."

Rifat led them through a maze of tiny streets until they became aware of the strong smell of a tannery somewhere nearby. At that moment a donkey laden with half-cured skins pushed past them and they followed it into a small warehouse full of piles of skins. The stench was now almost unbearable, and Yildiz was afraid she'd retch. The twins were also looking rather green and holding their noses, but Rifat didn't seem bothered by it, telling them to wait before disappearing up a ladder.

They heard clattering hooves arriving on the cobbles outside the tannery and looked round in vain for a place to hide, afraid it was Kizilbash in pursuit. They were mightily relieved to see a cavalcade of donkeys loaded with skins queuing to enter the tannery and completely blocking the alley. Karakachan gave them a noisy welcome, pulling on his tether and drawing unwelcome attention to his owners. They dragged Karakachan to a far corner of the warehouse while the line of tannery donkeys were unloaded.

"How do the men work all day in this pong?" whispered Osman. "It's the worst smell in the world. It's doing my head in."

"They're used to it, and I bet the donkeys love it." Iskander was nervously watching the ladder. "I wish Rifat wouldn't keep disappearing."

"I guess this is where he wants us to leave Karakachan. After all, the best place to hide a donkey is with dozens of others." Yildiz couldn't help yawning, despite the fact it seemed to let the stench go deeper into her nostrils. It had been a long night, and a long day stretched ahead. She was exhausted and her hands were throbbing from all the rowing she'd done. She looked at a pile of skins and ached to lie down and sleep.

"Iskander, I think we should look inside Baba's saddle now we've got a quiet moment." Osman drummed his fingers on the polished leather.

"You're right. Come here, Karakachan." Iskander undid the buckles, and laid the saddle upside down on the floor, out of sight behind a pile of skins. He undid some ties, and lifted a small leather flap on the underside of the pommel. He grinned at Osman as he felt inside, expecting to find the leather pouch full of gold coins he'd seen Ali stuff in there. His hand scrabbled about and his expression changed to puzzlement.

"There's nothing in there."

"Nothing?" Osman bent down and felt too. The space was indeed empty. The twins stared at each other.

"It couldn't have been stolen. No one would think of this hiding place." Iskander retied the flap and turned the saddle right way up. "Baba must have moved the gold himself. Typical Baba. He didn't trust me with the secret." As he put the saddle back onto Karakachan he couldn't help laughing about the fact that his uncle was on a false trail.

Osman rolled his eyes and with a resigned shrug started to laugh too. "It doesn't surprise me a bit."

"But the gold—" Yildiz was stunned that they seemed to think it was a joke their inheritance had disappeared.

"Is hidden somewhere else. We'll probably never find it."

"But nor will Amja Yacut." As Osman said this, their laughter built up again. "But the really funny thing is, I think I know exactly where it is!"

"Where?"

"Baba spent ages carving a new tent-pole, with a hollow section in one end. I wondered what it was for!" The boys hooted, doubled over with laughter.

"You're both mad. I give up trying to understand you." Yildiz sank onto a pile of hides. Her arms were so tired and sore she wished she could take them off.

Iskander put the empty saddle back on Karakachan, heartily relieved he didn't have to worry about the gold any more, but his amusement had already turned to anger. How dare Baba have so little faith in him.

"Here's Rifat," said Yildiz in relief.

Rifat came down the ladder followed by a small bandy-legged man with a skin like cured leather.

"Meet Yashar, my cousin. He promises he'll give your donkey a good home in return for having the use of him to carry skins. He's been supplying the palace with leather for years because of my recommendation and he owes me a big favour."

Yashar smiled and raised his hand in acknowledgment. "Karakachan will be safe here until you come and get him again."

The twins gazed at Yashar, who had slit eyes and high cheekbones and didn't look very honest or reliable.

"I have agreed to keep him only if he's a good worker, Rifat. Not if he refuses loads." Yashar inspected Karakachan. "Hum, you look fit and well cared-for, but are you one of those donkeys who kicks and bites everyone they don't know?"

"You must approach him from the front, then he's fine and you can load him with anything." Osman patted

Karakachan, praying he wouldn't nip the man, then turn round and kick him.

"He's very intelligent and he's also got a secret birthmark." This came from Yildiz, who had dragged herself off the pile of hides and was glaring in deep suspicion at Yashar. There was no secret birthmark, as the twins well knew. They hid their smiles.

Yashar wagged his head at her. "Don't worry, boy. I treat donkeys well. I couldn't run my business without them." He stroked Karakachan's ears in just the way donkeys like. "Don't I, old fellow? And you'll get him back as good as you left him. I'll never hear the end of it from Rifat otherwise." At that moment he was called away to check over the immense load of new skins.

Rifat stared at the three bedraggled and exhausted figures in front of him. "You all need food before you do anything else. Say goodbye to your donkey and give him some more feed while I find out where the donkey-drivers eat." He left them and they filled the nosebag, having taken their belongings from Karakachan's back. They then hugged him one at a time before tying his nosebag back on him and tethering him. Karakachan looked very relaxed and content, but they had tears in their eyes.

At that moment Rifat rushed up with Yashar. "Quick,

boys. Follow Yashar. Kizilbash is outside. I'll stay on guard here."

Tiredness forgotten, they pelted up the ladder behind Yashar, and not a moment too soon. Kizilbash and Yacut rode in noisily, causing the lines of donkeys to bray and try to break ranks. The overseer shouted at the newcomers.

"Take those horses out, they're upsetting my donkeys. If you've got business here, come in on foot."

"We're looking for two violent runaways with a donkey—" began Yacut.

Rifat sidled up. "With a black donkey?"

"Yes! Yes!"

"One boy taller than the other?"

"Get on with it, old man, have you seen them?"

Rifat didn't like Yacut's arrogant manner, or the way his eyes were set so close together they seemed to meet above his beaked nose. "I saw them in the square, Efendi. They didn't come this way – I could show you which street they took if—" He paused and rubbed his thumb and forefinger together.

"Show me exactly where they went and there'll be a tip for you."

"Follow me, Efendi."

They clattered out behind the old bostanji.

THE FINAL STINT

IFAT TOOK YACUT AND KIZILBASH to the area of the town full of butchers, before hurrying back to the tannery. He found the twins and Yildiz wolfing kebabs and bread.

"Shame on you, Rifat. These poor boys are starving. I've never seen food disappear so quickly! I've just sent for a whole lot more. You can pay for it this time." Yashar gave Rifat a slit-eyed grin and went back to work in the unloading area.

"Tell us what happened, Rifat!"

"They're searching for you in all those little streets in the butcher's quarter. It will take them a while to find they're on a wild goose chase. You've got a little time. Ah, here's the food."

Yashar had ordered large amounts, and as Rifat paid for it, he looked ruefully at Iskander. "I'm afraid

I'm running out of cash."

"I've still got plenty." Osman gave the old man enough to cover the meal and, as soon as they were alone, Iskander told him about the missing gold.

"Amja Yacut will never believe it wasn't in the saddle at all. He'll always think we took it. So it doesn't make things any easier – except we don't have to worry about keeping the gold safe." Iskander grinned at Rifat, who remained uneasy.

"Could someone have stolen it?"

"Unlikely. I think Baba moved it himself." He didn't mention Osman's theory – it was no more than a guess, after all.

There was a silence while they finished all the food. Yildiz felt much less tired, and sighed contentedly before she said, "One of us ought to find out about that ferry."

"I already have. It leaves at dawn tomorrow morning." Rifat stood up. "I asked the captain whether you could sleep on board tonight, and he agreed – but you'll have to pay extra. It's a pity about that gold, Iskander. Are you sure you searched the saddle properly?"

"Absolutely sure. Go and check it yourself."

Osman looked out of the doorway down the ladder. "It's too late. All the donkeys have gone, Karakachan too." Iskander and Yildiz joined him to look down.

Except for a handful of men stacking and shifting skins, the warehouse was empty and silent.

"Poor old Karakachan – he'll be so puzzled and hurt. I feel like we've deserted him," whispered Yildiz. All three felt bereft and fearful about the future.

"Can we wait here until this evening, Rifat?" said Iskander, breaking the long silence.

"I promised Yashar that when he got back from taking all the donkeys to the stables, we'd be gone. He doesn't want trouble." Rifat cleared his throat. "Now, let's plan the next move." He sounded tired.

The boys and Yildiz saw with a pang that he looked as tired as he sounded. He seemed even older than usual. Iskander touched his arm. "We can manage on our own now, Rifat. You rest. Just tell us where the ferry leaves from, and anything else we need to know."

"I'm all right, Iskander. I'll have plenty of time to rest when you've gone. I'll go out of the tannery first to see if the coast's clear. When I give you the signal, you must leave – separately – and stay apart until this evening. The jetty is just beyond where I dropped you, and the boat is called the *Dolphin*. Don't forget, *Dolphin*."

"What are you going to do, Rifat? Go back to the palace?" Iskander wanted to delay the moment of parting.

"Maybe. I'll see. I've been quite enjoying my freedom,

so maybe not. I might retire and claim my little bit of pension. I like the thought of an easy life, with a bit of fishing to help make ends meet."

Iskander started to fumble for something under his clothes, and brought out his half of the talisman. "Please have this, Rifat. Keep it safe and we'll all meet again. Osman's got the other half." His twin was already bringing his piece out.

Rifat took the two halves and clamped them together. They fitted perfectly. The little heads seemed to smile at him now their egg was whole again, and he smiled back. "People pick up idols like this in ancient places. Who broke the heads apart?"

Osman remembered the strange visitor, and how for a moment he'd mistaken Rifat for him. "I don't know, Rifat. I found them like that. But we'd like you to look after them for us."

"Can I see them?" Yildiz smiled at the odd little heads. "They're so sweet. They look happy together."

Rifat put the pieces in an inner pocket, "When you come back to fetch Karakachan, they'll be in one piece again. I'll get someone to rivet the back." He stood up. "Now, I must go. *Inshallah*."

"*Inshallah*." All three spoke almost in chorus as they followed him down the ladder. They watched him go with their fears over the next stage of their escape lightened a little by the hope they'd see their old friend again. When Rifat signalled the all-clear, Iskander ran away first, off to the left, Yildiz next to the right, and finally, Osman headed for the little market square and the fisherman's district.

Then they were gone. Rifat stood alone for a moment, feeling as bereft as they had felt when they saw their donkey was no longer there. Then something made him follow Osman. He saw him dodging through the market stalls with the bendy, graceful agility of a chengi, and it reminded him that Kizilbash wasn't going to give up his star dancer easily. Osman disappeared down a dark, noisy alley and as Rifat turned into it he heard a furious shout and sounds of fighting.

Osman had run into Kizilbash and his brother Bulent, who happened, by ill luck, to be walking down an alley that crossed his. Rifat could see that although the boy was putting up a valiant fight, he was being quickly over-powered by the two strong men. He'd managed to bite Kizilbash's ear, and blood was now pouring down the man's red beard and clothing. Rifat hung back – he could do nothing to help yet, but he could follow them. There was no sign of the uncle, Yacut.

Osman was dragged back to the karavansarai and

locked in Bulent's dark windowless office. Rifat had a good look at the layout of the karavansarai before being thrown out by one of Bulent's stewards.

"No vagrants. You pay to stay here or out you go."

Rifat needed help. He had no idea where Iskander or Yildiz were hiding, so he headed back to the tannery to find his cousin Yashar.

Iskander was already fast asleep under a wooden cart that had been pushed to the side of the road because of a broken axle. He was so exhausted he'd decided to spend the waiting time asleep, and was delighted to find this safe spot. Yildiz had had the same idea about sleeping, but couldn't find a suitable place. She decided she'd risk going near the harbour to see if she could crawl under an upturned boat and, as she crossed the big street near the mosque, was spotted by Rifat. They showed no sign of knowing each other, but as Rifat walked past her he muttered, "Osman's been captured. Make your way back to the tannery."

Her heart thudding, her exhaustion forgotten, she darted through side streets and reached the tannery just before Rifat. They went up the ladder and found Yashar doing his accounts in his lair.

"Now what?" He didn't look very pleased to see them

back so soon, but softened up when Rifat explained what had happened. He sighed.

"The only way in and out of Bulent's place is the main door."

"You know Bulent?"

"Of course – everyone round here does." Yashar gave them one of his slit-eyed looks. "I'll tell you something else. He wants to marry my daughter Ayesha when she's old enough."

There was a thoughtful silence.

Rifat eventually broke it, saying, "We've got to free Osman, but first let's rule out what's not possible. We can't go in and break that door down – it's too strong. We can't get him out by a window because I could see there wasn't one – it was more a cupboard than a room. Anyway, the place will be guarded. And once that uncle of his sees Osman's there—"

"What can we do then?" Yildiz was almost in tears.

"We'll think of something, Jem. Don't get too upset."

Yashar got up and stretched. "Well, it seems my accounts will have to wait. Let me think how to go about this. Somehow I have to get Bulent to let that boy out. He'll only do that if it's really going to benefit him." He went to the lookout point at the end of the room, from where he could watch the men working in the huge dye vats in the open yard beyond. There was a long silence before Yashar spoke.

"Here's what might work. I could tell Bulent that a rival tanner has fallen in love with my daughter, and made me a partnership offer I find hard to resist. Bulent will have to match it, and throw in the boy he's just locked up – otherwise he loses Ayesha."

"But will Bulent swallow that?" Rifat, looked as dubious as Yildiz felt.

"Bulent is totally obsessed with Ayesha, who's a charming little minx – she attracts men like flies. So, yes, he probably will, but I have to play it right. It's our only hope, unless you can think of something better."

Rifat made for the ladder. "Let's go. We need to hurry – I heard that someone had been sent to find Yacut, who's gone up the mountainside searching for his nephews." When they reached the floor of the tannery, Rifat stopped and put his hands on Yashar's shoulders. "Thank you for doing this for us, Yashar."

"You've made me a rich man by recommending me to the palace, Rifat. I like to pay my debts." He pushed Rifat's hands away with a smile. "Besides, life in the tannery is very predictable and you've certainly livened things up today, with more fun to come! And, I hope, a happy outcome for my little Ayesha."

He pressed his hands together. "*Inshallah*."

"*Inshallah*." They headed for the door.

As they walked past the mosque, Yildiz noticed that their black goat hair rug was lying folded on the wall, waiting to be claimed by its owner. She darted across to retrieve it and slung it over one shoulder, fixing it in place with her belt. It immediately changed the way she looked, making her broader and somehow older. She pulled the end of her turban over her mouth and nose, and hoped no one in the karavansarai would recognize her. She was to go in with Yashar as his servant; Rifat would stay outside keeping watch.

But they were told Bulent wasn't there – he had gone to the coffee house nearby. Yashar grinned. "Perfect. I need some coffee."

And indeed, it was a much better place for him to chat to Bulent, which he did for what seemed like hours to poor Yildiz, who nearly dozed off several times. Then she saw the two men grow serious, and put their heads close together. She watched, fascinated by Yashar's performance. Bulent was taking the bait, though clearly torn by loyalty to his brother. Then she heard him say as he leaned back away from Yashar, "Kizilbash knows that boy will soon be too old to be a chengi, so I don't think he'll mind much on that count if he escapes. The trouble is, Yacut has promised my brother part of some gold that apparently Osman has in his possession. I don't quite understand the ins and outs, but the upshot is Yacut hired Kizilbash to help capture Osman, and my brother hates to lose out on a financial deal."

"If you give me the boy I'll find out where that gold is and you shall have it as part of the dowry."

Brilliant, thought Yildiz. She saw Bulent weaken, and then stand up.

"All right, Yashar. I'll do it. There goes the muezzin for midday prayers. It's now or never."

The two men hurried out with Yildiz not far behind. She saw Rifat near the karavansarai gate, chatting to someone. Men were filing out of the karavansarai on their way to prayers, and amongst them she saw Kizilbash wave to his brother. Bulent made a sign he would follow, and then led Yashar through to his office. Yildiz followed, praying that someone like Ahmed wouldn't appear, recognize her and give the game away.

Bulent unlocked the door, but Yashar pushed into the office ahead of Bulent, making a quick warning face to Osman who began to grasp what was afoot when he glimpsed Yildiz briefly in the doorway. He was frogmarched into the now empty courtyard by Yashar, his hands still tied.

"Take his other arm, Jem. We don't want the little blighter running off again. Thanks, Bulent. I won't tell Kizilbash you let him out. And I'll keep my side of the bargain."

But Bulent had already locked his office and disappeared in order not to be seen with them, so they collected Rifat and headed away from the karavansarai. As soon as they had gone down a couple of alleys, Rifat undid Osman's ropes, then took Yashar's arm and said, "The adventure's over for us, Yashar. It's time to leave them. They have to go it alone now."

"What a pity – I haven't enjoyed anything so much for ages." Yashar beamed at Osman and Yildiz, his eyes almost disappearing behind his high cheeks.

His enjoyment ended abruptly. A horse galloped up the alley behind them and the rider brought his whip down on Yashar's shoulder, causing him to scream with pain.

"Out of my way!" It was Yacut. He raised his whip again to use it on Osman. Osman and Yildiz leapt in different directions, and the whip missed both. Yacut was now yelling with manic fury as he wheeled his horse and tried to aim again at Osman.

"You little fiend, I'm going to give you a beating you'll never forget!" The whip landed with a sickening thwack on Osman's back, causing him to double up with agony. Rifat managed to grab it and tried to pull it from Yacut. Yashar was still groaning and cowering at the side of the alley, in shock at the sudden turn of events.

"Oh, no, you don't, you wretch! Aha – you're the old man who sent me on a wild goose chase!" Yacut's mad rage seemed to give him superhuman strength, and he managed to pull the whip free, turn and bring it down hard on Osman so unexpectedly he didn't have a chance to avoid it as it slashed into his face and neck. Yildiz screamed at Yacut in rage, and the next moment she was whipped herself.

"Tell me where that saddle is, Osman, or I'll whip you again!"

With an extraordinary, almost animal, roar, Rifat launched himself at Yacut, pulling at his leg and trying to unseat him. The horse started to buck and rear, and looked as if it would bring its hooves down on poor Yashar, who managed to wriggle away just in time. Then shouts came from behind the onlookers who were rapidly collecting round the melee, and to Rifat's huge relief three janissaries appeared. Even better, he knew one of them. He hung onto Yacut in desperation until two janissaries took charge of the horse's bridle, and the third pulled the whip from Yacut and told him to dismount at once.

Once at street level, Yacut looked exactly what he was – a small weasel of a man who was now at a disadvantage. The janissaries and Rifat towered over him.

"What is the reason for this disturbance?" asked the senior janissary.

"I just want that little devil – he's my nephew – to return some valuable property of mine." Yacut was jabbering furiously as he pointed beyond his horse. The janissary looked over Yacut's horse's back.

"What little devil?"

"The boy I was beating—" Yacut couldn't see over his horse so he ducked round it.

The alley beyond was empty. Osman and Yildiz had disappeared. Yacut gave an agonized yowl before jumping up and down in rage and frustration. He then tried to mount his horse again.

"Let me get back on my horse! I must catch him!"

Rifat put his face close to Yacut's. "No point."

"Out of my way, idiot!"

"You listen to me, you wicked man. When they looked in the saddle for your precious gold, it wasn't there."

Yacut's mouth opened and closed. At last he got some

words out. "How do you know about that?"

"Never mind."

"You're lying."

"Why should I lie?"

"Because you're in league with those criminals!"

Rifat turned away from him in disgust, and took Yashar's arm. "I can see I'm wasting my breath here. Come on, Yashar. Let's go." As they turned to walk away, the janissary Rifat knew called after him.

"Before you go, Rifat – have you heard rumours of a runaway palace page anywhere in Uskudar?"

Rifat looked blank and scratched his head. "Why?"

"They say one has escaped, though I'll bet the truth is he's hidden himself somewhere in the palace complex. It's big enough."

"That sounds likely. And keep a sharp eye on that madman. He's dangerous."

Three figures crept onto the ferry after dark, paid the captain for their tickets, and bedded down for the night on deck under the black goat-hair blanket. Osman and Yildiz fell asleep at once, but Iskander, lying between them, was awake for hours, suffering over the fact he'd slept safely all day while very unpleasant things were happening to the others. The red weal on Osman's face and neck was bad enough, but they both said their backs hurt most. He listened to them groaning when they moved in their sleep, and felt increasingly guilty that he'd had such a calm, restful day.

He was also uneasy about this strange boy, Jem. First, why was he still with them? Iskander had expected the boy to leave them as soon as they'd landed and he'd been paid for his hard work rowing them over. But there was obviously no question of that – Osman, and even Jem himself, seemed to assume he was a permanent part of the family. His closeness to Osman and to Karakachan made Iskander feel the odd pang of jealousy despite himself.

Who was he? No one had explained, not that there'd been much time for it in the mad rush of the last twenty-four hours. How old was he? He looked much younger than the twins, but was as sharp and quick on the uptake as either of them. Look at the way he'd saved them earlier that evening. It was Jem who had spotted Yacut and Kizilbash going from boat to boat checking to see if the boys were on board, and then fast as lightning pushed them behind some bales of cargo and covered them all with the goat-hair blanket. It was a very near thing, and neither he nor Osman had noticed the danger, so convinced were they that their uncle would rule out ferries as an option for their escape.

They'd spent an hour hiding under that blanket, and the strong goaty smell of it evoked memories of home so vividly to Iskander it began to cancel out all the long months he'd spent in the palace. It also made him realize how much he wanted to be on his own with Osman to begin their new life together. He didn't really want a third person with them now, even a boy as nice, clever and helpful as Jem. He turned to look at Jem, whose sleeping face lay close to his own. The boy sighed and turned over in his sleep, revealing his arm and the top of his shoulder.

Iskander frowned and looked more closely at Jem's soft, smooth skin and long eyelashes, clear in the moonlight. A lock of dark hair had uncurled from Jem's turban. In that moment he knew for sure: Jem was a girl.

Startled and confused, Iskander stared up at the stars as he got used to this discovery. A girl. A girl was travelling with them. To his surprise, he found he didn't mind. He looked again at her profile. She was very pretty, as well as being brave and strong. He looked at Osman, and longed to know the story of their meeting and their travels together. At last, with the familiar comforting smell of goat hair right under his nose and the starry sky overhead, he fell asleep.

When Iskander woke, the *Dolphin* was sailing fast

through a sparkling empty sea. He sat up. The sun had just risen above the mountains of Anatolia, and Uskudar was a blur in the far distance. On the other side of the Marmara Sea he could just pick out the familiar outline of Topkapi Palace, and an unexpected pang ran through him. He'd left behind people he'd become very fond of, people he was most unlikely to see again. Dear Ismail, with his lop-sided grin and sweet nature. Prince Murad, who could have been such a good friend if their lives had been different. In his mind's eye he saw him galloping down the jerid pitch, urging on his team. Poor Prince Murad, trapped in his gilded prison.

Iskander lay back again and stared up at the blue sky. He'd miss his life in the palace, he'd miss the jerid, the lessons and the good food. But he was with Osman at last, and he'd soon see his mother and Gul again. And there was this mysterious Jem-girl, still asleep beside him. And when they collected Karakachan, Rifat would be there. A smile started to build until his whole face was filled with it. He'd escaped. He'd actually escaped from the palace. He could do what he liked. Life was going to be an adventure, and he was free.

It was time to wake the others.

Amnesty International

One Son Is Enough is a work of historical fiction, describing a system of slavery that ended a century ago. But slavery still happens in many parts of the world today and children continue to suffer due to the systematic denial of their human rights.

Human rights are basic principles that allow individuals the freedom to live dignified lives, free from abuse, fear and want, and free to express their own beliefs. Human rights belong to all of us, regardless of who we are or where we live.

Amnesty International is a movement of ordinary people from across the world standing up for humanity and human rights. Our purpose is to protect individuals wherever justice, fairness, freedom and truth are denied.

Youth Groups

We have an active membership of over 550 youth groups. Youth groups are gatherings of young people in schools, sixth form colleges or youth clubs who meet to learn about and campaign for Amnesty International. You can also join as an individual member and receive magazines to keep you up to date about ways you can help us. If you would like to join Amnesty International or set up a youth group, or simply find out more, please telephone our Education and Student Team on 020 7033 1596, e-mail student@amnesty.org.uk or visit www.amnesty.org.uk/education/youthandstudent/.

Amnesty International UK, The Human Rights Action Centre, 17–25 New Inn Yard, London EC2A 3EA. Tel: 020 7033 1500.

www.amnesty.org.uk